GOLDEN TOUCH

Golden Touch

SARINA BOWEN

Tuxbury Publishing LLC

CHAPTER 1
LIVIA

Every morning when I wake up, the first thing I do is listen for trouble. It's a lifelong habit, and today is no different. But all I hear this morning is birdsong. Lots of it. It sounds like a nearby blue jay and a chickadee have an ongoing disagreement.

Sitting up, I have to squint against the sunlight streaming through the windows. When I'd moved into this weird little apartment—carved out of the old pumphouse behind the Giltmaker Brewery—there'd been a set of faded curtains hanging from the windows. They were so tattered that I'd taken them down and hidden them in an upstairs closet.

Often, because I spend so much time alone, I mentally redecorate this place. New curtains. A cute paint job. A shower upgrade. A couch that isn't lumpy.

But this place isn't mine to redecorate. I'm only borrowing it. Lyle Giltmaker—the brewery owner—lets me live here for free. He's not a generous man in my experience, but he likes the idea that I'm always early for work.

The downside: I don't have a lease or any kind of job security. He could fire me and evict me in the same breath if he decided to. Still, it's the best deal in town, and I'm determined to practice gratitude. This has been a stressful year, and it's not every day

1

that you find a job where the owner doesn't ask too many questions, and also pays you in cash.

Lyle's a world-class grump, but nobody's perfect.

So I'm counting my blessings as I head for the tiny bathroom, pull back the rust-stained shower curtain, and crank the faucet. And I continue to count them, even though I'm not a morning person, and seven thirty feels stupidly early, and the water doesn't stay hot for long.

Less than twenty minutes later, I've got my makeup done, my heels on, and I'm ready to make the short walk to the brewery's office.

On my way out, I grab my phone from the charger in the kitchen and take a look at my notifications. And what I see there makes me pull up short—seven missed calls and a flurry of texts from my cousin. All of them from late last night.

Oh no. Even before I read her first text, I know it's going to be bad.

> JENNIE
>
> Where are you?
>
> Hell of a time for your stupid phone to die!!!
> There's some asshole pounding on my front door
> and yelling for you.
>
> Call me when you get this. Any hour. He's gone
> now because my crone of a neighbor threatened
> to call the cops. But we have to talk. I've never
> seen this guy before, but he's bad news.

There's more, but I don't read it, because I'm already calling her back.

"Hey," Jennie answers sleepily. "You okay?"

"I'm fine. But, God, I'm *so* sorry—"

"It's not your fault, babe. But I'm scared."

"I bet!"

"No, I'm scared for *you*, bitch. He was asking for you. And then he said…" She takes a breath. "'Tell that whore that somebody saw you two at the Busy Bean last week. Now I know which county she's in. Tell her that Razor hired me to find her, and I'm really good at my job.'"

I can't hold back my gasp. "Oh *no*."

"Yeah," Jennie says hoarsely. "I told him through the door that you refuse to tell me where you're living. And he was wasting his time bothering me."

"Did he believe you?"

"Probably. Yeah. But he made himself a nuisance anyway. Just to see what I'd do. So you have *got* to be really careful, okay? This man was a scary dude. I got a look at him through the peephole."

"What did he look like?"

"Like he could snap us in half. Big shoulders. Muscular. Lots of ink. Brown hair, dark eyes." She lets out a nervous laugh. "Honestly, he was exactly your type."

I bristle with resentment, probably because it's true. All the men I've dated look just like that. And it always ends badly. "New rule—no men, unless they weigh ninety pounds or less."

"Oh, please," she scoffs. "You like 'em big and rough."

This is unfortunately true.

"The worst part, babe?" she adds. "This means we can't hang out for a while."

"Oh *shit*." My heart dives, but she's right. We'll have to steer clear of each other, even though our rare meetups at bookstores and coffeeshops are the only thing keeping me sane. "He'll try to follow you."

"Maybe you need to get out of Vermont for a while. It's a small state."

"Maybe," I echo. But this is my *home*, damn it. And disappearing on a tight budget is not as easy as she makes it sound. "I'll think about it. Help me spot this guy—what was he riding?"

"Couldn't see the bike. Only heard the growl."

Damn. "Any other distinguishing characteristics?"

"I'll try to remember. But babe? I gotta get Henry to school."

"Go," I say immediately. "We'll talk later."

"Watch your back. Chin up."

"Love you! Don't worry! I'm fine."

We hang up, but I'm not actually fine. I'm freaked. My pulse is ragged. My hands are sweaty.

Razor strikes again. I was such a fool to get involved with him. And then I was an even bigger fool to think that leaving town would make him forget about me. I've been hiding in Colebury for *ten months*, and he hasn't given up. Instead, he's hired a guy to intimidate Jennie and try to find me.

My hands shake as I stash my phone in my pocket. This is exactly what I've been worried about. *God*. I'll never be free of him.

I'm extra cautious as I open the door and scan the back lot and the big brick brewery building. It's quiet, though. No cars except for my own. No sounds except the chattering birds.

I lock the door to my little apartment. It's just a doorknob lock, though. A child could break it with one sharp twist. And I feel so exposed as I cross the gravel parking lot to the back door of the brewhouse.

I use a different key to let myself inside. There's a cavernous hallway that runs front to back. Today it feels creepy as my footsteps echo off the tile floor.

But it's just my nerves talking. I pace to the front door and try the handle. Locked. I'm the first one to arrive.

In ordinary times at the Giltmaker Brewery, Lyle Giltmaker himself would be the first on scene. But the man had a massive coronary last month that almost killed him. He's temporarily recovering at a nursing facility, where he gets daily antibiotic infusions.

Ever since my boss was hospitalized, the brewhouse staff has been showing up for work later and later. And I happen to know that last night was poker night, so they'll be tardy and hungover when they bother to stumble in.

I pause at the threshold of Lyle's office and scan the big room.

The place feels oddly empty without Lyle behind his desk, barking orders at me before he even says good morning.

Can't believe I actually miss the old grump.

After opening a window to let in the morning air, I take his seat at the big old desk, because it has the best view out the window. And I pick up the stack of receipts that Leila—Lyle Giltmaker's daughter—left here for me yesterday. As the bookkeeper, it's my job to enter them into Lyle's old-fashioned ledger system.

If I had Quickbooks, this job would be done in five minutes. But Lyle is eccentric and insists on a strictly paper accounting system. Today I don't mind it. I need something soothing to occupy my thoughts, and numbers have always been my love language.

All is well in the land of bookkeeping for half an hour, and then I hear the low growl of an approaching engine. Even before I register that it's a motorcycle, I'm on my feet and peering out the window. I have a perfect view of a biker swinging into the lot and parking by the brewhouse's front door.

Oh my God. Oh God.

I can't see much of his face, because of the helmet and mirrored sunglasses, but there's something eerily familiar about the angle of his chin. He's just like Jennie described. Tall. Broad shoulders. He's got the cuffs unzipped on his black motorcycle jacket and I catch a glimpse of heavy ink.

I'm a dead girl.

CHAPTER 2
LIVIA

Wasting no time, the biker swings a leg over his ride and struts toward the door.

Holy shit. How did he find me?

Tell her I'm really good at my job, he'd said.

But I'm too young to die! I've never been to Hawaii. I've never had sex on the beach. (The cocktail totally doesn't count.)

My breathing shallow, I back away from the window and scurry into the corridor where nobody can see me. If he breaks a window in front, I can run out the back.

And go where?

Shit.

I'm light-headed from fear. The truth is that I only *look* like a badass. Don't let my tats fool you—I'm a lover, not a fighter.

I ease into the shadows at the rear of the long corridor. This is where I feel the safest—with one door behind me and another ahead. I try to listen for him, but all I can hear is my pulse thudding in my ears.

When the big front door swings open, I wonder if I'm hallucinating. That door was *locked* when I checked it this morning. But it isn't anymore. A piercing rectangle of light shines down the corridor as the man steps inside and removes his helmet.

I flatten myself against the wall out of his sightline and stop breathing.

"Hello?" he calls, easing down the corridor while I try not to pee myself with fear.

As I clench every muscle in my body, he pokes his head into the office, sees that it's empty, then turns around slowly.

This is it. He's going to drag me back to Razor, and I'll die before ever seeing Taylor Swift in concert.

But he doesn't notice me back here. Remarkably, he crosses the corridor and enters the brewhouse like he owns the place. I hear his footsteps echo in the wide-open space. "Hello?" he calls again. "Anybody home?"

Move, I coach myself. *Now.*

With terror in my veins, I ease toward the back door, fumbling for the knob. I open it as quietly as possible.

Inside my head, everything is loud. How much time do I have before he comes outside to look around? He'll recognize my car. Razor would have told him the make, model, and plate number. And if I start the engine and take off, he'll just hop on his bike and follow me.

After easing the door closed behind me, I realize I don't have many options. This feeling is entirely too familiar—I'm in trouble, and nobody is coming to save me.

Story of my life.

After another ragged breath, I hurry toward the pumphouse. But if I go inside, I'll be trapped again. So I double back and conceal myself against the brewery's back wall and pull out my phone.

"What is your emergency?" the 911 operator asks.

"I'm...I'm at the Giltmaker Brewery. An intruder has just entered the building."

———

The next ten minutes last forever. I listen to the thud of my heart and wait, shaking, for the police to arrive. There's a river at the very back of the property. Worst case scenario, I could jump in if he's chasing me. Not that I'm a great swimmer. But if he catches me, I'm probably dead anyway.

Finally, I hear the sound of tires on the gravel lot. I hold my breath and listen. There's a loud pounding of fists against wood. "This is the police! We're coming in!"

More than one voice starts shouting. I brace myself for violence, but the police must subdue this guy pretty quickly, because I hear a man say, "*Handcuffs?*" in an incredulous voice. "You're shitting me."

Only then do I emerge on weak knees, reentering the back door of the brewery just as the cops escort the guy out the front. I wave at the police, and one of them nods to me. "One second, ma'am."

As soon as the door closes on them, I hurry down the corridor to the front windows to see what's happening.

The scary dude is irate. Face red, and his cuffed hands curling into fists. He's arguing while they frisk him.

I notice that he's unarmed. All they find in his pocket is a wallet. No guns and no duct tape. Huh. Maybe he keeps his weapons in his bike's saddlebags.

Or maybe he's so highly trained he doesn't need weapons. There's plenty of muscle on him. And Jennie was right—he's just my type. My *former* type, that is. I'm done with men, for obvious reasons.

The guy looks up suddenly, as if he can sense me watching from behind the glass.

Those *eyes*, though. I know those eyes. Who is this guy?

Quickly, I step away from the window. I can't let Razor's evil minion get a good look at me. Even if this dude is carted off to jail, my ex will just send another one in his place.

I'm so screwed.

Two minutes go by before there's a soft knock on the door. "Ma'am?"

I open it to find a thirtyish policeman standing there. He's handsome in a cleancut way that many women would find attractive. If I were one of them, my life would frankly be easier.

"Thank you for getting here so quickly."

"We, uh, got a disagreement on our hands," the officer says. "Your trespasser claims that he's expected today. And I'm inclined to agree with him."

"Why?" I demand, an edge of hysteria in my voice. "I'm not expecting anyone new today."

"Well, I checked his ID, and his name is on the door." He grins. "And he gave me this business card for you."

The officer hands me a creamy ivory business card with embossed lettering. It says *NASH M. GILTMAKER. Chief Operating Officer, BrewCo Industries.*

"What?" I gasp. My heart starts pounding again. "That's impossible."

But maybe it's not. I think I've made a horrible mistake.

Did I just call the cops on Lyle Giltmaker's *son*? Holy…

"Omigod, I'm going to be fired."

The cop actually chuckles. "He's wondering who you are."

"I work here," I sputter. "For his father. Since last spring! And I've never seen him before in my life. There's a photo of Lyle's son on the desk in the office, and it looks nothing like that guy!"

The cop's eyes crinkle. "Lyle Giltmaker has two sons. Is it Mitch in the picture?"

I shrug in an exaggerated way. "How the hell should I know? Some guy in a hockey jersey. Lyle's daughter said Nash was arriving tomorrow."

"Huh. Well, I think you guys got your signals crossed. And Mitch Giltmaker is the professional hockey player," the cop says evenly. "Everybody knows that."

"Not everybody," I say through clenched teeth. My mind is spinning. "Apparently, the Giltmaker boys look nothing alike?"

The cop shrugs. "Look, I googled Nash Giltmaker on my phone as a failsafe and found this." He holds up his phone for me to see the results of a Google search.

When I see the photo, I practically grab the phone out of the cop's hands. "*This* is Nash Giltmaker?" I *have* seen him before. But only once, and it didn't end well.

Oh. My. God. This is getting more embarrassing by the minute.

The cop takes his phone back with a shrug. "Maybe take a closer look next time before you panic?"

"He wasn't supposed to arrive today," I gasp. This can't be happening. "And he had a helmet and glasses on, and he let himself in at eight in the morning. I was here all alone!"

"Simple misunderstanding," the officer says. "But it's not me you need to apologize to, yeah?" He pushes the door open wider, and I look outside.

There's Nash Giltmaker, leaning against a patrol car. He's talking to another cop and rubbing his wrists, probably where the handcuffs bit into his skin. He's facing away from me, but I can tell from the set of his shoulders that he's angry.

Honestly, I didn't know people could actually glower with their whole body. But here we are. And all that tension in that muscular body is weirdly appealing.

Stop it! I chide myself.

Maybe he can feel my eyes on him, too, because he turns suddenly in my direction. I react without thinking, ducking back into the darkness of the brewery, keeping out of his sight line.

I'm stalling. Not that it will help. We're about to have a very awkward conversation about what happened here today. And probably about that *other* time we almost met.

Maybe he's forgotten? We'd first encountered each other last November, almost five months ago. But if he remembers that night, it means I've seriously messed up with the Giltmaker heir *twice.*

Oh my God. I'm going to be fired by lunchtime.

CHAPTER 3
NASH

Who knew I had "start the day in handcuffs" on my bingo card?

"Sorry about that, Mr. Giltmaker," the officer says as he hooks the infernal things back onto his duty belt. "Big misunderstanding. She was just real good and panicked."

"Yeah. Gettin' that." I sigh. "Did she say why? This has always been a quiet part of town. Has there been a rash of break-ins or something?"

"Not to my knowledge, sir." The young cop looks nervous. "You're not gonna file a complaint, are you?"

"Against you? Nah. But she and I are going to have a conversation."

The guy winces. "Keep it friendly. And say hi to your sister for me. Leila is a great girl."

Speaking of Leila, I glance around the parking lot. "You haven't seen her, have you? She was supposed to meet me here."

"Can't say I have," he says. "Hope the rest of your day goes better."

"Thanks, man."

He heads back toward his cruiser, the other cop joining him after emerging from the brewery. I watch them pull away, take a few deep breaths, and try to regain my equanimity.

I'm an easygoing guy. The kind of person who doesn't get too upset when there's a kink in my day. Usually.

But coming home to Vermont is always a test of my patience. This trip is only a few hours old, and I'm already at the end of my rope. My sister has stood me up. My father's assistant called the cops on me. And I never even wanted this gig in the first place.

Maybe it's a sign. I should just get back on my bike and go home.

But I'd never bail on Leila like that, and her absence is starting to make me nervous. My sister is *very* pregnant, and now I'm worried that something's happened to her. I pull out my phone and try a text.

> Buddy, you late?

No answer.

With a low groan of frustration, I head for the door again and open it gently. It's quiet inside, just the way it was before.

"Listen up!" I call down the echoing hallway. "Whoever you are, I'm coming into the office. Don't shoot. And for fuck's sake, don't call the cops."

This announcement is met with silence.

Fuck.

I march down the corridor under a full head of steam, ready to get a good look at this shrew whose first impulse was to have me arrested rather than just ask me to introduce myself. She's probably an older lady—suspicious of motorcycles and tattoos. That must be it.

When I reach my father's office, the door is open. I lean against the doorjamb and scan the cavernous room. What I see is surprising.

First of all, the place is spotless. This room has been an office for over a hundred years, first for the mill that operated on this site since the late nineteenth century, and later for a trucking company. Eventually, my father bought the place for his many business ventures.

It's always been an interesting space, with floor-to-ceiling bookshelves made from oak and mahogany and a giant old desk. I used to hide under there as a child.

The bookshelves and the desk are still here, and since my father hates technology, the shelves are full of his old handwritten ledgers. What's different is that a century and a half of dust and huge piles of boxes and avalanching papers have disappeared.

I barely recognize the place. The floor seems to have doubled in size, and my dad's grand old desk is clear of debris and polished to a shine.

There's a second desk in the room now, closer to the door. And at this desk sits the second surprise—a stunning woman. Late twenties, probably. A little thing. White chick with dark, wavy hair and olive skin.

She's wearing an expression so defiant that I almost want to laugh. Her eyes are deep brown and *furious*.

But hang on—those brown eyes are tickling my memory. I blink, and her stunning face clicks into place. I've stared at this girl from across a crowded room. It was a few months ago. November, actually. I'd just survived Thanksgiving weekend with my family, and I was blowing off steam at the bar with a buddy from high school.

She was sitting catty-corner to me at the other end of the U-shaped bar, and for the entire night, we flirted across the space, our exchanged glances getting hotter as the evening progressed. By closing time, I was deep in lust with her.

But then she ditched me. I went back to Boston the next day, strangely sad and missing a woman I'd never formally met.

Here she is again, even prettier than before. Chocolate eyes that know too much, wavy hair I'd fantasized about running my fingers through, and nice tits under her sweater. *Really* nice. Sue me.

I clear my throat. "Well, look who it is. Honestly, I'm more confused now than ever. You saw me today for the *second* time in your life… and then immediately called the cops?"

"I barely saw you at all," she argues, her voice lower and smokier than I'd anticipated. "You were wearing a helmet and glasses—something a thief might wear—and all I saw was a biker breaking into the building."

"You got something against bikers?"

"Certain bikers," she says through clenched teeth. "Think of it like a special brand of PTSD."

I snort. "So you're Livia, huh? Nice to finally meet you."

Emphasis on finally. I guess I'm still salty about the night she got away.

"You must be Nash," she says in a voice you might use to say, *you must be a flesh-eating bacteria.*

"Oh, so now you know my name?"

She reddens slightly, but lifts her chin another few degrees, her gaze a challenge.

An incredibly sexy challenge, damn it.

She shrugs a shoulder, like the queen dismissing a servant. "I was told I'd meet you *tomorrow*. And there's a picture on Lyle's desk of your brother. I know now that he's the hockey player. But in my head, that's what I expected you'd look like."

Internally, I groan. Of course, the only picture on my dad's desk is Mitch. "So if we were identical twins, you wouldn't have called the cops? Can we talk about your quick trigger finger on 911?"

"Look." She crosses her arms across that gorgeous rack. "You're not in the clink, so I don't see why you're all worked up about it. There's been a lot of crime in the area."

"Oh yeah? I'll bet the scariest thing on last week's police blotter was a pack of raccoons in a garbage can."

She gives her hair a toss, revealing a creamy neck that I kind of want to bite. "You can't blame me for protecting your father's property. Honestly, you should be impressed."

I snort again. "Uh-huh. Do most criminals ride up to the front door in broad daylight and let themselves in with a *key*?"

"Can't be too careful." Her spine is straight, her shoulders square, her gaze defiant. She reminds me of a house cat I once took in. The damn thing was beautiful, but so aloof. Wouldn't come near me whenever I went looking for her. But later I figured out that she was willing to get close to me—but only when she thought I wasn't paying attention.

It's water under the bridge, since it turns out I'm allergic to cats. But now Livia is behaving just the same way. This woman and I had a lot of chemistry back in November. The whole fucking bar could tell.

She hit the nope button at the last minute. Fine. That's her choice. But we've got ourselves an awkward mess now, don't we?

Livia picks up a pencil. She scans the ledger in front of her, as if this conversation is over.

I'm just about to ask another question when my phone rings in my pocket. And since I need to hear from my sister more than I need to argue with Livia, I pull out my phone.

The screen says LEILA.

I answer immediately. "Hey! Where've you been? You won't believe the morning I've had."

There's an awkward chuckle, and it's not my sister's. "Nash? This is Matteo Rossi."

Hmm. Matteo is an old friend of my sister's. "Matteo? What's up?"

"Not Leila," he says with a chuckle. "Don't panic, but I had to bring her to the hospital after she fainted this morning. They're fussing over her now, but she's already improving. I just thought you'd want to know."

"The *hospital*? Oh hell. I'll be right there." I end the call and pocket my phone. "I have to go," I tell Livia. "We'll pick up this conversation later."

"Don't hurry back," she says, turning the page of her ledger.

She doesn't look up, and her straight spine is a study in feline haughtiness.

If I weren't so annoyed, I'd probably find it funny. "Whatever you say, pussycat."

I can feel the heat of her glare as I take my leave.

CHAPTER 4
LIVIA

The moment Nash leaves the office, I throw down my pencil and cradle my head in my hands.

How much bad luck can one woman have? Serious question. I can't *believe* I called the cops on Lyle Giltmaker's son. If I hadn't panicked, I might have noticed that he looks a little like Lyle—with the same thick brown hair, and the same cheekbones.

I also might have noticed that he was *that* guy. The one from the bar. The one I flirted with for three hours last fall.

Fuck me. What are the odds?

Okay, now that I think about it, they're not so remote. It was a holiday weekend, a time when wayward sons come home to see their parents. And I was at Speakeasy—a property partly owned by the Giltmakers. Too bad I never let the man get close enough to introduce himself.

Now that seems like a mistake.

I let out a little moan of stupidity. And, fine, lust. The night we never met was, bizarrely enough, one of my happiest memories from the past year. And Nash Giltmaker really is *exactly* my type. Which is why I ultimately decided not to let myself get sucked into his bad boy aura.

That night was a fun time, though. A unicorn night. I was out with my cousin. She's married with a small child, so our nights out together are rare.

Furthermore, when you're on the run from your violent ex, hanging out in bars is something you just can't do whenever you feel like it. I can't take the chance that one of his guys will spot me and tattle.

Or worse. They might slip something into my drink and I'd wake up back at Razor's place, handcuffed to a piece of furniture. Just like the first time I tried to run away.

So I'm very careful. That's why my night out last November was a special treat. I'd risked it because I knew that the Valkyries Motorcycle Club was having their biggest bash of the year that night. It's a Sunday-after-Thanksgiving tradition. First they take a long ride during the daytime, while the roads are still clear of snow. Then they follow it up with a big bonfire and a barbecue.

It was one night when I knew *exactly* where Razor and all his evil friends would be, so I didn't have to worry. Going to Speakeasy with Jennie was a safe choice.

Safe, and fun. But not smart.

That night, Jennie was a little late joining me, so I'd waited at the bar, my coat draped over the back of the stool beside mine. I nursed a beer and enjoyed being out in the world and feeling mostly unafraid.

Then I spotted *him* across the bar—broad shoulders, impressive ink where his biceps bulged from his T-shirt, and a hot smile that was beaming my way.

Just my catnip, damn it. So I'd flirted a little. I'd held his gaze a little too long. It didn't take much.

A minute or two later, the bartender—a cute, slender man with an Aussie accent—slid a beer across the bar to me. "Me mate over there wants to shout you a drink. And he nicked my phone to spin a tune for you."

"And you let him, did you?" I'd laughed, and the bartender had shrugged.

Looking back, the encounter makes even more sense. Nash's

family is a part owner of that bar. Of course the bartender handed over his playlist.

The song that came on made me smile, too. It was "Can't Take My Eyes Off of You"—the sexy Lauryn Hill version.

Okay, fair. He basically read my mind. But then he escalated things by following that song with "Dibs" by Kelsea Ballerini and "Damn I Wish I Was Your Lover" by Sophie B. Hawkins.

It wasn't subtle, but I'd be a liar if I said I didn't enjoy it. Every time I glanced toward his end of the bar, his bottomless gaze found mine.

When Jennie arrived, I told her what he'd done, and she was deeply amused. "Lord, that man is hot," she said with a giggle. "You're gonna hit that, right?"

"Doubt it," I said. "In fact…" I beckoned to the bartender. "Any chance I could add a track to the playlist?"

He gave me a smirk. "Hell, yes. Keen to see where this goes."

I chose "No" by Meghan Trainor, and the bartender just about burst a gut laughing.

I couldn't take my eyes off McHottie, though. He didn't get mad. He gave me a slow smile, his dark eyes shining with humor. Then he licked his generous lips. "Well played," he mouthed.

I felt a shimmy right where it counts. Who doesn't love a man who can take a joke?

He didn't back off. His next song was "I Want You to Want Me" by Cheap Trick.

My cousin howled with laughter. "Oh, I *like* this guy," she said, raising a glass in his direction. "Well done, sir."

I shot him a flirty smile. It had been so long since I felt desirable to anyone. After too many months with a man who only tried to break me down, the low-stakes attention from across the bar was like a beautiful gift wrapped up in a bow.

"This is how it's supposed to feel," my cousin said. She's always been able to read me like a newspaper. "Not every man is a control freak, you know."

"I know," I agreed, just to shut her up. But I really didn't believe her.

"Go home with him," she whispered. "I worry about you being lonely."

"God, Jennie. You realize he only wants a couple hours of my time, right? I'm not going to start dating him, or anyone else. There's really no point."

"There's totally a point! Maybe he'll make you feel like a queen for one night. You should remember what that's like. A few hours of fun can change your whole outlook."

I already felt the glow of attraction, my resolve weakening. I felt that shimmer. That spark. The promise of something new and beautiful. It reminded me why I'm alive.

After a terrible year, I wanted to believe life had more in store for me than hiding from my ex and working my office job.

The next song my hottie chose was "It's Gonna be Me" by NSYNC, sending my cousin into another fit of laughter, while I gave him a shy smile across the bar.

He gave me a cocky grin, but his wink was as warm as it was sexy. I let myself wonder what kind of kisser he was. And whether his hands were rough or smooth…

Meanwhile, he seemed to get a lot of attention from the rest of the bar. People kept stopping by to say hello. In between well-wishers, he spent a lot of time chatting with his friend—another heavily tattooed man occupying the barstool next to him.

This guy had brought a sketchbook with him. The two of them were having an animated conversation about the drawings. Hottie's friend was a tattoo artist, maybe?

I was intrigued. It made me want to meet them both. And you have to admire a man who has friends, a hobby, and amusing taste in music.

And, fine, really great biceps with intricate designs all over them and a smile that lit me up inside.

Then Jennie waved the bartender over and requested a song. "Go for it, love," he said, handing over his phone.

She chose "Yeah Boy," by Kelsea Ballerini, which made me roll my eyes even though I love Kelsea Ballerini.

By then, we'd been there for a couple hours. My hottie's tattooed friend went to the men's room, leaving him alone to request one more song as he gazed at me from across the bar.

His final play was "Send me a Sign" by the Thirst Traps. Such a plaintive song, with a deep, sexy beat. And the lyrics are full of humility.

So I sent him a sign by slowly unbuttoning the top button on my blouse.

"Omigod, yes!" my cousin squealed. "You're my idol."

Without even a glance in his direction, I took in my cousin's bright smile. "It's just that you're married," I pointed out. "This seems like a big adventure to you, when it's really just dangerous."

She'd rolled her eyes. "It's not dangerous at all. The guy knows half the people in this place, including the bartender. And look—he's closing out his bill with a credit card, which means anyone could track him down. He's obviously a member of this community."

She made a few good points. "Well, fine. But if he murders me, avenge my death."

She slid off her stool. "My work here is done. Have a blast. Thanks for meeting me here tonight. It makes me happy when you're happy."

I put my hands on her shoulders. "You shouldn't worry about me. I'm going to be okay."

"Sure, but there's a difference between okay and great." Her pretty eyes searched my face. "I appreciate you. But I don't want you spending the rest of your life paying for one silly mistake." She'd kissed me on the cheek. "Call me tomorrow. I want details."

Then she left.

I closed out our tab and watched the two men across the bar give each other a back-slapping hug.

My hot new friend glanced over at me. He held up a finger in the universal sign for give me a moment. Then he pointed himself toward the corner of the bar where the bathrooms are.

I watched him go, and even as his very fine ass receded into the crowd, I started to feel very foolish. What was I thinking? The world is full of hot men.

My ex had been hot, and I'd met him in a bar much like this one.

Well, maybe not so much like this one. It had been a seedier place southwest of here with a sticky floor and a rougher crowd.

But he made me feel like a real princess at first. They all do. That's how this works. He'd been smart, great in the sack, and he did the whole roses-and-dinners thing for a couple months after we met. I thought that meant he loved me.

Then he started finding fault with everything I did.

And then the violent outbursts started…

As I slid off my stool in Speakeasy, I realized I was about to repeat the cycle. I'm old enough to know that the shiny glow of male attention doesn't last. Not with the guys I'm attracted to, anyway.

Sure, some of them keep up the pretense longer than others, but if you play with fire, you're going to get burned. After spending months trying to extract myself from Razor, with only mixed results, I still had the scorch marks.

So before he returned from the men's, I made the smart choice —the only possible choice—and grabbed my purse and jacket and headed for the front door. I'd trotted across the gravel parking lot and jumped into my crappy car. The one I couldn't afford to replace, because I had to leave everything of value behind when I left Razor. Including my bank account.

I'd gone home to my little hidden apartment behind the brewery, thinking that was that. Or so I'd thought.

Sitting at my desk, I let out a loud groan. I've pressed the panic button twice on Nash Giltmaker. He's going to think I'm unstable.

Given the circumstances, it will be hard to argue otherwise. And when he fires me, I'll have no safe place to go.

CHAPTER 5
NASH

After visiting my sister, I walk out of the hospital and dial my elusive little brother.

For once in his life, he answers immediately. "How is Leila?" He's several states away, and probably feeling even more helpless than I am.

"She's going to be okay," I tell him. "She has some kind of pregnancy-related, high-blood-pressure condition. They're taking good care of her, but they might have to induce labor."

"Leila has high blood pressure? She's too young for that."

"I told you—it's a pregnancy thing. Have you ever heard of preeclampsia?"

"Fuck no," he grumbles. "What do I know about pregnant women? A whole lot of nothing. As it should be."

"Same, bro." We both snicker. "Good thing the hospital has it under control. Matteo is there with her. Mom is on the way back from Montreal to be here, too."

"Matteo, huh?" Mitch asks. "I wondered if he was the daddy. But Leila wouldn't say."

"Doesn't seem like a secret anymore. He told me he flew back here to be with Leila. Permanently."

"Well, that's something," my brother says with a sigh. "Good for Leila. Always liked that guy. So what are you doing in Cole-bury? Thought you weren't willing to run the brewery."

"I'm not very willing. But Leila needs me for six weeks until Dad is back at the helm. I had to take a leave of absence from BrewCo."

"Thoughts and prayers. Working for Dad is my worst night-mare, and I say that as the favorite son."

I laugh, because at least he acknowledges it.

"So how's it going?" he asks.

"It isn't yet. Haven't even seen the old man yet, and my tenure at the brewery is off to a rocky start."

"Oh God. Why?"

When I tell him about my morning, my brother howls with laughter. "Please tell me there's body-cam footage. I got a high school buddy in the sheriff's office. I could ask him..."

"Fuck no. I will end you."

He snickers. "So who is this Livia? I gotta meet her."

"Well..." I hesitate. "Remember last November, when I told you I spent a whole night DJing tunes for this chick at Speakeasy? And then she bailed on me?"

"Oh, I heard all about it," my brother says. "You drunk-dialed me that night from Leila's sofa. You were so bummed."

"Well, it's her. That's Livia."

First a silence. Then more loud laughter.

"Yeah, yeah. I know. Hell of a coincidence."

"I gotta meet this chick. She sounds like a good time."

"Feel free to fly your ass back here and take my place." Leaving my job and my home in Boston for six weeks is a huge inconvenience. I still can't believe I agreed to it.

"Why'd she call the cops?" he asks. "Serious question."

"Fuck if I know."

"She must be afraid of something," my brother says. "You don't get that jumpy by accident."

I'm too annoyed to admit that he's probably right. "Who

knows? The whole thing is awkward as hell. And I'm only here because Leila begged me."

"I wish I could help," Mitch says. "You'll keep me updated on Leila? I'm gonna worry."

"Yeah, same."

Leila is the oldest of the three of us. She's always been the competent, infallible one. I'm the forgotten middle child. Mitch is the baby of the family—the charmer. The one who gets away with everything. He also has an ironclad excuse for not pitching in to help the family business—his hockey team is about to tackle the playoffs. Depending on how well they do, we might not see him until June.

"You *are* going to show up this summer, right? To meet your new niece or nephew?" I ask.

"Of course," he says, even though it isn't really a given. I'll bet Mitch spends fewer than four days a year in Vermont. It's been like that since he left for college. "How soon is Leila having this baby?"

"Not sure. Could be a couple more weeks. Could be tomorrow."

"It's a good thing you're there," Mitch says. "Just at the right time."

I make a grunt of acknowledgement. Leila and my father are both hospitalized, and I'm the obvious one to step in during this disaster. I'm a brewer by trade.

My sister, on the other hand, is a preschool teacher. And she's about to have a newborn to care for. *There's no one else, Nash*, she'd said. *The brewery is your family's legacy.*

Except that's not really true. The Giltmaker Brewery is my father's legacy, not mine. He made it impossible for me to feel any love for the place. Early on, when I'd tried to embrace the family business, he'd made it clear that all I'd ever be was an enlisted man. Never an officer.

Then, when I quit to work for the competition, I was suddenly a traitor. A corporate sellout, too. I can't win with that man, and I dread the job of running his precious business for the next six weeks.

"Is there anything I can do for Leila?" Mitch asks me. "Anything I can send her?"

"Doubt it," I assure him. "Unless you know what kind of baby gift she wants. She's in good hands, though, and I'll keep you posted. I'm on my way back to the brewery. Hopefully nobody will call 911 this time."

"Hopefully," Mitch says with a snicker. "I got bail money if you're hard up."

"Good to know," I grumble.

We hang up, and I buy a sandwich at a Montpelier deli. Then I swing onto my bike for the trip back to the brewery. It's located just north of Colebury—the town where we went to high school.

At least it's a pretty ride out of town. The road winds between the river and a pine forest. The air is clear, and there's no traffic. Just me and the bike and the road and the springtime sunshine. I feel my mood lift.

By nature, I'm a happy guy, and these are my old stomping grounds. I raised hell in these hills as a teenager. My fondest memories are sneaking a case of beer and a radio into the woods with my friends. We'd drink and party until the batteries and the beer ran out.

It was cheap beer, of course. We could never afford Daddy's beer, and I wasn't stupid enough to steal it. My friends used to tease me. "All that beer. A whole warehouse full. Where's ours?"

They didn't understand. Who wants the specter of his father at a party? Not me. And the people who say that the beer is my legacy ought to remember that legacies can be both bad and good. The Giltmaker Brewery is a source of family pride, but also the source of our pain. So many sacrifices. So many arguments.

By the time I was twenty-one and legal to drink my father's prized beer, I decided I didn't want a thing to do with it. Still don't.

But here I am, gunning it toward the place. There's a million things I need to do. Meet the brewers. Study the recipes and the brewing schedule. Take samples of the beers in the tanks. Check the supplies on hand and report it all to Dad.

Then I'll have to listen to him chew me out for one thing or another. Unlike Mitch, I'm always failing him.

But first things first. I need to eat my sandwich and stake out the bunkroom in the pumphouse. The plan had been for me to stay at my sister's place tonight and then move into the bunkroom tomorrow. I don't even know if the place is ready.

I could have stayed at a hotel in Montpelier, but the commute would suck, and six weeks is a long time in a hotel room. I can't stay with my sister and her man. That sounds crowded, especially if there's a new baby in the picture.

Leila had told me that Dad's assistant lived in the pumphouse apartment. And that she wouldn't mind if I kipped upstairs in the bunkroom. Maybe my sister didn't think this all the way through, though. Livia did *not* look happy to meet me.

I roar up the two-lane road and try not to notice how sweet the Vermont air smells. I don't want to miss this place. I don't want to feel the pull.

Six weeks, and I'll be history. It's better that way.

CHAPTER 6
LIVIA

By noon, I'm taking a lunch break in my apartment, poking at the salad I made for myself and wondering if I'll be here long enough to use up the groceries in the fridge.

Yesterday, my greatest fear was that Lyle Giltmaker would die of his heart condition and make me jobless and homeless.

But now I have a new fear. Lyle's stupidly attractive son hates me now, and if he decides to do a little digging in my employee file he'll probably fire me on the spot.

Then I'll really be out of options. Few people are willing to hire a woman for cash, and also give her a place to live. I can't use my social security number or any of my credit cards, because they're potentially traceable by my ex, who's both smart and devious.

If I lose my place here, I'll be living in my car or asking a women's shelter to help me get a fresh start. Except I'm not an innocent woman with children to shield. I'm someone who's made a lot of mistakes and has to pay for them. Charities aren't meant for women who should really know better.

In the middle of this mental doom loop, I hear a motorcycle approaching. My stomach lurches, and I put down my fork.

It's probably Nash. I'm not so eager to see him, but I'll take Nash over my ex any day. Even if Nash doesn't fire me, I'm still in danger. The scary dude Jennie found on her porch last night is still out there somewhere.

The noise grows louder and then stops when the engine cuts outside the window. I rise from my chair and watch Nash Giltmaker swing his leg over the bike.

Okay. Well. At least he isn't one of Razor's minions.

A moment later, he knocks twice on the door, then tries the knob. It's locked, of course.

I cross to the door and open it. And I'm immediately jolted by his larger-than-life attractiveness. Those clear brown eyes. That strong jaw.

For a split second, my heart pauses on *what if*. What if I hadn't ditched him that night? Would that be a fond memory? Would we have become friends?

He frowns. "Can I come in?" he asks. "My sister said I could stay in the bunkroom upstairs."

"Starting *tomorrow* night." I'm clinging to this detail, because I'm trying to get my head around the idea that this sexy creature and I are supposed to be roommates for six weeks.

He grins suddenly, and his face transforms from hot and grumpy to hot and devastating. "Sure thing, pussycat. You call my hospitalized sister and ask for her keys so I can stay at her place tonight like we planned."

"Hospitalized?" I yelp.

"Yeah. They're trying to figure out if she needs a c-section."

Oh! Poor Leila. And of course I'm not going to bother her right now. "Maybe your dad's place, then?"

"Uh-huh," he says with a smirk. "Dad has a cat, and I'm allergic."

"Oh." I sigh. And then I have an alarming thought. "Wait— who's taking care of Smokey?"

Nash tilts his head to the side and smiles again. "Aw, Livia. It's heartening to know that you care about our animal friends. My mother took in the cat. But the dander is still all over Dad's house."

"Right," I say, stepping back from the door and waving him in. My kitchen area is *very* small all of a sudden. "Look, I'm sure you're used to nicer digs than this. Maybe you'll find yourself a nice Airbnb."

His grin widens. "Doubt it. I took a leave of absence from my job to volunteer for my dad. Not hurting for money, exactly, but it would burn me up to spend a lot of cash while I'm here. And I'm not a picky guy. Even if it's a disaster upstairs, I plan to give it a whirl."

"Fine. It's your funeral."

He chuckles. "You seem awfully eager to get rid of me. Can I ask why you offered to host me upstairs?"

Because I don't really have a choice?

And because it never occurred to me that a successful brewing executive would look anything like him. I'd expected a nerd in a suit. Not a muscular bad boy with ink showing at the V-neck of his T-shirt.

I don't feel like sharing either explanation with him, so I say between clenched teeth, "Just feeling neighborly."

His smile fades, and his intelligent brown eyes dart around my kitchen and living areas. "This place was a crumbling dump last time I was here. You must have spent some hours fixing it up, yeah?"

I shrug. He's right, but I don't really want to discuss it.

"My dad probably likes having you on the property," he says, rubbing his chin. "You're always at his beck and call that way."

"It's convenient," I grudgingly agree. "And it saves both of us money."

"I bet," he says. "Cheap place to live, and he probably pays you less as part of the deal, right?"

That's exactly right. I just nod.

"Huh. Wonder how the tax accountant feels about that." He frowns, and I quail inside. Then he pats the saddlebag over his arm. "Just gonna drop my bag upstairs. Back in a jif." He turns to head up the stairs on long legs.

I shouldn't notice how his ass does an admirable job of filling out his jeans, but I'm only human. He's the hottest man I've laid eyes on in years.

It's so unfair.

I sag into my chair and stare down at my salad. Why is God testing me like this? Why did he put a hot, snarky, motorcycle-riding bad boy in my path?

Stop whining. Just get on with it.

I cover my salad bowl and stow it in the refrigerator. Then I carefully wash my fork and put it away in the drawer.

Nash reappears about a minute later, a startled look on his face and a deli bag in his hand. "Was Dad fixing up that space to rent it out? It's spotless."

I just shrug.

"You could perform surgery up there. Even the bathroom sparkles. Is that your doing?"

"No," I lie. I don't like a mess. In my spare time, I've thrown away the old junk from upstairs and cleaned the whole place out.

"Huh. Just my good fortune, then." He sits down at my table as if he owns the place.

Which, I remind myself, he does.

"Listen up," I say in a futile attempt to regain some control over the situation. "You see this clean kitchen? It's going to stay that way. Tidy up after yourself. Every single time."

"Yes, ma'am," he says.

But men don't keep their word, so I drive the point home. "Any messes you leave on my table, you will later find on your pillow upstairs."

"Fair," he says with a shrug. "I'm not going to be all up in your space, okay? I just need somewhere to crash for six weeks. We'll both be counting down the days."

"Is Leila okay?" I ask.

Concern etches his features for a quick second before his handsome face smooths out again. "She will be," he says, pulling a sandwich out of his bag and unwrapping it.

"From now on you'll keep me up to date on her progress, and you'll let me know if there's anything I can do."

He pauses his sandwich on the way to his mouth. "You know, pussycat, for someone so hot, you have kind of a militant streak."

As soon as he says "hot," my stupid body reacts, and I imagine those hands on me instead of a hoagie sandwich. Old habits die hard, I guess.

But then I pull myself together. "I hear that a lot. And I'm not your *pussycat*."

"Meant it as a compliment." He takes a bite and chews thoughtfully. "Big eyes, big attitude."

"I didn't ask for compliments," I say coolly. "I will tolerate you for six weeks, because I have to. But there is nothing I want from you."

He chuckles. "Just keep telling yourself that."

I bristle.

"Now what's on the agenda this afternoon?" He takes another big bite, and I look away. No man should be attractive while stuffing his face. But miraculously, this one is.

I can't believe I have to share a roof with him. "Leila told me to introduce you to everyone who works in the brewhouse and get you up to speed. And then drag you off to see your father. Her words."

He winces. "I can handle the brewhouse tour by myself. I'll do it after I make sure there aren't any crumbs on the table, so you don't sneak upstairs in the night and murder me in my bunk..."

"Good plan."

"You'll have to fill me in on what my father expects when I visit. How hands-on has he been?"

"Very." I clear my throat. "First, he wants you to sneak samples into the care center. Leila couldn't get it done. But he can't stand the idea of bottling anything he hasn't personally tasted."

"Yeah, okay," he says thoughtfully. "I hear that. We'll just pack them into a briefcase or something."

"Leila says they're strict," I tell him. "She tried carrying a six-pack in, and they freaked right out."

He smiles again, and honestly I'm unprepared. The smile takes his face from handsome to blinding. "I love my sister, but she has a good-girl complex. Something tells me you and I are better at espionage."

I find myself smiling back at him, but I worry that his big, dark eyes see too much of me. How can he tell that I have a bad-girl streak that runs a mile wide?

Turning my back on him, I pick up my bag and prepare to begin my afternoon. "We'll get those samples to your dad first thing tomorrow morning."

"Sure."

"I'm going to run to the hardware store and make you a copy of the front-door key. I need you to keep this place locked up at all times. And I mean that literally. I have a zero-tolerance policy for leaving the door open."

"Yes, ma'am. That old button lock isn't much of a barrier, though. A thief could open it with a dirty look."

Like I don't know that? "Lock it anyway." And with that frosty statement, I take my leave.

CHAPTER 7
NASH

Interesting.

I watch Livia go, wondering what's got her so scared. Or *who* has her so scared. Locking the doors is a good life skill, and so is calling the cops on an intruder.

But the woman is seriously skittish. There's got to be more to the story than she's let on. And if she thinks she's hiding it, she's wrong.

Something's happened to her since that night at the bar. Something bad. And I mean to find out what.

———

But not right away, it seems. After lunch, I spend a lengthy afternoon in the brewhouse. That means introducing myself to the staff, and pitching in with the day's brewing work. The best way to earn everyone's trust is to strip down to my T-shirt and clean out the masher with the rest of them.

It's sweaty work, but I don't mind. Moving my body is good for the soul. And I know better than to jump in with a lot of opinions about the operation. These men are loyal to my father, and God only knows what that man says about me behind my back.

So I concentrate on enjoying the scent of yeast and barley in my nose, and the rhythmic pump of my muscles as I shovel another load of spent grain into a wheelbarrow.

As we work, I'm listening to Badger, the youngest brewer, tell a tale about last weekend. "So then she said, 'Let's go to my place,'" He pauses for dramatic effect. "And I think I'm getting lucky, right? But it turns out that when she said, 'I'll teach you how to play D&D,' she meant right then and all night."

The other guys guffaw, and I find myself chuckling.

The phone in my pocket vibrates with an incoming text. I break the rhythm of my work to see if there's any news about my sister.

But nope. It's another text from BrewCo. I've gotten a dozen of them so far today. I'm getting the sinking feeling that nobody at work knows what a *leave of absence* actually means.

"Any word on Leila?" Badger asks.

"Nope." I slip the phone in my pocket. "Want me to dump out the wheelbarrow?"

"Roger's turn," Badger says, his cheeks flushed from exertion. "I'll get the hose, and we'll mash in a new batch of Meadow Gold —the spring special."

Roger takes the wheelbarrow away, and I take a moment to glance around the brewhouse. These guys are working hard enough, I guess, but half the brew tanks are empty. It wasn't lost on me that Livia had been the only person in the building when I arrived this morning.

A well-run brew cycle starts early, and I suspect the guys have been slacking while my dad is away. So that's something I'll need to address.

It's not the only thing I'm noticing about this place, either. All this manual labor is good for my soul, but it's not very good for the bottom line. I can't believe that Dad's brewing process hasn't been updated in thirty years. It boggles the mind. The mash is manually heated to the optimal temperature. Tanks are monitored with old-school thermometers. Spent grain is shoveled out of the masher by the brewers.

What a colossal waste of time. I'm surprised they're not filling the hot liquor tank with an old-fashioned handpump and working by candlelight.

"Hey, Badger?" I casually inquire of the chatty brewer with the quick smile and sleepy eyes. He's worked here for five years and seems to know more than anyone. "How come so many of the tanks are standing empty?"

He shrugs. "Ask your sister. She was supposed to tell us what to make next."

"Huh. Right." There's no way I'm bothering Leila right now, but it seems like she's been more overwhelmed than I realized. "I think I'll take an inventory and plot out a brewing schedule for myself. If I have questions, you'll help, yeah?"

"'Course," he says with a friendly shrug.

Out of the corner of my eye, I spot my father's prickly assistant as she sashays down the main corridor.

"Yo! Livia!" I holler across the brewhouse before she can get too far.

She stops walking, turns slowly, and lifts her chin. There's a challenge in her eye. "Does your lordship require something of me, sire?"

Badger snorts.

"You got an extra notebook and a pen somewhere I could have?"

She turns around without another word to head back toward the office.

Badger is explaining another of my dad's outdated brewing procedures, when Livia reappears a few minutes later. She's carrying a brand-new notebook and three pens that she brandishes like weapons. "Pick your poison," she says, trying to avoid my eyes.

I don't let her. I don't look at the pens. I trap her gaze and we have ourselves a little staring contest—my cynical eyes locked onto her prettier ones.

And as a faint blush paints her cheeks, I win the contest easily. Her gaze slides away, nervous about what I might see in it.

I take a pen from her hand. "Ooh, a G2. I knew I liked you. Thanks, pussycat."

She gives me a final, chilly glance and stalks away. And I admire the sway of her ass as it disappears into the hallway again.

"Why does she look like she wants to either kill you or bang you?" Badger asks.

"Don't limit her options. Could be both at the same time," I point out, clicking the pen.

He laughs. "Just don't do anything to piss her off, dude. She practically runs this place."

"Noted." Can't help it that she's attracted to me, though. It's nobody's fault. Women often find me irresistible.

"Let's show you the bottling line," Badger says. "Needs some maintenance. It's kinda behind the times."

I hold back a sigh. Then I follow him over there.

———

When the workday ends, I invite the brew team out for beers and pizza at the Gin Mill in Colebury. Then I pay everyone's tab. Not only does this win me some much-needed goodwill among the brew staff, but it keeps me out of Livia's hair for a few hours. She needs to get used to the idea of sharing her space with me.

"Can I get one more pizza to go?" I ask the guy behind the bar at the Gin Mill. "And I'll close out the tab."

"Sure, man."

I choose a margherita pie, because I don't know what Livia likes. And while I'm waiting for the order, I text Matteo Rossi.

Any news?

MATTEO

Labor induced! We're counting contractions and
watching TV. Baby will probably arrive tomorrow.

Need anything?

Thanks, but your mother is buzzing around
making sure we've got everything we need. She
says hi BTW.

Good to hear! I'll be thinking about you guys.
Give Leila my love.

He returns a thumbs up.

I sip my beer, mentally sending good vibes to my sister. It's
hard to wrap my head around the fact that tomorrow there'll be
someone in the world who calls her Mommy. It's almost like we're
supposed to be grownups now.

Although *Uncle Nash* has a nice ring to it, I suppose.

I finish my beer and listen to the soundtrack of bar chatter and
music. And I can't help but think about Livia and our flirtation in
the bar next door. Even now, in spite of the disappointing
outcome, the memory makes me smile.

I feel unsettled about our interaction today, though. And not
because she called the cops. I'm over that already.

But Livia seems so different from the first time we met. She's
wary. There's fear behind her brown eyes.

Fear of what, though?

"Here you go—one margherita pizza and the check," the
bartender says.

After leaving him a nice tip, I head back out to my ride. It's a
cool spring evening, and I can hear the peeper frogs singing as I
secure the pizza on the back of my bike and then swing my leg
over the seat.

I fire up the engine and head out. The country road opens up
before me, and I can admit that it's more fun to ride my bike here
than in Boston. Vermont has its moments.

But I still don't belong here.

CHAPTER 8
LIVIA

At nine o'clock Nash knocks on the door, after I'd half convinced myself that he'd changed his mind and gone to a hotel.

From my spot at the stove, it's only a couple paces to the door. So I twist open the knob and then go right back to ladling chili into clean deli containers.

Or I try to, anyway. But Nash is a difficult man to ignore. He's a big person, and magnetic in a way that I can't really explain. The kitchen feels really small all of a sudden.

And hot. It feels hot. I could blame the chili, but the truth is more like a hormone rush. This man just does things to me. It's those flashing brown eyes, and those square shoulders.

I wish he'd turn around and walk back out again. I don't need this in my life, and it makes me grumpy.

"You cook?" he asks by way of greeting. "Smells good."

God! Men. I turn down my Kelsea Ballerini playlist and tell him how it is. "Look, I cook so I can eat. It's cheaper than buying pizza." I point at the cardboard square in his hand. "If you're still hungry you can help yourself, I guess. But go easy, because this has to feed me for a week."

He blinks. "That was just a compliment, pussycat. And this is for you." He sets the box onto the table. "Didn't go crazy on the toppings, because I don't know what you like. I know it's a little late, but I treated the brewers tonight, and thought I'd bring you something so you wouldn't miss out. Could make a nice lunch for you tomorrow."

"*Oh*," I say, as my cheeks burn brightly with embarrassment. "Thank you. That wasn't necessary."

He grins. "You're welcome. I'm not going to eat all your food, lady. But when I get sick of takeout, I might ask to borrow your skillet, if that's okay."

"No problem," I say quickly. "As long as you're not one of those men who doesn't know how to do dishes. And did you lock the door?"

He turns his back on me and clicks the button into place. "There we go. Sorry I forgot. Crappy lock there, too."

"It's all I've got. Not my door to upgrade."

"Okay. We'll work on it," he says.

I look up from my ladle. "We will?"

He shrugs. "You seem a little jumpy. Figure you have a reason. And the lock is a real POS."

I don't know what to do with that. "Thank you for the pizza. The Gin Mill does nice work."

"Don't they? Didn't want to leave you out, but I was after some bonding time with the brew boys. Need them to trust me so they'll answer all my questions."

"Yeah, I get that." I put the lid on the last serving of chili. "I don't go out to bars, anyway. You're visiting your dad tomorrow, right?"

"Right," he says in a grudging voice. "I'm going to need you to go with me."

"Me? Why?"

"Leila says he likes you." He takes off his leather jacket, and I hate myself a little for admiring the shape of his body beneath a clinging waffle-weave shirt. "And I need him all calm and reasonable, two qualities he usually lacks whenever I'm around."

Interesting. "All right. Remember that you need to bring him some samples."

"I know. Gotta sneak those in. Do you have a big purse or something?"

"Sure. No problem."

He gives me a hot smile. "Thanks. I'll be upstairs, questioning all my life choices." He turns toward the stairs. "And I'll be up there all alone." He stops, one hand on the banister. "Unless you had a mind to visit me."

"I do not," I say a little too quickly. "Not, uh, at this time."

He actually laughs. "Let me know if you decide to fit me into your busy schedule. You know you want to."

Heat climbs up my neck, because he's right. My attraction to him burns brightly. But it was a bad idea back in November, and it's a much worse idea now. "I'll keep you in mind."

"You do that, pussycat." He climbs the stairs, still smiling. "Nightie night."

Not two minutes later, I hear the song "Call Me Maybe" playing upstairs. Loudly.

And I have to laugh as I put my chili away. I'm a sucker for a man with a sense of humor.

His music gets quiet after that, and I hear the sound of the upstairs shower running.

As I settle myself in for the night, I try not to picture water sluicing down his inked body. And I try not to wonder what he looks like wearing nothing but a towel.

I get into bed and check social media. Some women use Instagram to follow celebrities. I use it to keep tabs on a motorcycle club that's trying to kill me. Two of the members' girlfriends post a lot of pictures, and every time I see my ex in one of them, I feel nauseated.

But it's useful information. Tonight, I copy the links to some photos and share them with Jennie.

Do any of these guys look like the scary dude
who came to your house?

If someone is hunting me, I'd like to know who.

Then I text my brother to feel out whether he's had any violent visitors to the front porch of the house he shares with some other guys in Winooski.

Hey Brady. Everything good with you this week?

He replies immediately. And when I read what he says, I roll my eyes.

BRADY

I could use $100. I'm out of groceries.

Hell. That's what I get for vague-texting.

Something happen to your paycheck?

I quit the grocery store. Manager was an asshole.
I don't have time for that kind of negativity in my
life.

My brother, ladies and gentlemen. Too good for this world. Or at least too good to work in it.

Next week I'll fill out some more applications.
But I'm down to a couple cans of soup. Can you
help me out?

God. He really needs to learn how to adult. But I hate to think of him going hungry. We've *been* hungry, and it isn't fun.

I'll send you a check tomorrow.

You're the best sister I ever had!

That joke has gotten old, seeing as I'm the only sister he's ever had. So I roll my eyes and put down my phone. I shut out the light, and roll onto my side. And I find myself holding my breath, just listening.

The house feels different with someone else in it. The ceiling creaks occasionally under the weight of Nash's footfalls upstairs. That ought to make me feel unsettled, but it doesn't. Most nights I'm alone on the property, hyper vigilant every time I hear an engine on the road. Some nights I feel like the last woman alive.

Tonight feels entirely different. I curl up, listening to the low, unintelligible male voice upstairs on the phone. And I wonder who he's talking to.

But it doesn't matter. For once, I'm not completely alone. You won't hear me admitting it out loud, but it eases me. Not that it makes any sense at all, but I feel more at peace than I have in a long time.

Maybe I'm just exhausted from all the upheaval in my life.

That must be it.

I close my eyes and try not to dream of hunky tattooed men with slow smiles.

———

I wake early the next morning and listen, as always. The birds are at it again outside my window. Otherwise, the house is silent.

Just in case Nash is an early riser, I carry my clothes into the downstairs bathroom. There's another one upstairs for him, luckily.

I'm already dressed and putting on my face by the time I hear his footfalls on the stairs. Although he stops halfway down. "Knock knock. Everybody decent? Not that it's a problem if you're naked."

Poking my head out of the bathroom, I roll my eyes. "Coast is clear."

"Unfortunate," he says, striding the rest of the way down the stairs. "I slept surprisingly well, thanks for asking."

"We're all relieved," I mumble, wondering if I'm supposed to offer him breakfast. That's what a nice girl would do.

Too bad I'm not a nice girl.

"Gotta love this commute across the parking lot," he says cheerfully. "See you over there."

"Right. What time do you want to see your father? I thought we'd leave here at ten."

"Works for me." He turns toward the door.

"Hey, Nash?"

He swivels back toward me, surprise in his expression. "Yeah?"

"Did you hear any news from Leila about the baby?"

He shakes his head. "Last night I spoke to Matteo, and he told me that Leila was receiving IV drugs to induce labor. But it could take a whole day."

"Wow, okay." I send out a silent prayer of strength for Leila.

"I texted both her and Matteo fifteen minutes ago, asking how they're doing. No response, though."

"I'm sure everything's fine," I say quickly.

"Yeah. Of course." He gives a quick nod and then leaves the pumphouse, taking care to depress the button lock before he shuts the door.

I sit down at my breakfast table alone. The way it's supposed to be.

CHAPTER 9
NASH

After a quick cup of coffee from the brewery's breakroom, I set myself up to do an inventory. That means carrying a clipboard into the malt room to tally up the supplies.

Like the rest of the mill, the malt room has high ceilings and old wooden floors. Antique soda lamps hanging from the rafters cast a soft glow, and the place smells *divine*. Like toasty grain and magic.

Gun to my head, I'd admit that the Boston brewery where I work lacks charm. At BrewCo, the storage room is a nondescript, climate-controlled cinderblock warehouse. The grain comes off tanker cars and moves through the brewery via a system of chutes and hoppers, never touched by human hands.

It's soulless, my father likes to say. *Shouldn't even call it beer*.

That's exactly why I don't come home very often. There's more than one way to make beer, and he likes his with extra judgment in the glass.

It still stings, though. When I was a young man, I thought my father and I would work side by side. He'd claimed to want me to join the family business, and I'd believed him. With his blessing—not to mention financial assistance—I got a business degree with the goal of adding more firepower to our combined skill set.

Those were the early days of the Giltmaker Brewery. My father hadn't hit the big time yet, but I believed in him.

Unfortunately, he didn't have the same belief in me. It only took me a few months after college graduation to realize that he'd never see me as an adult. He'd never accept me as an equal. Our partnership was doomed from the start. He hated all my ideas. He belittled my efforts.

But I didn't give up entirely until the day we had a horrible fight right in the middle of the brewery. He *fired me* in front of the staff. Most embarrassing moment of my life.

Later, he claimed he didn't mean it. But the damage was done. I took the first brewery job I was offered, and I didn't look back.

Or I tried not to anyway. But then my father surprised us all— including himself—when, seemingly overnight, Goldenpour became an outrageous success. One week my dad was just another small Vermont brewer, and then *Beer Magazine* gave Goldenpour the first perfect score they'd ever awarded to a beer. There's a plaque in the brewhouse with the score gilded onto it. *100*.

That's when the crowds started to show up. From my desk in Boston, I saw photographs of the line out the door—beer tourists queued up by the hundreds for the chance to buy a four-pack of the world's most esteemed New England Ale.

Fast forward a few years, and Dad's beers haven't just won awards—they've won *all* the awards. This building makes some of the most vaunted beers in American brewing. If I'd stayed on, I might have been a full partner in the brewery.

If only my father had let me.

After all these years, it's hard to acknowledge that I was once in love with the family brewery, before our painful breakup. Coming back home is like a visit to The One Who Got Away. Only it's not a girl, it's a job.

That's why I was so hesitant to come back and help out, even in a time of crisis. But here I am, clicking the button on my pen and counting up the bags of grain and hops. Trying not to feel sentimental about this place.

And every ten minutes or so I pull out my phone and stare at my texts. BrewCo employees seem to text me every ten minutes, but the text thread with my sister and Matteo remains silent.

Any sign of the baby? Everyone okay?

No response. Maybe they're resting.

Or maybe something terrible has happened, and they're rushing Leila into surgery.

Thanks, brain. Thanks a lot.

With a grunt of frustration, I stow my phone and go back to work. It's hard to count bags of malt when you're worrying about your sister.

After finishing in the grain room, I head over to the storage area. It's not as atmospheric, because most of our products have to be kept refrigerated. To accommodate plenty of chilled beer, dad built a state-of-the-art cold room between the loading dock and the tasting room.

It's forty-two degrees Fahrenheit in here, so my clipboard practically freezes to my hand as I write down how much of every kind of beer we've got in stock.

The answers are frankly troubling. How could we be so low on inventory when half the tanks are standing empty? I head back to the brewhouse to get some answers.

"Hey, Badger?" I have to call out to him a few times before he hears me over the sound of the water sprayer he's using to clean out the masher.

The water finally cuts off, and he turns around. "Yeah, Nash? Something wrong?"

I hold up the clipboard. "Just doing a little inventory. Do you know why we're so low on Goldenpour?"

"Yeah," he says slowly. "Because your dad makes that one."

"By himself?"

He nods, and his expression seems to imply that I might be a little slow on the uptake.

"Okay," I say, "but could you make it if I asked you to?"

"Well, sure," he says with a shrug. "I'd need the recipe."

"Of course. Let me double check the ingredients and maybe we'll start a batch later today, all right?"

He gives me a curious look before nodding again and turning back to his work.

I head back to my father's office, working out the math in my head. I recall that Goldenpour is a twenty-two-day beer from mash to can. That's a *long* time. We're going to run out before then.

And my sister didn't notice? Poor girl must have been more overworked than I guessed.

When I walk into the office, Livia is up on the rolling ladder that slides the length of the floor-to-ceiling bookshelves. She's got one of Dad's many binders in her hands. This one says *Unpaid Invoices*.

"Hi," I say in greeting. "It's me again."

"Who else?" she murmurs without looking up from her page.

"Can you tell me which of these books has my father's recipes in it?"

"In a moment," she says, taking her time. She scans the page before making a careful note in the binder.

I hold back my sigh. I can't believe we're about to run out of Goldenpour. A smart business does not stall sales on their most lauded product.

Livia gets down off the ladder. After retrieving keys from her desk, she walks to the antique safe in the room's corner. She unlocks the old metal door and rifles through the safe's contents.

"Under lock and key?" I snort. "Really?"

"My idea," Livia says. "Sometimes we find the beer tourists wandering around this place, looking to snap a picture of the recipes. But also? Your father is paranoid." She pulls a set of folders out. "And that man won't digitize *anything*. One fire is all it would take to destroy forty years of records."

"Ah. Interesting." All elite breweries try to keep their recipes a secret. But you can't really lock away a recipe—it lives in the minds of the employees.

She passes me the folders, and I quickly flip through them. There are eight beers that I recognize and another eight that might have been seasonal one-offs or perhaps ideas that my father has yet to produce. There's one huge problem. "Where's Goldenpour?"

Livia snorts. "You're kidding, right?"

"No. Why?"

She lifts her flashing dark eyes to mine. "He doesn't share that one."

I blink. "No kidding. Trade secret. But I need to see it in order to brew."

"You don't understand," she says quietly. "He doesn't share it with anyone. Not even Badger. Why else would we be running so low?"

"With *anyone*," I repeat slowly. "Literally anyone? That's *crazy*."

She throws her arms out to the sides, as if to agree with me. And I'm even too stunned to admire her cleavage.

It's like my father *wants* to go out of business. "Huh. I guess I know what he and I will be discussing later this morning. But before that, I need to look at ordering supplies. Can you show me an inventory sheet from before he got sick? So I can duplicate it?"

Wordlessly, she moves the ladder to another location on the wall of binders and climbs up again.

I can see how this is going to go. Even if Livia would rather push me off a cliff than help me, she literally holds the keys to running this business, and I'll have to figure out how to work with her.

She pulls down an unlabeled binder from the center shelf. "Here. This is the one you need."

"How could you tell?"

"Because I work here." She tosses me the book, while I try not to admire the creamy V of skin above the top button of her blouse. "It's chaos, but familiar chaos."

"Like it would kill my father to use a spreadsheet?"

She gives me a catlike smile. "It might, according to him." With an elegant leap off the ladder, she plucks a sticky note off her desk and slaps it onto the binder I'm holding. "Although I already did the math. Your next malt order should probably look something like this."

I squint at the note. The handwriting is so small and precise that I wonder if robots printed it. But the list contains varying quantities of three different hops, three different malts, and several canning products.

When I scrutinize my own inventory and mentally compare it to the one in the binder, I can already tell that my shopping list will look a lot like hers. Almost exactly. "Livia? Do you usually do the ordering?"

She shakes her head. "Never once."

"Then how do you know what we need?"

A shrug. "I'm observant. But go ahead and do the math yourself, if you'd rather. Aren't we leaving soon to see your dad?"

"Yeah." I'm still staring at the sticky note. "You have a lot more of the Californian hops on here than the Idaho."

"That's because I'm inferring that you'll need the Californian for Goldenpour. But only your father really knows." She gives me a smug little smile. "Now go pull samples for the old man. Can't wait to watch you try to convince him to give up the recipe."

"All right, all right." I stuff the sticky note in my pocket. "Let me get some jars out of the tasting room."

"No sir." She frowns at me. "They'll clink together in my bag, and the nurses will escort us off the property." She points at my father's desk. "Use those plastic snack cups and label them with that Sharpie."

I eye the containers. She has a point, except for one problem.

"Dad can't stand the scent of plastic in his nose while he tastes," I say quietly. "Your idea is great, though."

Livia's shoulders sag. "Dude, don't patronize me. I didn't consider the plastic issue." She lifts her chin and taps it slowly. "Fine. Clearly, we have to be a little more creative."

Then she turns on her heel and heads for the door.

"What did you have in mind?" I ask as she passes me.

"You'll see. I'll be back in fifteen."

CHAPTER 10
NASH

An hour later we're striding side by side into the Serenity Hills Nursing Care Center. I've got a four-pack of organic kombucha in my hand. At least, it looks like kombucha.

Livia bought the stuff at the food coop, and then she and I poured three of them down the sink. After thoroughly washing the bottles, we refilled them with beer and used the brewery's bottling equipment to put new caps on them.

The fourth bottle is still kombucha, just in case we're stopped and frisked. That detail smacks of overkill to me, but Livia has big opinions about pretty much everything, and I'm just trying to roll with it.

"This place is pretty nice," I point out as we cross the lobby. The atrium is sunny, and the front desk has been fashioned from upcycled barn wood. I see signs for a therapy pool, a yoga studio, and a meditation room. "I've stayed worse places."

"You'd think it was a Siberian prison camp for how he talks about it," she says quietly. "Your father does not practice gratitude."

"No," I agree. "He does not."

Livia leads me down a bright hallway to room 109. She taps on the door before pushing it open, and I try to make my face pleasant as I mentally brace for seeing my father.

"You're late," he says immediately, scowling at us from an easy chair. "I thought you said ten."

"Is that the way you greet your family?" asks a sour-looking nurse who's taking his pulse.

Great question, lady. "Hi, Dad. Sorry to make you wait."

He grimaces. Then he gives the IV pole beside him an evil look. "Guess it doesn't really matter, does it? I'm trapped here in this building all day."

It's true. After heart surgery, my father had an infectious reaction to his stent. The course of treatment is a grueling six-weeks of intravenous antibiotics, administered four times a day around the clock. That's why he's stuck here.

The nurse finishes checking the IV and turns around. Her name tag says *Alice*. I watch as she fixes her gaze on the four-pack in my hand. "What do you have there? We don't allow any alcohol or sugar sodas."

"Oh, I would *never*," I gasp. "This is kombucha. It's terrific for the gut biome. It will build him back up like that." I snap my fingers.

"It had better," Alice says. "I don't know how much more I can take." Then she marches out of the room.

Yikes.

"Making friends again?" Livia asks my dad. "Kinda risky being rude to the people with the needles."

"She started it," he grumbles. "Nash, close the door."

God, his tone. I close the door, but I do it with gritted teeth. It's stupid, but I spent my whole adult life wishing my father were happier to see me. I shouldn't even care, but I don't know how to stop.

He lifts his chin and looks me straight in the eye. "Never get old," he says. "It's a trash fire."

This asshole. It's no one's fault but his that he had an untreated heart condition. And now the man wants a pity party? He'd have to be nicer first.

"I'm looking forward to getting old," I say. "It really beats the alternatives."

My father raises a hand and beckons like a king on his throne. "All right. Let's taste."

I want to throw the bottles at him, but Livia explodes first.

"For fuck's sake, Lyle. Say a proper hello to your son. He brought you three beers to taste. And more importantly, he left a good job to come up here and help out. If you don't fake a little gratitude, he's going to hightail it back down highway 89, and you won't see him again until the holidays."

The room fills with a stunned silence, and I practically swallow my tongue. And then I nearly swallow it again when my father turns to me with a contrite expression.

"It's good to see you Nash. I appreciate you bringing in those samples. Your sister couldn't figure out how to do that. She got busted on her second attempt. Scared her silly."

Figures he'd throw my sister under the bus while paying me a compliment. But I let it slide. "I always enjoy a good caper. Especially since it was all Livia's idea. Are you sure you even need me in Vermont? Livia seems to run the place already."

"I'm not a brewer," she says, waving a hand at the four-pack. "I know how to keep the books clean, but not the beer tanks. And, unlike you freaks, I don't have the nose for it. All beer tastes about the same to me."

My father rolls his eyes. "I used to think she only said that to wound me. But we gave her some blind taste tests, and it did not go well. It's her only real flaw. That and her bitchy mouth."

"Hey—that's a feature, not a bug." She pulls a beer opener out of her pocket. "Now are you going to taste this stuff, or what? I've got a full day planned."

"Yes, ma'am."

Yes, ma'am? Wow. If Livia got my father to perform a musical number and a tap dance, I'd only be marginally surprised.

I take one of the beers out of the pack and remove the top with the church key. "Here, Dad. This one is—"

"Don't tell me."

I sigh.

He sniffs. "Meadow Gold. Day four?"

"Uh, yeah." I guess that's how it goes when you devote your entire life to the pursuit of the finest craft beer in America.

"Let's see." He tastes. "Okay. Yeah. Has a decent body already. Yeast seems happy. Malt character is solid. No hints of diacetyl, but keep an eye out for that."

"Of course." Avoiding off-flavors is, like, day one of brewing school.

"I guess things aren't a total train wreck, then." He hands the bottle back to me. "Let's have another one."

He tastes the other two beers and doesn't find much to bitch about. So that's something.

I pull out my clipboard. "Now we've got to discuss Goldenpour. Look at this—there's nothing left to ship. Even serving it in the tasting room is going to tap us out after a few more weeks. Did you know that?"

My father's face falls. "I'm the only one who brews Goldenpour."

"Heard that this morning," I tell him. "So if you ever get run over by a bus—" *Or die from an untreated heart condition.* "—the beer dies with you? Is that the plan?"

He gives his head a stubborn shake. "My lawyer has a copy of the recipe. Sealed. Your mother inherits if I croak."

I blink. "Okay. Well. You've thought this through some, yeah? But I still don't get it. What do you think is going to happen to the brewery if nobody can mash in the beer before you're out of here?"

He looks down at his hands, and I'm startled by how old they look. "Your sister didn't want to learn to brew, and I thought they'd parole me by now. The infection is all cleared up."

"That's not how antibiotics work," Livia mutters. "Nobody listens when I talk."

"Okay, okay," my father says. "How about this? I'll call you up and tell you the grain bill. You can mash it in. Then I'll call Badger and give him the hops formula. Bob can monitor the fermentation…"

"Yeah, okay," I say, following along. "I think I understand. If it's a team effort, no single person knows the whole recipe."

My father snaps his fingers. "Exactly."

"Right." I rise from the windowsill where I'd perched myself. "Then good luck with the rest of your life. I'm out."

"What?" His eyes practically bug out. "Why?"

"Because that's *idiotic*," I snarl. "Either you trust me, or you don't. End of."

His face reddens with anger. "This is *not* about trust."

"Christ." My laughter is bitter. "How can you say that with a straight face?"

"Boys," Livia warns. "Take it down a notch."

But my father doesn't know how. "Now listen, son. You're employed by one of the biggest breweries in the world," he sputters. "Big companies exist to use people up and spit 'em out. Hell, the terms of your employment probably require you to share any and all pertinent knowledge—"

"Bullshit!" I holler. "Everyone at BrewCo knows who I am, and who *you* are. And I have *never* been asked about your product. Not once."

He opens his mouth to argue, but I'm not done. "I'm thirty-four years old, but you've always treated me like a child. We could have discussed this like adults. You could have said, 'Nash, I'm in a bind. Let's talk about a thorny question of intellectual property.' But you didn't do that. You just treated me like a hostile witness. And the worst part is that you don't even realize how fucked up that is."

Having said my piece, I leave the room.

CHAPTER 11
LIVIA

Lyle doesn't say anything until the door clicks shut on his son. And then he lets fly a string of curses. "That boy just storms out! He never listens!"

"Who could?" I shout back. "You straight up told him you don't trust him with the family recipe. What kind of loving message does *that* send?" I grab the three beer bottles we opened and carry them over to the sink, where I pour them out and rinse them.

Lyle just stews in his chair, hamstrung by the IV tube, resentment rising off him like mist.

I count to one hundred in my head.

If a job interviewer asked me to describe my greatest skill, I'd tell him that I'm a kickass bookkeeper. The best of the best. And that's the truth.

But I have another superb skill, one that I keep to myself. I am the world's foremost expert on Man Moods ™. It's a survival skill I honed out of necessity over a lifetime of dealing with difficult men.

And by difficult, I mean unreasonable. It's a skill I've needed since birth. Difficult men are everywhere. One of them is glaring at me right now.

Lyle Giltmaker is an interesting case. He's a rare breed of yeller. He's not proud of his anger, and he appreciates being contained. That's why I've learned to push back with him.

"Look," I say firmly. "If you want the brewery to go tits up in the next six weeks, that's your choice. But give me and the rest of the employees a heads-up so we can find another job." I put the bottles back into their carrying case with three angry plunks.

"You done?" he growls.

"Depends." I sweep my bag off a chair and nail him with a stare. "Are you gonna make this right?"

His expression turns sheepish. "Tell Nash I'll call him tomorrow with an ingredient list. And then after the delivery arrives, we'll reconvene another morning. He can put on those damn earphones everybody wears these days, and we'll brew a batch together on the phone before anyone else shows up."

I pause by the door. "That actually sounds like a fine solution, if only you'd said so ten minutes ago. Nash will probably be halfway to Boston by lunch time. Who could blame him?"

"Fuck." He tips his head back against the chair. "He's a hothead, too. That's why we don't work together. Will you talk to him? Try to talk him off the ledge?"

Like it's my job to solve the Giltmaker family drama? Then again, I don't want to be unemployed. "You'll owe me. Big time."

He gives me a grouchy look, but we both know he needs me. Lyle is recently divorced. His wife left him a year or so ago, and I suspect that Mrs. Giltmaker used to be the one who knew when to rein him in. The men in the brewery don't. Some are too afraid of him, and some simply don't care if he acts like a toddler.

His daughter claps back, though. I've seen Leila in action. Watching her is how I learned to handle Lyle. "I will give Nash your message. It might not be too late."

"Thank you," he says, giving me a wobbly nod. He's a proud man, but a tired one. There are dark smudges underneath both eyes. You can just tell that he isn't healthy. Not yet.

"See you soon," I add quietly. "Ping me if you need anything. Anything reasonable, that is."

He snorts. I exit the building and find Nash leaning against my car and scowling.

Behold: grumpy male, exhibit number eleventy billion.

I slow my roll, taking a moment to study him. Maybe I've learned to handle Lyle, but that doesn't mean his son isn't dangerous. There's so much tension in that strong body. I don't know Nash well enough yet to know whether his frustration will boil over and splash me.

There's a dark energy rising off him as I approach the car. When he spots me, he straightens up and smooths his expression. "Could I drive?" he asks tightly.

No, my senses scream. It's not safe to get in a car with a driver in a rage. Plus, my car is a heap of junk. He won't enjoy the driving experience, and it might make him even angrier.

But this man and I have to share a roof. I've already pissed him off twice—first by rejecting him and then by calling the cops on him. How many more times can I emasculate him and live to tell about it?

So I do that thing that women have been doing for centuries. I weigh one danger against another. And then I hand over the keys.

"Thank you," he says gruffly.

Wordlessly, I climb into the passenger seat. I know better than to get chatty with an angry man, so I clip my seatbelt into place and wait.

He starts the car and warms up the engine. He frowns at the indicator lights, and my pulse jumps when I remember that I'm almost out of gas.

Shit. My ex would backhand me for that. No question. As a reflex, I grip the door handle and prepare to duck the slap.

But Nash is already backing my car out of the parking spot. Then he looks both ways before pulling carefully through the parking lot and then out into the flow of traffic.

Okay. Well. I start to relax. A little, anyway. You don't get to be a world-class reader of men's moods by letting your guard down.

Everybody knows that driving can soothe a person's soul. It's that illusion of control. Like you don't actually have to drive back to your shitty job or your scary home. You could just keep on rolling if you needed to.

I'm hoping it soothes Nash. But instead of flooring it on the open road, he turns into a little country store and parks in front of their ancient gas pump.

When I check the price of gas, I have to hold back my sigh. Twenty cents higher than at a chain? That's robbery. Nonetheless, I reach for my seatbelt the moment the car comes to a stop. "I'll pump it." I'll stop at half a tank and finish the job somewhere else.

"Sit," Nash barks, giving me a macho frown.

My hands freeze on the seatbelt buckle.

"Arliss has it."

Who? But I'm smart enough to keep my trap shut as Nash undoes his own seatbelt and gets out of the car.

That's when I notice the FULL SERVICE sign on the pump. I didn't even know that was still a thing. And sure enough, a guy about ninety years old limps up to Nash, wearing a gap-toothed smile. They shake hands. Nash disappears into the store.

Okay. Whatever. I seethe as I calculate the cost of a full tank. The up-charge will only be three bucks, but I'm still going to resent the hell out of it, mostly because Nash didn't check with me first.

And then I notice that the old man is pumping premium gas, and I recalculate again, damn it. I'm getting all worked up into a Lady Mood ™ by the time the tank is full. Nash still hasn't emerged from the shop, which is really flipping convenient, because that leaves me to pay this man a tip, too. I pull out my credit card. But the old man limps back to the building without telling me my total.

Nash shows up a few minutes later carrying a bag. He stashes it in the backseat before reclaiming his spot behind the wheel. Then he starts the engine to let her warm up again.

"Um, I don't have cash," I admit. "You should have let me put it on my card."

"It's on me," he says, his voice a low, sexy scrape.

Ignoring the flutter in my lower belly, I ask, "What's in the bag? Because if you're already planning your escape back to Boston, there's something I need to tell you. Your father had a change of heart."

"About what?" Nash asks.

"Goldenpour. He wants to call you one morning after we order supplies. He'll give you the recipe for mashing in a batch. The whole recipe."

There's a grunt from the driver's seat.

"I basically threatened to quit if he was going to let the place go to hell."

Another grunt. "Okay."

Okay. What does that even mean in this context?

He puts the engine in gear. But then his phone chimes with a text. He puts the car into park again and pulls his phone out of his jacket pocket. "Sorry. Gotta know if it's Leila."

Something tight inside my chest loosens up by a fractional degree. "Of course."

He opens his phone and reads a text. Then he leans his head back suddenly and smiles at the ceiling of my crappy car.

"What?" I demand.

"Baby girl," he says. "Everyone healthy. Born right around the time my dad and I were shouting at each other."

A baby girl. I sit with that a second. I picture ten tiny fingers and two chubby little feet. "That's some good news right there."

"It is," he whispers. "And that's why I'm here, yeah? Not just to be Dad's punching bag. But to take Leila's mind off the business, so she can have her baby in peace. I gotta remember that."

He puts the car in gear and pulls out onto the road. There's a moment of silence, and I finally relax.

"Hey, I'm sorry," he says suddenly.

"For what?"

"I made you come to see my dad, because I thought he'd be less of an asshole, and then I'm the guy who stormed out. Didn't mean to put you in the middle of it all."

The apology stuns me into silence. I'm used to men's tantrums, but they *never* say they're sorry. "It's fine," I murmur. "No harm done."

He sighs.

"What's the deal with you two, anyway?" I hear myself ask.

He taps his thumbs on the wheel for a moment, thinking. "I worked for him for a few months after college, until we burst into a fireball. The last straw was when he humiliated me in the middle of the brewhouse. But even without the theatrics, I wouldn't have lasted in the job. He was never going to listen to me."

"Ouch."

"I've had my job at BrewCo for over ten years, and he never misses a chance to tell me how poorly he thinks of the company."

"I noticed that," I murmur.

"He can think whatever he wants, right? But it's just rude to put my job down all the time."

"True." We lapse into another thoughtful silence. And I realize I'm thinking about my pizza in the fridge and not worrying about Nash's anger anymore.

"Son of a biscuit," he says as the brewery comes into view. "The place is mobbed."

I check the time. "Yeah, that's normal. The tasting counter opens at two, but they get in line early. And aren't you on the schedule to help out in there today?"

"Yeah. But it's only twelve thirty!"

"You really haven't been around here much," I observe. "It's always like this. Only the first hundred customers are guaranteed a four-pack."

Nash shakes his head. "The grumpy old man got everything

he wanted, yeah? He's famous. You'd think they were giving away Taylor Swift tickets here."

I've had that same thought many times—about the concert tickets. But I'm not so sure Mr. Giltmaker got everything he always wanted. In fact, I know he didn't. To me, he seems like the loneliest man alive.

Nash grumbles under his breath as he navigates the busy parking lot. He pulls the car past the loading dock and parks beside the pumphouse.

"You should grab some lunch," I tell him as I climb out of the car. "The counter shift starts early, because you'll have to do some crowd control."

He tosses me my keys. "Eh, lunch can wait. Thought I'd top up your oil first."

"Come again?"

He pulls the bag from the backseat. He retrieves a bottle of motor oil and sets it on the hood. "Your car probably needs a complete oil change. But I'm in a hurry, and I don't have my tools. So I'll just top it up. Take me fifteen minutes."

I look at the bottle, trying to make sense of this. "You bought oil for my car? Why?"

He gives me a look like I might be stupid. "Because the oil light is on, pussycat. Figured drivin' it might be more fun if it didn't burst into flames."

"It wasn't going to *burst into flames*." I sound defensive, but I'm embarrassed. I've been too busy to learn basic car maintenance, and—I can't explain this to Nash—I'm afraid to take the car to a garage. Razor knows an unholy number of mechanics, and it's possible he has spies watching out for my vehicle.

Nash pops the hood and locates the dipstick. He pulls it out and squints at it. "You happen to have a funnel?" He snaps his fingers before I can tell him no. "Actually, never mind. I can use an empty plastic water bottle. I saw one on the floor of your car."

My humiliation complete, I retrieve the discarded bottle from the car and hand it to him. Then I unlock the pumphouse and go inside. In the kitchen, I take a bowl of chili out of the refrigerator and put it in the microwave with an inverted plate on top.

A few minutes later, I pop outside again. Nash has removed his motorcycle jacket and rolled up his sleeves. His forearms flex as he carefully adds oil to my engine. He stops whistling and turns his head suddenly, catching me staring. Slowly, his generous mouth forms a smile. "See something you like?"

"Thank you for doing that," I force myself to say. "I, uh, made you a bowl of chili."

His smile grows, and he chuckles lightly. "Aw, pussycat. It's almost like you like me." He recaps the empty oil bottle.

"I don't *like* you," I lie. "I'm just feeding you so you can show up and help out Connor in the tasting room. He's probably holding back the hordes on his own right now. And I don't work in the tasting room."

"How come?" After setting the empty oil bottle by an exterior trashcan, he follows me into my kitchen.

"Because I just don't. I'm an introvert. It's too people-y in there for me."

He frowns. "If you say so. Hey—doesn't this look great." After washing his hands, he sits down in front of the chili.

And it does look great. I've added shredded cheese and sour cream and a side of corn chips.

"You pulled out all the stops for me."

"Don't let it go to your head," I snip. "My chili is excellent, and it deserves to be served properly."

He picks up his spoon and grins. "Yeah, this is a hell of a good sign."

"For what?"

"That it's still happening between us. A woman doesn't make a meal like this for a guy she doesn't want to bang."

"This is thank-you chili!" I sputter. "It's not I-want-to-bang-you chili."

"Can't it be both?" He winks. "I can picture it."

"I can't," I lie.

"Need me to draw you an illustration?" he asks. "I'm handy with a sketchbook."

My younger self would sit right down and flirt with this man. I used to be a fun time, and I used to enjoy the company of men like Nash Giltmaker. But then I grew up and got smarter.

I pull the pizza he brought me last night out of the fridge, and I head for the door. "I'm going to eat lunch at my desk. There's work I need to do. Don't forget to lock up."

"Yes, ma'am." He gives me an appreciative glance before I go.

I still have the warm flutters. And it's *very* inconvenient.

CHAPTER 12
NASH

Livia wasn't kidding when she warned me about the hordes. By five minutes past two, the tasting room is slammed with customers, and the line is still out the door. They all want a tap beer to drink and a four-pack to take home. I'm pouring pints and making change, and I can't even see the back of the line.

Never mind making it another two weeks with our stock of Goldenpour. I wonder if we'll make it two hours.

It's absolutely too people-y in here. The girl did not lie.

The handy thing is that my dad's cold storage opens right into the tasting room. Every half hour or so, a brewer enters the walk-in from the brewhouse floor and moves the merchandise closer to where Connor and I can reach it.

It's a good thing I ate lunch, because the line never quits. I'd already known that Dad was successful. I'd seen pictures of the line wrapping around the building. But until today, I didn't really understand how fans *feel* about Goldenpour.

"Drove six hours to buy this," one man says, adjusting the fishing hat on his head.

"Yeah? Well, I drove *twelve*," someone pipes up behind him.

How about that, Dad? You're a rock star. That's why it's such a damn shame that you're too much of a grouch to enjoy it.

If I'd stayed in Vermont, I could have been a part of all this.

Then again, if I'd stayed, I might hate my life.

My father would make sure of it.

***

It's a long afternoon. I hope nobody expects me to do this four times a week—which is exactly how often the tasting room is open.

"You can leave the cleanup to me," Connor says after the door finally closes after the last customer. "Sure you have better things to do."

"Nah." I gather up the last of the dirty glasses. "Not gonna be that guy—the owner's son who can't wash a dish."

Connor chuckles. "Suit yourself. Nobody thinks of your family that way, though. Your dad rolls up his sleeves in the brewhouse every day. Cleans the tanks with the rest of us."

"That's not because he's humble. It's because he's a control freak."

Connor laughs, as if I were joking.

I'm not.

When every glass sparkles, I hang up my dish towel and see Connor off. The brewhouse is quiet, all the brewers having left for the day. There's a light still on in the office, though, so I head back there. Somehow, it doesn't surprise me that Livia is the first to arrive in the morning and the last to leave.

After stepping into the office, I don't immediately see her. Then I crane my neck and spot her high on the library ladder, holding an open cigar box. "Oh. There you are."

She startles violently, destabilizing her balance. She wisely chooses to grab the ladder to save herself, but this makes the box wobble, and suddenly it's raining cash. Tens and twenties flutter down from above, and she lets out a startled noise, something like "yeep!" And then "fuck a duck," a moment later.

I laugh. Who wouldn't? Then I start to gather the bills from the floor. "Wasn't trying to scare you. Awfully jumpy, aren't you?"

She growls and hurries down the ladder. "I can pick those up."

"I'm sure you can, but I'm a helpful kinda guy. Is this the petty cash? Wouldn't a bank deposit be a better idea?"

Livia hesitates. "The deposit is already in the safe. Connor brought it to me a half hour ago. It's locked up."

Huh. "Then what is all this?" I wave a stack of money at her.

"It's my money," she says quietly. "I keep it in a box on the top shelf. It's safe there. And today was payday."

I did hear two of the brewers talking about picking up their paychecks. "No automatic deposit for you?"

Guiltily, she shakes her head. "Your father pays me in cash. I can show you the ledger entry. And I can show you the math on the bank deposit. You can count it before I take the money to the bank tomorrow morning."

"I don't need to check your math," I say carefully. "Does everyone get paid in cash?" What a strange arrangement.

She shakes her head again. "Just me. By special agreement. I know it's weird. He doesn't check my math, either, which I think is awfully trusting. But I can't exactly tell him I think so. It would seem…"

"Guilty?" I try.

"Well, yeah. And you know he doesn't take advice very easily."

I snort. "He's an odd duck. Just tell me this—is he lucky to have you on his side?"

"Hell, yes," she says immediately. "I'm a fantastic bookkeeper. I caught a bunch of mistakes during my first month here. The last guy's work was garbage."

"All right. How about you put this away, then?" I hand her the stack of bills I'd collected off the floor. "Seems like the bank would be safer, though."

"I'll take it under advisement," she says in a voice that tells me she has no such plans. "He called, by the way."

"Hmm?" I'm busy admiring her cute ass in those jeans as she climbs the ladder again.

"Your father called. He had me read out the inventory, so you two can plot your order."

"Yeah, okay. And?"

"He asked me to put in an emergency order for hops. So I did. You'll have it in the next few days."

"Ah." I guess that makes sense. "Thought you were going to say he had second thoughts about trusting me with the recipe. And meanwhile, he's trusting you with all his material wealth."

She gives me a tiny smile. "I guess we won't know for sure until he actually shares the recipe with you, will we?"

"Nope. Guess not." I jam my hands in my pockets. "Want to go out for dinner? My treat. You fed me lunch."

"I…" A shadow passes over her face. "I can't. Sorry."

Hell. Shot down again. "It could be just a friendly meal." We have to work together. I can't let this be awkward. "Or I could even get us some takeout."

She perks up. "I could do takeout."

"Huh. Okay. What's good around here besides pizza."

"The burrito place in Colebury. Or the Skinny Pancake in Montpelier."

I can't understand why she's willing to eat takeout with me at a tiny kitchen table, but she won't go to a restaurant.

"Why the long face?" she demands. "You can pick something else if you want."

I shake my head. "It's not that. I'm just trying to figure you out, is all. You want my body, but you won't admit it. And you won't be seen with me in a restaurant…"

"That is not true!" she sputters. "I just…don't like going out. It's too people-y. I'm an introvert."

"You keep sayin' that. But you didn't seem so introverted that night at the bar," I point out.

Her face falls, and I want to kick myself for bringing it up.

That night still bothers me, though. It's not the sexual frustration, exactly. The missed opportunity feels bigger than that. She had a certain…presence. A *glow*. Not sure what to call it, but I could sense it all the way across the room. Whenever she laughed, she threw her head back. I wanted to hear that laugh up close. I wanted to know her, if only for a night.

She's watching me a little warily. "That night was…" She lapses into silence "It was almost special. But I couldn't take the risk."

"The risk," I repeat slowly. "Why?"

She gulps.

———

LIVIA

"I understand that a woman has to be careful," Nash says, his tone patient. "But you didn't even *meet* me. Didn't give me a real shot, did you?"

He's right. I didn't. Nash doesn't seem like an abuser, but Razor didn't either. Not at first. And once you make that mistake, you shouldn't ever make it again. "Look, I didn't think you were going to murder me. But a woman can never let her guard down."

He spreads his hands in a conciliatory manner. "If you'd asked me my name, you would have known that I have deep roots in this community. Just saying. Would've been nice."

He's got me there. But that's not the point. "I realize you knew half the people in the room, which helps. But in my case, it just didn't matter. I'd recently gotten out of a bad relationship. Really bad, okay?"

He has the good manners to wince.

"I've made so many bad decisions that I might not ever get out from under them," I explain. "And guess where I met my ex? In a bar. So even though you were cute and most likely harmless, and I was lonely as all hell, I couldn't do it. I couldn't go home with you. It felt too much like starting the whole cycle over again. I've made new rules for myself. They're very strict."

Oh God. I've said way too much. Empathy fills his big brown eyes. "That sounds rough, girlie. I'm sorry to hear that."

"Don't be." I step back behind my desk and gather up my things. "It's fine. I'm fine. It was just bad timing. We couldn't have our thing, and I didn't mean to disappoint you."

He chuckles softly. "I'm a big boy. I'll get over it. But I'll admit I was curious. Thought maybe one of the songs I chose was wrong. Or maybe you were intimidated by my obvious sexual prowess. Not everybody can handle my very big…" He clears his throat suggestively. "…personality."

I snicker in spite of myself.

"But I think you've got what it takes, Livia. You're a girl who likes a challenge. Good thing we're getting a second chance, yeah?"

"No," I say, grabbing my bag and my keys. "We're having takeout food together. We're not getting naked afterwards."

"Is that one of your rules?"

"Yup."

He tilts his handsome face, considering me. He doesn't look smug; he looks thoughtful.

"What if it's a sign?"

"A sign? Of what?"

He crosses his muscular arms. "Maybe we've met a second time because the first one didn't quite work out."

"You mean like…" I almost can't say it. "*Fate*? You're joking."

"Not joking." He shrugs. "Just seems like getting a second chance to know each other is a gift from the universe. We shouldn't turn it down."

I feel like I'm being punked. Inked bad boys don't believe in fate. "This is all very fascinating," I say, making a little shooing motion. "Now let's get out of here, before we both get hangry." I turn around and step past him, heading for the door.

He makes a low, sexy sound behind me.

"Are you ogling my ass?"

"Oh, absolutely. Since you asked, I was just imagining how it would feel in my hands. Is that also against your rules?"

"You know it is," I growl.

But I have the warm flutters again, damn it.

———

That night, we eat burritos together at the kitchen table, washing them down with some Corona and lime.

"Would your father break out in hives if he knew we were drinking an inexpensive mass-produced lager on his property?" I ask.

"Absolutely," Nash says with obvious glee. "That must be why it tastes so good."

I take another sip, and he isn't wrong. This feels surprisingly festive. Nash has a playlist going on his portable speaker again. The current song is "You Look Good" by Lady A. and I don't know if that's a coincidence or more flirting.

And I can't ask, because I'll sound like I'm fishing for compliments.

When I admitted to Nash that I was lonely, it was the truest thing I'd ever said. And I never blast music in this house, because it deafens me to outdoor noises, and I'm fearful that I'll miss something.

Even the simple pleasures of music were stolen from me when I ran away from Razor. But right now, I have food and beer and the company of a man who might—at the very least—behave as a deterrent to anyone who wanted to grab me and return me to Razor's clutches.

After dinner, Nash declares that he's going to shower and call his sister.

"Tell her congratulations from me!" I call as he heads for the stairs. "Can't wait to meet the baby."

"I will give her your love," he says, pausing. "But I hear they aren't accepting any visitors for a little while. Except for my mother. It's a germ thing."

"I get it."

"Would you, uh, help me find the right gift?" he asks. "I don't know anything about babies."

Ooh. I can think of nothing more fun. Shopping for babies is always a joy, but I can't pass up this opportunity to push back on Nash's assumptions. "Wait. You think a single woman just naturally knows what to buy for a baby? Like it's part of having two X chromosomes?"

He leans on the banister. "Well, yeah."

I snort.

"Livia." He fixes me with his hot, caramel gaze. "You made the pumphouse livable on zero budget. Pillows on the old couch. Bright dishes in the cabinet. Your clothes fit you like they were designed for your rockin' body. Your earrings match your top, two days in a row. Clearly you know a thing or two about shopping."

My breath catches. I can't believe he noticed the pillows. Plus, my earrings? And my thrift-store dishes?

He slowly smiles. "But never mind. I'll ask someone else for help," he says. "No big."

"No, I'll do it," I say quickly.

His grin widens.

We both know I can't wait to spend some of his money on a glorious baby gift. "I'll find something special. What's your budget?"

"Keep it under a grand," he says, and I hear him chuckling as he disappears upstairs.

CHAPTER 13
NASH

The baby gift Livia ordered with my credit card arrives a few days later as we're getting lunch on the table. At the sound of the truck's rumble, Livia slips into the corner beside the fridge.

"UPS," I explain, hating how her cheeks have paled and her smiling eyes have gone stark and wide.

Swear to God, I'm going to punish whoever frightened her like this. She hasn't shared more about her situation with me. But I see her expression change whenever strangers wander into the brewery's back lot.

Even now, she's carefully staying in the corner as I open up for the UPS guy and sign for the package.

As soon as he's gone, she pretends like nothing's happened, sliding into her chair and picking up her fork. Today, Livia has made us a chicken pasta salad with pesto dressing and blistered cherry tomatoes.

I never expected her to cook for me, but I'm not going to turn it down. And I've done my part by filling the refrigerator with groceries and cleaning up the kitchen to her exacting standards after every meal.

Back in my chair, I take a bite of my delicious lunch, and give her a nudge. "So... I bought the baby a blender?" That's what the photo on the outside of the box looks like. "It looks kinda cool, but I didn't know babies drank protein shakes."

She gives me an arch look that just makes me want to kiss her senseless. "It's not a blender. It's a European food processor that also cooks the food. Leila is really interested in eating organic. Six months from now, she'll be making all her own baby food in that." She points at the box. "I'm going to wrap it after lunch. You're welcome."

I give her a wink. "Thanks, pussycat."

She rolls her eyes.

This is our way now. We've gotten used to each other. Although Livia is careful to maintain the facade of being annoyed with my presence, in spite of all the hungry looks she throws my way when she thinks I'm not paying attention.

The energy between us burns a little brighter every day, even if she needs more time to be sure I'm not a threat. "This is really good," I say, taking another bite. "I get by in the kitchen, but you take it to a whole other level. When did you learn to cook?"

She gives me a thoughtful glance. "I've been cooking my whole life."

"Yeah? Big family tradition?"

Livia takes another bite, and for a moment, I think she won't respond. Then she says, "Sometimes when people ask about my family, they're not really prepared to hear the answer. My life has been complicated."

As if that's not a hundred percent obvious. "I'm not scared of you, lady."

She gives me a challenging glance. "Well, we didn't exactly have any family traditions. I never really knew my dad. He left before I turned two. And my mom, well... Sometimes I hear people say, 'She did the best she could.' And I suppose that's true of my mom. It's just that doing her best meant barely scraping by and resenting us for it."

This breaks my heart, but if I let it show, I know Livia will clam up. "She sounds fun."

Livia gives me a wry smile. "She was volatile and occasionally scary. She loved telling me that I was her biggest mistake. 'Can't get ahead now,' she'd say, a cigarette dangling from her mouth. 'Not with you kids in the way all the time. Now move your fat ass. I can't see the TV.'" Livia rolls her eyes, as if this is funny. "In a cage match between my mom and your dad, I'd put my money on my mother."

I chuckle uncomfortably. "Do you still talk to her?"

"Hell no. She left the state the minute Brady turned eighteen, and we haven't heard from her since. Neither of us was surprised. She made herself as scarce as possible as we grew up. When I was ten and Brady was nine, she quit her daytime job to work nights at a boyfriend's bar."

"Odd choice for a single mom," I point out.

"Definitely," Livia agrees. "We'd come home from school, and she'd show me what there was to eat and then leave for her shift. She told me to make sure that Brady had a bath and did his home-work. So that's what I did." She shrugs. "And when I got sick of eating canned soup, I taught myself to cook. Pasta with sauce came first, because the instructions were on the labels. Then scrambled eggs and toast, because I saw a soap-opera character prepare breakfast for her lover on TV."

"So educational."

She laughs. "Don't worry, I eventually discovered cooking shows. I couldn't get the same ingredients, but I really learned a lot. I wanted to go to culinary school, but Vermont only had one, and I couldn't afford it. So I chose bookkeeping instead."

"It's never too late," I point out.

She shakes her head. "I actually like working with numbers. And restaurant hours are terrible. If I ever got the chance to go back to school, I think I'd become an accountant. It's not sexy, but it's a good living."

"Oh, please. Like you couldn't make accounting sexy? You're halfway there already. A pencil skirt and some fuck-me heels. I'd want to do you on your desk. Just saying."

She puts her face in her hands and laughs. "Stop it. You have a one-track mind."

"Two tracks. Don't forget the beer."

There's nothing sexier than Livia laughing. She gets this exasperated expression on her face, like she doesn't know whether to kiss me or kill me. "Okay, fine—two tracks. Beer and women."

"Beer and *you*," I correct. "I'm picky. And you're the first woman who's made me this crazy in a really long time." I might as well just lay it out there. Gotta shoot my shot.

She sobers up immediately. "That's just because I said no. You're probably not used to hearing it."

I put down my fork. "Sorry, but you're wrong. First time I ever saw you smile, I said, 'I have to get to know her.' And, sure, it's only been a week, but everything I see of you I like. You're fierce. You make a mean chicken salad. You're smarter than most of the population, and you don't take any shit from anyone. Your body makes me hot, but your smiles make me hotter. And I spend a good portion of every day trying to figure out how I can get more of them. You understand?"

Her mouth parts with surprise, but she doesn't say anything.

"Think it over," I say, pushing back my chair. "I've got to go spend the last ten minutes of the lunch break with the brewers, so they don't have a chance to get stoned before we mash in another tank of Meadow Gold."

CHAPTER 14
LIVIA

After lunch, I'm so distracted that it takes me two tries to wrap Leila's baby gift in pink paper.

The baby's name is Reina, for "queen," which is what Matteo calls Leila as a pet name. I've always found it incredibly romantic. I've met Matteo on several occasions, and I think the world of him.

It's funny how I trust Matteo to be an excellent partner to Leila, and an excellent father to Reina, too. I'm as sure about him as I am that the sun will rise tomorrow.

But I firmly believe that no man will ever love me like that. I don't doubt that fact, like I don't doubt that mud season will arrive in Vermont.

No man has ever made a speech to me like Nash did at lunch. I couldn't even make a snarky comeback, I was so surprised. I appreciate the compliments he paid me. Because I *do* make a mean chicken salad, and I am smarter than most people realize. It's nice of him to say so.

But it doesn't change how I feel at a gut level—that there's a fundamental glitch in the universe between me and functional relationships.

It probably has something to do with my childhood. Nash had

looked startled when I told him about my mother. But I only told him half the story. Sure, I learned to cook and do the shopping. I did those things because I was trying to please her. I thought if I were a little more competent, she'd finally love me back.

The result was just the opposite. My hard work seemed to fill her with rage. "You think you're so special," she loved to say. "So high on yourself."

She's the reason I became a people pleaser. The teacher's pet. The friend that everyone calls when they're in a bind.

It's also why I've been so stupid when it comes to the men in my life. My ex is the perfect example. For a while, he made me feel beautiful *and* useful, he hooked me like a fish.

Then he broke my life and left me with scars—both literal and figurative—and I finally learned not to blindly hope someone will be good to me just because I'm me.

I can't risk my job, my livelihood, and my sanity for a fling with Nash, no matter how much fun it would be. But as I carefully tape the wrapping paper into place, I still hear his voice in my head. *You're the first woman who's made me this crazy in a long time.*

It doesn't mean much, but it sure was nice to hear.

———

At quitting time, I cross the parking lot with my usual furtive glances to make sure nobody's ready to pounce. I don't see anyone, and as I unlock the door, my thoughts turn to dinner.

It's weird the way Nash and I have settled into a homey little pattern for lunch and dinner. I cook, or else he buys takeout. Tonight, I'm thinking of wowing him with my homemade guacamole. And fish tacos, maybe?

In the kitchen, I find a note on the counter.

L—

I got the summons to meet my baby niece.

Thanks for wrapping the gift. Don't worry—I will be telling Leila exactly who chose and wrapped the gift because my sister would never believe me if I tried to take credit.

Will bring back pizza because Leila lives over the Gin Mill.

Text me your topping choice if you don't want margherita.

—N

P.S. Feel free to go without toppings on your body. Naked is always an option.

I snort.

I make my guacamole, because the avocados are ripe, and it would be a crime to let them turn brown.

Then I also make a pitcher of sangria with a very cheap bottle of red wine and some oranges, because it's a crime to eat guacamole without a fun beverage to go with it.

After leaving the pitcher on the counter to let the flavors combine, I paint my nails a color called Fiesta Red because I'm bored and lonely and why does the pumphouse seem so flipping *silent* when Nash isn't here?

When he goes back to Boston, I'll get used to the silence again, right?

Two hours later, Nash unlocks the door and steps inside, carrying two small pizza boxes. "What's up, pussycat? Is that sangria?"

I eye the jaunty pitcher on the table and wonder if I'm trying too hard. "It is. I also made guacamole because of those ripe avocados."

"Score!" he says. Then he crosses the room in three strides and…hugs me?

I'm suddenly pressed against a sturdy, hard chest. He smells of fresh air and leather. The feel of strong arms around me is so good that I lean into it and lose myself for a moment.

Then he steps back and reality blinks back into place. "What was that?" I demand.

"Anyone who makes sangria and guacamole gets a hug. I'm in a fantastic mood."

"Leila and the baby okay? Or is everyone exhausted?"

"Both," he says. "They're great, and they're also exhausted." He takes off his jacket. "I held the baby. You'd be proud."

"Let me just alert the media."

He snickers. "She was so tiny." He tosses his jacket on the back of a chair. "I didn't realize they made 'em that small. Let's eat. I'm starved."

He sits down at the table, and I grab the plates.

"Gotta say—you were right about the food-processor thing. Leila was very excited. You'd think I bought her a private jet." He chuckles. "I'm her favorite brother this week. Thanks for that."

"Told you so," I say, because I just can't help myself.

"Cool," he says, opening one of the pizza boxes and taking a slice. "It's fine to say, 'I told you so,' just as long as you don't mind me saying the same thing back to you."

"Pfft," I say, passing him a plate and a napkin, because we have a routine. It feels natural to end each day right here at this little table. Not that I'd admit I look forward to it. "Can't think of any reason you'll be telling *me* 'I told you so.'"

"Sure I will," he says, picking up a slice of sausage pie. "One of these nights, right after orgasm number three, you'll be on your back in bed. And you'll look up at me and tell me I was right about everything."

My breath hitches. Orgasm number *three*? The kitchen is suddenly too small again. I find myself studying him like I've never seen him before, trying to imagine it. In my experience, a man's got maybe a fifty percent shot of hitting a single. Forget a triple.

Then again, after breathing the same air as Nash Giltmaker for a week, I can admit he's the sexiest man I've ever met. I can't pinpoint why, even though I've put a lot of thought into the matter. Some days I'm sure it's the shape of his smile, or the way he walks—shoulders back, chest out, like he could take on the world.

Earlier today I'd decided that it's not even the way he looks, but some kind of magical juju that rumbles through me whenever I hear the deep sound of his laughter.

Whatever it is, Nash has an X factor that most men lack. A magnetism that's got to be good for, say, half an orgasm all by itself.

But *three?* That must be an exaggeration.

"You're staring, pussycat." He winks at me. "Eat your pizza. Keep your strength up. When you finally give in, you'll need energy."

I manage to roll my eyes while I help myself to a slice of pizza.

After dinner, Nash sets his laptop on the coffee table and asks me if I want to watch a movie. "It's either that, or I'm going to spend all night returning emails. My job doesn't seem to know what *leave of absence* means."

My heart twists in an uncomfortable way. "Are they mad at you for leaving?"

"A little," he hedges. "But you know what's sad? I can practically do my whole job from here. I'm one hundred eighty miles from the beer, but everything I need is right here." He pats the computer.

"Well, that's at least convenient?" I suggest, refilling our sangria glasses.

He picks up his glass and frowns. "I guess. But it makes me realize that my dad is kind of right about my job. I call myself a beermaker, but I don't ever touch the beer. I don't even get close."

"Your dad also thinks he could outthrow most of the Sox's pitchers. I don't think I'd take his advice on this."

Nash throws his head back and laughs, and the sound rolls through me like a wave. Then he sets his computer on the coffee table and pats the cushion beside him. "Come on, movie night."

"What movie?" I ask, weighing the risks of sitting close to him.

"You can pick. I need a break, and you look to me like you're all up inside your head. Pick something funny, maybe."

I'm not a funny girl, not lately anyway, and when I sit down beside him and lean over the keyboard, I search for *The Witch*, because I've heard good things, and Anya Taylor-Joy is cool.

"Whoa!" Nash says when he can see the screen again. "Did you open my playlist?"

"No? Was I supposed to? I'm not in the mood for a comedy, and I thought you could handle this. Was I wrong?"

He leans forward and clicks back to the menu—then chooses "Nash's Playlist."

The Witch is the first thing on it. "I've been meaning to watch this."

"Then why didn't you suggest it?" I prop my feet on the edge of the coffee table.

"Didn't want to scare you. But you know what this means, right?" He gives me a smug grin that shouldn't look hot, but somehow is.

"That we both like scary movies?"

"It's fate," he says, nudging me with his knee. "This movie is at least five years old, and we both want to see it."

"That's called a *coincidence*," I point out.

"That's called a *sign*," he argues. "Now hit play, pussycat. Let's see if you're tough enough for some scary witches."

It's possible I'm not. Apparently woodsy New England witches are very scary. The cinematography is bleak. There's a creepy shed. And a possessed goat.

But, hey, at least I'm not thinking about triple orgasms.

Instead, I'm slowly sinking into the sofa and trying not to cover my eyes.

"You doing okay over there, honeybunch?"

"Uh-huh." I take another gulp of sangria so I don't scream.

He reaches over and smooths my hair back. It's a friendly gesture, but I like the warmth of his hand more than he could know. When it's gone, I miss it, but he doesn't touch me again, or take advantage of my nerves.

It's tempting to climb into his damn lap, but I stay strong. The credits finally roll, and I'm filled with relief. "That was fun," I gush. "Thanks for being a friend and watching that with me and not doing the age-old slither-closer until oops-my-arm-is-around-you bullshit."

When he closes the laptop and turns to face me, I expect him to laugh, but his face goes all warm and sweet, and his voice drops into a low and sexy range. "Still don't know which real-life demon has got you so spooked. But I don't play games, honey. I see you need a little space, so I'm giving it to you. When you're finally ready for me, that's when we'll happen. Count on it."

Then he gets up, checks the locks, and goes upstairs, murmuring "goodnight" on his way.

Count on it.

Oh boy.

I get up and brush my teeth. I take myself to bed alone, like always, but I hear Nash moving around upstairs and feel safer knowing that he's in the house.

And, fine, a little turned on.

The next morning, I hear my phone ringing when I shut off the shower. *Hell.* My blood pressure spikes, because only Jennie would call at this hour, and only if it's important.

After wrapping up in a towel, I scurry out of the bathroom and collide with a cinderblock wall. "Oof!"

"Easy, lady," Nash says. "Your phone has been ringing since you went into the shower. Thought you should know."

I manage to take a step backwards and grab my phone from his hand. "Thanks. Sorry if it disturbed you."

"Wasn't a problem. I was up making coffee. But now I'm unsettled."

"Why?"

His gaze heats as it drops to my cleavage. Specifically, the swell of my breasts over the edge of the towel and the place where my tattoo curls down one shoulder and ducks beneath the terrycloth. "You, soaking wet, in a towel. That killer ink on your chest..."

I do, in fact, have killer ink. But I can't really take credit.

"Fuck. Who needs caffeine?" he growls. "You need any help drying off, you come find me."

"Right." The heat of his gaze makes it difficult to think, but I manage to turn away and head for my room.

CHAPTER 15
NASH

Livia disappears into her room, and I need a moment to get myself under control. She has no idea what she does to me.

As I wait for the coffee to brew, I hear her side of a telephone conversation echoing in the quiet building.

"What did he look like?" she asks frantically. "And please tell me *exactly* what he said."

If I'm not mistaken, her voice is shaking. Somebody is bothering my girl. She'd give me a swift kick to the balls if she heard me call her that. But we're close now, whether she acknowledges it or not. The spark between us just refuses to die.

The coffee finishes brewing, and I'm pouring it into two travel mugs when her bedroom door opens. She enters the kitchen, fully dressed, and says, "Please tell me one of those is for me."

"Of course it is." I hand her the mug that has a quarter cup of almond milk in it, just the way she likes it. "Something going on? Is there a problem?" There must be. She looks pale and unhappy.

She averts her eyes. "I got an email from UPS. The hops you needed are arriving today, so tomorrow you can get your dad on the line and make your first batch of Goldenpour."

I stare her down. "Pussycat, whatever phone call has you

freaked out and shaky before eight a.m. was *not* about a UPS delivery."

Livia looks down at her cup. "Oh, that. It's nothing for you to worry about. A friend called. I'm having, um, some family issues."

"Okay. Anything I can do to help?"

She shakes her head quickly. "I got it under control."

Bullshit, darlin'. But she's not in a sharing mood, so I'll have to be patient.

———

The day flies by in a blur of work. I spend my morning on the canning line. It's very satisfying to see a finished batch of Meadow Gold roll off the conveyor belt, each can labeled and grouped into four-packs.

Between batches, I find myself sketching a more efficient, two-track canning setup with a better oxygen reduction system. Just because a beer is handcrafted doesn't mean the canning process has to be so damn slow.

For lunch, I eat a BLT with avocado that Livia made for me. I find it in the fridge with my name on it.

It's thoughtful, and also tasty. Just like Livia. On my way to the tasting room for another grueling shift behind the counter, I poke my head into the office and find her seated at her desk, bent over one of my father's ledgers.

"Hey, girl."

Livia startles, drops her pen, and pushes her chair back from the desk. It's the office-worker's version of fight or flight. Not until her wide eyes find me in the doorway does she relax a little. "H-hey," she says. "Problem?"

I shove my hands into my pockets and take her in. She's wearing a kickass top in a wine color that accentuates her chest, and her hair is swept into a silver clip. She looks phenomenal, but

I know her well enough to see the stress she's trying to hide. "I came by to thank you for the sandwich. That was really nice of you."

"Oh." She clears her throat. "You're welcome. Thanks for buying groceries, roomie."

Roomie. That little joke is her way of keeping me at a distance. It won't work forever, though. I saw the way she looked at me during our little movie night, and it's not the way roommates look at each other.

But that's not our issue right now. I stalk into the room and park my ass against the side of the desk. "You want to tell me what's got you so jumpy?"

"Nothing," she says quickly. "I'm fine. Your hops delivery arrived, by the way. I checked the bags myself. And your father is all set to call you tomorrow morning at seven. He'd like you to arrive in the brewhouse by then."

"Yeah, okay." But I noticed that abrupt change of subject. And now she's fidgeting with her pen. "Anything else?"

She shrugs guiltily. "Morgan called in sick. He was supposed to refill the walk-in during your shift in the tasting room. So I guess I'll grab a jacket and fill in for him. Unless you've got a better idea."

"No, ma'am," I say. "We need somebody back there."

"I know." She rises from her seat and walks past me toward the door. "I'm on it."

"Livia?"

She turns expectantly. "Yes?"

"I can't make you tell me what's got you buggin' out. But I'm here if you want to talk. And if you don't, I'm also really good at stress relief."

For a second her eyes darken. But then she shakes her head, and her lips quirk as she tries not to smile. "I'll keep that in mind." She strolls out of the room, swinging her hips as she goes.

———

The tasting room is the usual madhouse. Beer enthusiasts in a line out the door.

I've made the executive decision to stop selling Goldenpour in cases so I can hoard the last of our supply to serve it a glass at a time to the tasting-room customers.

Scarcity is part of the brand's image, but I don't want people driving all the way up here next week to taste the most celebrated beer in America, only to leave without "seeing the face of God," as one journalist described his first taste of Goldenpour.

There are some grumbles, but I don't get too much pushback. Judging by how often I have to reach into the cooler, the fans are buying up our seasonal brews instead.

Bonus—half the time I turn toward the refrigerator, I get a glimpse of Livia through the glass doors, hustling to restock the beer so that Connor and I can reach it. She's wearing a puffer coat, and the chill has pinked up her cheeks.

It's not a glamorous job, but Livia doesn't complain. And whenever fate conspires to put us nose to nose in the refrigerator, she gives me a little smile before shoving a four-pack of beer onto the shelf in front of my face.

I'm just ringing up another four-pack of our spring brew when a familiar voice rasps my name.

"Nash Giltmaker! I got a bone to pick with you."

I look up to find Poppy, an old friend from high school. We've known each other for twenty-five years, and she looks much the same in her thirties as she did as a school girl—dark-blond curls, blue eyes, and a big smile. Plus, a husky voice that was weird on a little girl but is just plain sexy now.

"Hey girl!" I lean forward to clasp her shoulder.

She actually hops up onto the counter and flings her arms open. "Where is my hug? More crucially, where is my text message telling me you're in town? Wait—is your phone broken?"

With an awkward chuckle, I give her a tight hug. "Sorry, Popps. I know I should have called already, but it's been crazy."

"Oh, please." She gives me a look that tells me what she thinks of this weak excuse. "Nash, if you're struggling, I'm your first call, not your last. And I can't believe I had to hear you were in town from Corky and his crew. Did you hear Corky's wife left him?"

"*Hell*." I hadn't heard that about our old friend. "I'll ask him out for drinks. Now get off the counter before the customers decide it's a good idea to riot for cases of Goldenpour."

"Fine. But beer me," she says, hopping down and grabbing an empty glass. Then she cocks her head and frowns. "Who's that? You're keeping a pretty girl in the refrigerator? She looks unhappy."

"She does?" I twist my head and catch a glimpse of Livia before she disappears.

"She looks annoyed. And maybe I'm the reason?"

"Interesting." I chuckle.

Poppy's eyes twinkle as she pushes her glass toward me. "Nash, I'm so impressed! In town for a few days, and you've already got a girlfriend? That's quick work, even for you."

I open my mouth to say that Livia isn't my girlfriend, but somehow nothing comes out. Because it's hitting me that I wish it were true. It's been a while since I wanted to date anyone, but that's what I want from Livia.

Too bad she's ten paces behind me on this revelation.

Reading me, Poppy cackles. "Aw, Nash has it *bad*. Better tell her we're just friends. What do I owe you for the beer?"

"Nothing, Popps. Thanks for hunting me down. And I'll be a better friend. Want to have dinner tonight?"

"Can't." Another shrug. "Going dancing in Montreal with the girls. But we'll hang out soon, you hear? If you're only in town a few weeks, I need to see more of you."

"Yes, ma'am." I give her a mock salute. "You can talk me off the ledge my father has me out on."

She winces. "I can only imagine. That old coot doesn't appreciate you, and I'm betting he's not a very grateful hospital patient."

"You got that right." This is why Poppy and I have been friends since grade school. She gets me.

"But hey—call Corky, okay? Like, *immediately*. He misses you, and he's in a bad place."

"Okay, I will. I swear."

Poppy takes a gulp of her beer and flicks her eyes toward the cooler again. "Your girl is nervous, so I'm out of here. Bye, handsome. Tell her I want to meet her. We'll hang out."

"Sounds like fun."

After we say goodbye, I grab my phone out of my pocket and steal a few seconds to text Corky.

> **I'd love to see you. Drinks tomorrow?**

"Yo, can I get some service?"

I glance up, irritated, to lock eyes with the next person who's stepped up to the counter. He's a big, rough-looking guy with a biker jacket on his broad frame. He's got a beard that never sees a trimmer and a dangerous look in his eye.

"Sure. What are you drinking?" I reach for a tasting glass.

"Need help," he says. "But I don't need a beer."

Then you're in the wrong place, pal.

"I'm lookin' for a girl. Name's Ivy. I think she works here. 'Bout yay big." He holds up a hand about five and a half feet off the ground.

My brain jumps right to Livia. "Ivy, you say?"

"That's right." He crosses his arms. "We're old friends. I need to have a chat with her."

The back of my neck tingles mightily. Even when I'm drooling over a glimpse of Livia's kickass tattoo, I'm not too far gone to notice the ivy leaves. "What's this girl look like?"

"Dark hair. Pretty. Good with numbers. She work here? Maybe in the office?"

Instinctively, I shake my head. "Can't say I remember anyone like that. Sorry. There's only one woman who works here, and she's in the shipping department."

"She hot?" he asks. "That could be my friend."

"Well, sure, if you like 'em about seventy years old," I say. "Or maybe seventy-five."

The dude grins. "Huh, okay. Thing is? Her car is out back. Dark red. Old Subaru. Kinda shitty. But I don't see her anywhere." He swings his big head around to scan the tasting room.

While he's busy, I aim a glance through the glass doors of the freezer.

Livia is conspicuously missing.

"Here's the thing," I tell the guy when we face each other again. "This property backs up to a nice spot on the river, and people like to park their cars in our lot and take a walk. Maybe your friend is on a long, romantic stroll out back with her boyfriend."

He scowls. "Huh. Maybe."

"Yeah, if I were you, I'd walk down to the river and poke around some. If you think you saw her car, and she's not here in the shop, then that's your best bet."

He nods his big, bearded head. "Alrighty. Will do."

I watch him walk out the front door. Then I turn to Connor. "Can you cover us for a few minutes? I got something to do."

"Sure," he says, tapping a beer. "Just hurry back."

The tasting room has a back door, and I use it to duck into the brewhouse, where I find Livia standing with her back against the solid metal door to the walk-in. She's hugging herself, like she can't get warm. And, sure, when you've been working inside a refrigerator, you might have a chill. But I think something else is going on.

"Livia. Keys."

Her chin jerks up, and she takes me in with jumpy eyes. "What?"

"Give me your car keys. I gotta move your car. Unless that bearded guy really is your friend, and you'd like to say hi."

Her lips part, and then slam together again in a grim line.

I put my hands on her shoulders and look into her frightened eyes. "Livia, you trust me?"

Her eyes widen with surprise. "Yes," she whispers.

"Then I need those keys," I repeat. "Right now."

CHAPTER 16
LIVIA

I'm spiraling. One glance at Razor's henchman—they call him Rotty, as in Rottweiler—and I felt my flimsy little world collapse.

He found me. It's over. I'm going to have to run. *Again.*

But before I do, I have to deal with Nash Giltmaker. He's still standing in front of me, demanding my keys. I shove my hand into my pocket and produce them, if only to shut him up.

Panic is loud inside my head. Where am I going to go? How did this even happen?

"Livia," Nash barks. "Stay with me. Listen."

I raise my eyes and find his caramel gaze locked onto mine. His hands are a warm weight on my shoulders, and it grounds me back into the present moment.

"Go to the loading dock and look out the window," he says briskly. "Wait there. And when you see your car turn the corner, open the bay with the ramp. Got it?"

The ramp. Oh.

"Got it?" he repeats. "I need you to focus."

"Got it," I say softly.

His hands fall away, and without another word, he takes the keys and strides toward the exit.

I watch him go, and then I force oxygen into my lungs. With

his instructions still ringing in my ears, I point my feet towards the loading dock, taking care to stay as far from the windows as humanly possible.

Rotty is still out there, and he has a bead on my location. All he'd have to do is lurk around this place a few days in a row. He'll spot me for sure.

This is a *complete* disaster. I'll never be able to relax again in Vermont. But I don't have enough money to leave. And I'd miss Jennie and my brother. Besides, even if I flee, I'll always be looking over my shoulder.

Near tears, I make it to the loading dock, where I hover at an oblique angle to the window, keeping out of sight as I watch the back lot for my car.

The Subaru doesn't appear. The minutes tick by, and I'm swamped with dread. Where's Nash? Did something happen?

The longer I have to think, the worse it gets. Rotty is Razor's surliest henchman. He has a mean streak and a quick temper. I've always been afraid of him—even before I was smart enough to be afraid of Razor.

I'm almost physically ill by the time my old car appears out the window. I lunge for the button to open the door, and then duck out of view as the mechanism begins retracting the door up and out of the way.

My car rolls up the ramp, and as soon as it's clear, I hit the button to close the door. I watch Nash park the car, wondering if he managed to pull this off without Rotty noticing.

Nash's eyes are full of unanswered questions, and I realize that if he figures out the truth about me, I'll have to leave, regardless.

Nobody wants a criminal working for their family business.

Nash closes my car door with more care than it warrants and then stalks over to me. "All right. Let's hear it. Why do you look like you just drank a poison milkshake?"

I shake my head. It's a gross image but not a bad metaphor for how I feel. "That guy is not my friend."

"Got that, darlin'." He folds his arms and sizes me up. "But who is he?"

My breathing is still shallow. I'm not over the fear I felt when I spotted Rotty in the tasting room, standing only a few yards away from me. He was probably armed. He'd have to neutralize me or threaten me to get me onto his bike.

If he'd seen me, who knows what he would have done. Pulled a gun on me right there in the tasting room? Or—no—he'd probably hide on the property, waiting to catch me alone after work. He could easily subdue me, and then drug me or just toss me into the trunk of a car.

I'd be completely at his mercy. And then Razor's…

Without thinking, I place the palm of my hand over the scars on my arm—the ones I got the first time that I tried to leave Razor.

Nash frowns. Then he takes a step forward to grasp my wrist for a closer look.

His grip is entirely gentle, but it still causes the air to seize up in my lungs. And I make a noise of terror.

At the sound, Nash drops my hand instantly. But his frown only deepens. "What is *that*?" he demands, pointing at the mess of white, clawed marks on my forearm.

"A scar," I say curtly. "We all have them."

"Huh," he says. "Fair. But I'm thinkin' someone helped you get that one. Was it that guy?" He jerks a thumb toward the door.

"No." I sigh. What can I say that will end this conversation? "He's just a friend of my ex. They've been, uh, looking for me for a while."

"Define a while," Nash growls.

"Um…a year?"

His eyes practically bug out. And it's not like I blame him. I don't know whether to be surprised that they almost found me, or surprised that it took this long.

"A year," he says slowly. "Can I assume that neither your ex nor his skanky friend are looking for you out of the kindness of their big, generous hearts?"

Slowly, I shake my head. "Do you think he saw you move the car?"

Nash grins suddenly, and the heat of his smile startles me like always. "He went for a little hike. I followed him down to the river then ran back and moved the car. He's going to assume he missed you."

"The *river*? How'd you get him to do that?"

"When he started asking for Ivy, I figured it was you. I told him a true story about how people often park here to walk along the river."

"Oh," I say, swallowing hard. "Thank you."

"Ivy, huh?" His brown eyes look appraising. "It suits you."

"My legal name is Livia, it's just that nobody ever called me that before I ran…"

Oops.

"Ran *away*?" His eyes get feral again. "Let's hear more about why you needed to run away from those pricks."

"Let's not," I say quickly. "We just had a…difference of opinion." I shrug with as much nonchalance as I can muster. "They wanted me to stay, and I wanted to go. Seems like they're, uh, not over it yet."

"*Pussycat*." All the muscles in his upper body go tight. They're almost popping out of his appealingly tight shirt. "Explain."

I shake my head. "Listen, I appreciate your trick with the car. I really do. But you can't help me with them. And you shouldn't ask me any more about it. Trust me when I tell you that ignorance is bliss."

He lifts a hand to rub his eyes. "Then how come I don't feel so much bliss right now, with you turning white and cowering in the brewhouse?"

Once again, the breath leaves my lungs. I'm not used to anyone noticing all the strange things I do to stay invisible. Living in the margins is a skill I've perfected. It keeps me alive.

Nash sees through me, and it's entirely unsettling. And then it gets even worse when his gaze turns warm and patient. It's tempting to just step into his arms and spill the whole story. I'm so tired of hiding. Tired of running. It would be a relief to share my burden for a minute.

But I can't do that, for at least two reasons. One, my past isn't his problem. It's mine. I brought my troubles upon myself. And two, if Nash knew the whole story, he'd be obligated to call the police and turn me in.

Those are very good reasons, so I bite back my impulse and cross my arms. "Connor needs you in the tasting room," I say. "And the beer needs restocking. I, uh, can't do it myself right now." Not with Rotty wandering the property looking for me.

Nash glances towards the front of the building, realizes I'm right, and curses under his breath. "Okay, pussycat. We'll talk about this later," he says. Then he strides away, while I try not to admire his ass in those jeans.

——

For the rest of the workday, I hide beside the fireplace in the office like Cinderella. I crouch against the stones, seated on the floor, my laptop on my knees. It's the only way I can concentrate, because in this spot there aren't any sight lines through the windows.

This morning, when Nash brought me my ringing phone, the caller was Rory, a guy who did some bartending for the Giltmakers this past summer. He's got a new bartending gig in town, and he called to say that a customer showed up flashing a photo of me, and asking him if I looked familiar.

"I said no, Livia. But I dunno if I'm a good liar. And this guy was a real piece of work."

Rotty must have figured out that he was getting close. So he drove all around Colebury today, looking for my car. Then he found it. I'm so screwed.

Not until six o'clock rolls around am I brave enough to get up and stretch out my sore limbs. Then—after a careful glance out the window—I slide the ladder to my favorite location on the bookshelf, and I climb up. I grab a cigar box from the highest shelf. After removing the lid, I hastily count the bundles of money inside. Four thousand one hundred twenty-five dollars.

It's my entire net worth at the moment. It sounds like a wad of cash, but when your car is practically dead, and you need to start your life over in another state, it's not really enough. And I've made things worse with frequent handouts to my cousin and my brother. Because they need the money more than I do.

Or so I'd thought, until about three hours ago.

Feeling defeated, I tuck my money back into its hiding place, climb down off the ladder, and gather up my things. Then I head for the back door and scan the parking area.

Late-day sunshine washes over the gravel lot. The property backs up to a stand of fir trees. Beyond that, there's a path to the river, where the grassy slope runs down to the water's edge.

Unfortunately, there are lots of shadowy places to hide, and I can't see in every direction. So I feel horribly exposed as I close the brewery door, check the lock, and then hustle across the open ground to the pumphouse, where I unlock the door before shutting myself quickly inside.

As soon as the lock is depressed, I stand stock still, my back against the door. And I listen for any footsteps.

It's quiet, except for the thudding of my heart. How can I go on like this? If I stay, I'll be running around like a little mouse, afraid to poke my head out of my hole.

But if I leave, I'll suddenly have a host of new problems. Razor's private investigator will track me down via my social security number if I can't find another all-cash job. When my driver's license expires, I'll need to give the DMV a legit address. Yet another way to track me down. I need an ID to buy a plane ticket, rent a car, apply for a lease...

My best bet would be to go so far away that Razor wouldn't bother to fetch me if he found me. Except bikers move around a lot. Road trips are kind of their thing. And Razor has a network of biker friends that extends hundreds of miles in every direction.

So I'd need to go to Alaska to escape his grasp. Or Hawaii.

Or Mars.

My thoughts heavy, I get to work making this place a little safer for the night. Those tatty curtains I'd removed from the windows when I moved in? I find them where I left them upstairs in a closet folded into stacks.

They've been stored a few months, so naturally I have to wash and dry them again. And iron them. Because even a desperate girl likes a job done right.

Once they're ready, I choose the least ratty pair, and I thread them onto the rod in my bedroom. Then I peer outside to make sure nobody is watching me work.

For now, at least, the coast is clear. And by hanging the rod back up, I've made it harder for a violent, nosy biker to see inside my bedroom.

The light is starting to fade by the time I tackle the kitchen window. I'm standing on a kitchen chair, adjusting another curtain when I hear the sound of a key in the lock. My heart leaps into my throat as Nash steps inside.

He clocks me immediately, pale-faced and clinging to the refrigerator with one hand and a curtain rod with the other. "Hey there," he says. "Doing a little redecorating?"

"You could say that." I turn away from him and hastily place the rod back onto its brackets.

"Interesting taste you have in curtains," he rumbles. "What is that style called—shabby chic?"

We both know it's just shabby. Nothing chic about it. So I don't bother to answer.

"Want to go out and grab a burger at the diner?" he says.

"No, thank you," I say quickly. As if showing my face in a diner is even a possibility for me.

"Thought you'd say that," he says. "So I got us both one for take-out." And sure enough, he's pulling a paper bag out of his rucksack and placing it on the kitchen table.

"Then why did you ask?" I demand, even as the delicious

scent of cheeseburgers and fries hits my nose. My stomach rumbles.

"Curious what you'd say." He pulls out a chair at the table. "You told me once that you don't work in the tasting room because it's too people-y. But I'm thinkin' you don't mean it like an introvert does. You're not trying to avoid all people. Just a few people in particular."

"So?" I grab the last curtain and circle the table, heading for the living room window. "That's my business."

"You say that. But we're working together for a while here. It's pretty obvious that I can't do my job without your help. So I better figure out what we're up against. If Mr. Ugly Beard gets his mitts on you, the whole brewery will grind to a halt."

"That's an exaggeration."

"Not really."

"You're just trying to bribe me with a cheeseburger, so I'll tell you all my dirty secrets."

"No way, lady," he purrs. "I'll know *all* your dirty secrets when I finally get you under me in bed. This is different. This is survival. Now sit down at this table and eat your food."

Have I mentioned that anxiety is exhausting? That must be why I actually do what he says. I drop the last set of curtains on the sofa and return to the table, where I plunk down in a chair.

He pushes a wrapped burger toward me, and I can tell without asking that it's an Everything Burger from the Colebury Diner.

Maybe I'm just weak. But I start to salivate before I even take the first bite.

We eat in silence for a couple of minutes, and I can almost feel my soul rebuilding itself bite by cheesy bite.

I'm watching Nash arrange an order of fries *and* an order of onion rings in the middle of the table when he asks, "So...what's the deal with your ex and his flying monkey? I got his license plate, by the way. I'll be asking a friend to run it later."

"No!" I gasp, in spite of the fries I'm shoving into my mouth.

He quirks a bushy eyebrow. "Problem?"

"Look. I appreciate the way you helped me today. And I appreciate the *hell* out of this dinner. But you cannot antagonize that guy. It won't help me. My only two choices are hide or run."

He sets down his burger, and that's when I know I've said too much. "Livia," he says quietly. "That's not an answer. That guy lied to my face today when he told me why he was looking for you, and I had no trouble lying back. But what if next time he asks Badger instead? You think Badger is quick enough on his feet to cover your very fine ass the same way I can?"

I slump into my chair. "I guess I better run, then, because hiding isn't working out so well anymore."

He pushes the onion rings toward me. "Eat some of these, because it's either you or me. And I got a six pack to protect."

I take an onion ring and bite it. Viciously. My traitorous eyes go right to the waffle knit shirt that's stretched across his tight body, because I'm only human, and I wish I had x-ray vision.

"All right," he says calmly. "Please tell my abs why you feel you need to run away. I'm not trying to dig into your past. But you're the only person left standing around here who knows how my father's business operates. And when you talk about running away, I've half a mind to chain you to that chair."

The moment he says it, the food turns to ash in my mouth.

CHAPTER 17
NASH

Until this minute, I've never seen anyone turn white in front of my eyes. But the color drains from Livia's face by the time I finish the sentence. Somehow I've triggered an awful moment from her past.

Way to go, Giltmaker.

Cursing under my breath, I push back my chair. In two paces I'm across the room and grabbing a glass for Livia. I fill it with ice cubes and some Coke I'd stocked in her fridge. Then I place the glass in her hand. "Drink this."

She takes a sip, and I root around in my rucksack again, coming up with my flask. "Want a splash of rum?"

Livia shakes her head.

"Okay. I get it. That was poorly stated. I'm sorry."

She shakes her head again. "Nothing. It's... You were just making a joke. Never mind."

But this isn't a *never mind* kind of situation. Livia is strung out, and I just made it worse. "Look, I understand that you're in a tight spot right now. But within these walls, nothing bad is going to happen to you."

Her eyes flick toward the flimsy door lock, and then back to me. "If he saw my car, he'll be back. What was he riding, anyway?"

"Not riding. Driving. No bikes in the lot at the time."

She flinches again. "Shit. If he was in a car, that means he was ready to grab me."

But why? I want to shout. Not that I'll get answers. And she's too shaken up for me to press it. "How about you stay at my dad's house for a few nights? He's up on a hill. Nobody for miles."

If possible, this idea seems to terrify her even more. She actually shivers. "Nobody to hear me scream? No thanks. Besides, Lyle hates people in his space."

Too true. "Finish your burger. Then we'll switch bedrooms. You'll feel safer upstairs, I'll take your room."

She takes a deep, steadying breath. "No. I'm a big girl. Don't inconvenience yourself any more than you already have. I'm fine." She pops up out of her chair and begins tidying up the kitchen with nervous hands.

I watch her, thinking. There must be a way I can make her feel safe enough to relax. If she has to leave, I'll deal with it. But it would be better if she didn't. Besides—running scared with no plan usually doesn't play out so well.

Ignoring me, Livia finishes wiping down the counter. Afterwards, she hangs the final set of those hideous curtains over the living room window, before retreating to her bedroom, where she shuts the door.

I sit down on the living room sofa and contemplate the awful curtains. They're familiar—a piece of my past.

When I was a little boy, I had the run of this whole property. My father was the kind of man who was always working. Always hustling. Always full of new ideas. It's fair to say that he was a decent dad to me when I was small. He wasn't the kind to play with us for hours, but he humored all our questions and brought us to work with him. And he didn't mind when we were underfoot.

The pumphouse was one of our favorite spots on the property. The two bunkrooms upstairs—and the big old shower room—had been outfitted for millworkers a century ago. But the downstairs apartment was crafted during the decade I was born. My sister thinks my father furnished the place during one of the difficult patches in our parents' marriage. When he needed someplace to go.

I don't know if she's right, but it's plausible.

As kids, we'd play hide and seek within these walls. But nobody was really taking care of the place. It must have been a dusty wreck when Livia moved in. She'd have worked for weeks to bring it up to her exacting standards.

And now she wants to flee?

I look at the flimsy lock on the door. Then I glance toward the back of the building, where there's no strip of light under the door. Either she went to bed at seven o'clock, or she's too nervous to turn the light on.

This can't go on.

I get up, find my keys, and fetch my extra bike helmet. "Pussycat!" I call through her door. "Get your cute little ass out here. We're going for a ride."

A moment later her door opens on a scowl. "What are you going on about?"

"We need to take a little trip. Let's go. You'll need a jacket. It's cold on the bike."

She blinks. "I'm not riding bitch on your bike, Nash."

"Scared?"

"No!" she yelps, offended at the idea. "Those days are over for me." She crosses her arms, and I almost get distracted by the excellent new view of her cleavage.

But a man's got to keep his head. "Look, I got something to shop for at Home Depot. Round trip, it'll take me an hour and a half. We can't take your car for obvious reasons. And I can't leave you here alone. That leaves my bike. Get your shoes on." I tap my foot. "Time's a wasting."

I hand her the helmet, and she makes a shocked, irritated

noise. I turn my back and busy myself with washing out my glass and putting it on the drying rack. By the time I'm done, she's standing there in a riding jacket, the helmet under her arm. Her face is pure irritation, but I don't gloat.

"Okay, Livia. Nice night for a ride. Let's go."

After locking the door, I put on my helmet and throw a leg over my bike. Then I wait.

A moment later, Livia slides onto the seat behind me, fitting her feet onto the footpegs like a pro.

I'm only human, so my pulse quickens as her arms slide around my waist. I start the bike, and after letting the engine warm up a moment, we scoot off toward the open road.

Soon we're flying down the highway together, her curvy body tucked against my back.

It's heaven and hell at the same time.

———

Living in Vermont means anything you might need requires a trek. It's more than a half hour trip to the Home Depot, but that's the only place that's open late enough for my needs.

"What are we here for, anyway?" Livia asks as she removes the helmet and shakes her hair.

I wrap an arm around her small body and lead her through the double doors. "Got a long list. Extra bolt for the front door. Window locks. Maybe a paper window shade for the office."

"A…what?"

"You'll see. Follow me."

I march her all around the store. I find a new deadbolt for the pumphouse, plus a swingarm door latch for the inside of the door—the same thing they have in hotel rooms. I can install it tonight.

There are a dozen things in my cart by the time we check out, including a couple accordion-style paper window shades for the office. "The ugly curtains will do for now in the pumphouse," I murmur. "Not sure Home Depot sells real curtains."

Livia's gaze drops to her shoes. "I'll take care of the curtains. This is a lot you're doing for me."

Except it isn't. A couple hours work on a substandard dwelling that my family owns isn't a big deal.

When I look at Livia, who's smart, fierce, and beautiful—the whole package—I wonder who made her feel like even a little bit of trouble is too much.

CHAPTER 18
LIVIA

The wind licks my body as we shoot up the highway toward Colebury again. I tuck my face against Nash's strong back and inhale leather and springtime air.

I've been here before, and I don't mean the back of a bike. I've been *emotionally* here before—clinging to a strong man who's taken the reins of my life in hand. How easily I've handed them over tonight. I didn't even put up a fight when he told me to come along with him to the store, because I didn't want to be alone.

That's the worst reason to do anything. But I'm tired and scared. I needed a timeout on my life, even if only for a few hours.

It wasn't until we were standing in the aisles of Home Depot that I realized everything Nash set out to buy was for *me*. He'd done a quick but entirely accurate assessment of the brewery's worst security flaws, and he'd set about to do his best to fix it. And just thinking about it brings the unwelcome sting of tears to my eyes.

I'm not a crier. I can't afford to be. It's got to be the wind on my neck. I haven't ridden on a bike in so long that I'm not used to it anymore.

That must be it.

Nash takes a smooth, banked turn to exit the highway and I

instinctively lean into it. I miss the rush of a motorcycle ride. The high. But I can't forget the last time I felt it—on the back of another guy's bike. One who would just as soon strangle me as love me.

I can't lose sight of the facts. It doesn't matter if a guy is hot or fun, or if he pretends to play the role of the hero. That means nothing in the long run.

It's even possible that Nash is the real thing. But he's not going to be *my* real thing. I've already made all the mistakes I can afford, plus a few extra beyond that. I've already lost too much to men who treat me badly.

So what if riding on the back of his bike feels like flying?

And so what if he's making sure the locks on the doors will hold up past a sharp lurch of Rotty's shoulder against the doorframe? Nash is the landlord, more or less. If he wants to improve the property a little bit, I shouldn't let it go to my head.

Nash takes an unexpected turn before we reach the brewery. He starts winding the bike up a hill, and for a moment I'm confused. But then I realize this is Lyle Giltmaker's road. He moved into a log cabin after his divorce, and I've never seen the place.

Five minutes later we come to a stop in front of the dark house. Nash kills the engine, and I let go of him and sit back.

"All right, we need a vehicle. So I'm borrowing my dad's truck. You want to drive the truck or the bike back to the brewery?"

I stare through the helmet visor at him. "You're kidding, right?"

"No?" He lifts his helmet off and frowns at me. "We need a vehicle, for groceries and such. Your car has to stay hidden."

"I got that part." I take my helmet off, too. "But you aren't seriously offering to let me ride your bike."

"Sure I am." He frowns again. "I drove your car. Fair's fair. Are you saying you can't handle it? Took you for an old pro."

I just blink. Because Razor would rather lose a testicle than allow a woman to ride his bike. Any woman. And here's Nash offering me the bike. *Fair's fair.* "Actually, I'm a little rusty on the motorcycle. I'll drive your dad's truck."

"Suit yourself. Let me grab the key out of his kitchen."

I take it from him when he returns, and I open the driver's side door.

"Livia?" He's still holding his helmet under one arm. "Give me a five-minute head start, okay? I want to look around the property before you show yourself."

I give a little shiver in spite of myself. "Okay, sure. Good thinking."

————

Ten minutes later, I pull into the lot. Nash is waiting in the pumphouse doorway for me.

"All clear, pussycat," he says cheerily when I reach the door. "Now let's MacGyver some shit. I'm going to grab some tools from the main building. You okay here a second?"

"Of course." But I make sure to scoot my nervous ass right into the kitchen and lock the door behind myself. And then I turn all the lights on downstairs, one by one, just making sure I'm alone.

Damn that Rotty. And damn Razor most of all. I used to feel relatively safe here, and now I don't.

Luckily, Nash returns only a couple minutes later with a toolbox. Then he wastes no time screwing the hotel-style security device onto the door. "It's not foolproof," he says. "And I'll need a locksmith to drill the deadbolt holes as soon as possible. But this will slow 'em down if they try to force the door."

He measures a piece of scrap wood, cuts it to size, and inserts it above the window sash in the bedroom, preventing anyone from opening the window from the outside.

He's not just making an effort; he's making a thoughtful effort.

I *will* feel a little safer knowing that I can't be taken by surprise in my bed.

A guy who goes to this much trouble deserves to be thanked, but I don't have the proper means to do so. Except, of course, with my naked body, and that's not happening.

But hang on. "Would you like a cocktail?" I hear myself offer. "You deserve a treat after all that."

A naughty grin steals across his kissable mouth. "Sure thing, pussycat. Whatever you're offering, I'm accepting."

Honestly, that smile gives me the warm flutters. So I turn away from its brilliance and head for the kitchen, where I scare up a couple of limes and some simple syrup. I've got tequila and Cointreau, so I mix up a couple of margaritas on the rocks.

"That looks special," he says, coming up behind me as I tap some flaked salt into a saucer to rim the glasses.

Suddenly, I'm all too aware of how small the kitchen is, and I remember how closely I'd pancaked my body onto his on the back of his motorcycle. When I inhale, it's an intoxicating mix of lime and jacket leather. "This is nothing special, really. Back in the day, when I was fun, I made some elaborate cocktails."

"Hmm," he says. "If you're making a cocktail right now, doesn't that mean you're still fun? I mean—I'm already having fun."

I turn to face him and catch the teasing smile on his face. "Nope," I insist. "I gave it up. This is just a random cocktail between friends. It's not a trend."

He tips his head back and grins, as if I said something funny. "Sure thing, honey. Can't wait." And the way he says *can't wait* implies more than a margarita.

But whatever. He can dream if he wants to. I slice a wedge of lime for a garnish and pour our two drinks. "Here we are. Cheers."

Still smiling, he picks up his drink and carries it over to the sofa. "Come toast me right here."

"On the sofa?" I clarify.

"Something wrong with the sofa?"

I shake my head, even though I don't trust myself on it with him.

But this little party was my idea, so I follow him over and sit down. "To your health," I say, lifting my glass. "And mine, I guess, since you've made it harder for Rotty to terrorize me."

Our glasses touch, and then he takes a sip. "This is delicious, sweetheart. You are a fun time, whether you admit it or not."

"Thanks, I guess. But it needs to be said—this is not an attempt to get you drunk so I can take advantage. We're not sleeping together tonight."

Wizened brown eyes give me an assessing look. "I like how you put that qualifier on there—not *tonight*. I like the cocktail, too. And every time I look at you, I get ideas. But I don't take a woman to bed only when she's too scared to go alone."

"I'm not scared," I argue reflexively.

"Uh-huh." A sexy grin slides across his mouth. "We both know you're a tough customer. And now that I've gone more than a week without the cops showing up to put me in handcuffs, I can admit that it's your best feature. You're *fierce,* darlin'. You don't take any shit from anybody."

Something cracks apart inside me when he says this. Because Razor only wanted me to sit down and shut up. Nash sees me for who I really am, and it's a huge compliment.

Except it has the unfortunate effect of completely disarming me. I'm mute on the sofa, my drink forgotten halfway to my mouth, my gaze locked on Nash's handsome face.

He takes the drink out of my hand and sets it down on the coffee table. Then he hitches closer to me and takes my face in two roughened hands. "Hold still, pussycat. There's something I gotta do."

The kiss seems to happen in slow motion, like a beautiful clip from a film. There's plenty of time for me to dodge it, but I don't even try. I don't have the will.

Instead, I just soak in the sensation of Nash's smile tilting as he brushes the tip of his nose over mine. It's a show of confidence, building up the suspense.

His generous mouth covers mine with a press that's commanding yet gentle.

Warm flutters rise up and engulf me. When he deepens the kiss, my tummy does a swoop and roll as I grip his shoulders and part my lips.

He tastes like lime juice and danger—the good kind, the kind I suspected on that first night when we were two strangers across the bar. I knew it would be like this—one of his bold hands skimming down my back to palm my ass, and my traitorous body thrumming with anticipation.

Suddenly, I'm lifted off the sofa and deposited onto his lap. The kiss becomes a full body experience, and so it's hard to think when I'm surrounded by a hard-bodied man who's sucking on my tongue and teasing my nipples through my clothes.

Thinking is overrated anyway. I can feel the need rolling off his body, and we're in such perfect sync it almost hurts.

Until everything suddenly stops. The kiss ends as abruptly as it began, and I'm deposited gently on my own side of the sofa.

Panting, I stare up into his flushed face, too revved up to pretend indifference.

"You said we weren't sleeping together tonight." His voice is pure gravel, and his color is high. Like I've done the same thing to him that he's done to me.

"Okay. Right." My sluggish brain fights for the proper response. "I meant it, too." Although this statement is dubious coming from a woman whose bosom is literally heaving right now.

He grins. "Make no mistake, lady. Someday soon, I'm going to bang you like a screen door in a hurricane. But you said that wasn't happening tonight, so I'm going to turn in. I got a call at seven a.m. with that asshole who calls himself my father, so I'm gonna need my Zs."

"Right," I say, my mind a beat behind as I straighten my clothing.

I *did* say I wasn't going to seduce him. And he listened, which is a rare thing for a man to do.

So why am I suddenly so disappointed?

Shake it off, Livia. I grab my drink off the coffee table and get up. "Sleep well," I say. "And, um, thanks for the extra locks."

"My pleasure," he says in a deep voice.

I drop my glass in the sink and head to the bathroom, where I stare into the mirror. The woman who looks back has windblown hair and kiss-bitten lips. I whisper to her, "Don't be an idiot. We're swearing off men."

She replies, "Even the super-hot ones?"

"Even those," I whisper back.

"We never have fun anymore," she points out. "Like, never. A little fun wouldn't kill us." But then she frowns, because she knows that's not true.

A little fun with Razor turned into some very big regrets.

I look away from the mirror and brush my teeth.

When I finally emerge from the bathroom, Nash is still on the sofa, but now he's reading a paperback novel, a book light clamped to the cover. "Night, pussycat."

"Night."

He shuts off the book light and sets the book on the floor. Then he closes his eyes.

And doesn't move, except to raise his inked arm over his head and make himself more comfortable.

"Nash...?"

"Mmm?"

"What are you doing?"

"Sleeping," he says. "You should try it."

"But why are you on the couch?"

He opens his eyes. "Because your bed is off limits. And some asshole wants to get his hands on you. He wants to take you somewhere you won't tell me, but it has something to do with your ex and those scars on your arm. And possibly something to do with chaining you to a chair. And so I gotta take this threat seriously."

My eyes practically bug out. "But the doors are locked. You fixed them yourself."

"Never know," he says sleepily, closing his eyes again. "If he comes around, I'll be ready. Night, Livia."

I stare at him for another long beat. I've never met anyone like him. "Goodnight, you stubborn man."

He grins without opening his eyes.

CHAPTER 19
NASH

I do not recommend the pumphouse sofa for a good night's sleep.

Then again, maybe it isn't the sofa's fault. I spend half the night having dirty dreams about a certain bookkeeper with a smart mouth and a smile that makes me want to push her down onto a bed. Or a chair. Or any nearby surface. I'm not picky.

I eat breakfast and carry my coffee cup into the brewhouse a few minutes before seven a.m. I'm wondering if my father is really going to call and tell me his precious recipe.

My phone rings at exactly seven o'clock. For all the old man's faults, he is prompt. "Morning, Dad," I answer, adjusting my air pods. "How are you doing today?"

"Still trapped in this damn hospital. You got the mash tun all cleaned out and ready?"

I guess we're skipping the small talk. "She's ready. The water is heating. What temperature you want?"

"One fifty-two on the mash temp. You ready for the grain bill? I need you in the storage room. Don't write this down…"

I roll my eyes. "I'm going."

When I get to the storage room, he starts calling out types of grain faster than I can load the bags onto a battered old industrial cart. Each bag contains fifty pounds of milled grain, sealed tight. The mix he gives me is about eighty-five percent English pale malt, five percent caramel malt, and the rest is white wheat and dextrose.

I write that shit down on a sticky note in my own personal shorthand. Fuck his paranoia.

"Got it all?" he asks as I steer the cart toward the masher. "Better count twice."

"Oh, at *least* twice," I grumble. Getting the world's favorite cult beer wrong is not on my bingo card today. "You want to call me back in fifteen? It's going to take me a while to slice all these bags open and pour them into the hopper."

"You get started and we'll talk."

"Fine. It's your funeral."

"It almost was, so…"

I grin at my dad's trenches humor and grab a utility knife from my apron. Then I heft the first bag into the grist hopper's open window and slice the end of it off.

And, fine, it's satisfying to hear the dry sound of grain running through the hopper. The toasty scent of malt hits me like a memory.

"One down. A million to go," I grumble.

"Cheaper than a gym membership," my father says. "Why do you think I still have guns?"

This also makes me grin in spite of myself. I keep up the pace, emptying bags of grain, counting them again as I go. "Is this a bad time to point out that this part could easily be automated?"

"It's always a bad time for that," he growls. "People don't wait in line for beer that's automated."

"Depends on what you're automating," I say carefully. "Your canning line doesn't affect the brew process at all. And yet you could improve the efficiency of your end-stage process by, like, seventy percent—"

"No," he clips. "I know you mean well, but I can't make any changes to the building."

Hell. I should have known he wouldn't listen, even if I have years of experience with things like this. In fact, he probably won't listen *because* I have those years of experience. His ego is too fragile.

"Concentrate on the beer, son. And be careful with the hose from the hot liquor tank. There's insulated gloves for this."

Unfortunately, I've already scalded one hand on the very hose he's referring to. Not that I'm going to admit it. "What are we doing to balance the water?" Come to think of it, I didn't see any calcium sulfate, calcium chloride, or lactic acid in the storage room.

"Nothing," he says.

I pause in the middle of cutting open the last bag. "Nothing? Is the liquor tank treated separately?"

"No. I use the water just as God gives it to me."

"No shit?" Last night I googled the hell out of *how to make Goldenpour*. I wanted to know what the internet knew about my dad's recipe. Foamies love exchanging secrets about their favorite cult brews.

Sure enough, I found several reddit threads speculating on the Goldenpour recipe, including photos taken through the mill's windows. And zoomed-in shots of the temperature gages on the tanks.

Turns out the base of Dad's famous recipe is just plain old, untempered well water. I want to laugh as I open the valve that starts the flow of water into the mash tun.

"Did you preheat the masher?" my father demands.

"Doing it now."

"All right. Fill 'er up. Then you can start to add the grain. Slowly, now. We don't want dough balls."

I feel like I'm twelve again, because that's how old I was when I learned how to brew beer. "I'll go slow."

"See that you do."

When the tank is full, I shut off the water and then climb up onto the mash platform. I start the flow of grain from the hopper and grab a wooden paddle so I can stir it up.

This part makes me feel like a cartoon witch with a cauldron. *Bubble, bubble, toil and trouble…*

"How's it looking?" my father asks. "No clumps?"

"Looking good. All clear."

"Time to recirculate. Open the pump valve just a crack and let the wort circulate through the grain bed."

Yes, master. I send the wort circulating back through the grain bed.

"Let it recirculate for about 15 minutes, then we'll start the sparge. You remember how to set the sparge arm?"

"It's like riding a bike, Dad. And I'm handy with a bike."

He mutters something about cocky sons under his breath. But this conversation isn't nearly as irritating as I'd imagined it would be.

I'm actually having fun, but I'll take that secret to my grave.

"Good. Call me back when you're ready for the next step. Don't mess this up; it's our legacy in that tun."

"No pressure, huh?"

"None at all. And Nash? Don't get fancy and try to 'optimize' this. It's perfect as is."

That was unnecessary, and it takes my mood down a notch. "I'll call you when I'm ready for hops."

"See that you do."

We hang up, and I tuck my device away. I don't want to be that guy who dropped his phone into the tun and poisoned a whole batch.

By now, the other brewery employees are trickling into the brewhouse. Including Livia, who's wearing a dark-green, off-the-shoulder sweater. And I can see the edges of her tattoo trailing across her collarbones.

Something primal stirs inside me. I'd like to peel those clothes off her and inspect all her ink.

With my tongue.

It will happen eventually. The girl wants me, and I'm pretty irresistible. But it's not going to happen this morning, so I'd better get a move on.

There's beer to make, grain to order, and a business to run. The fun can come later.

CHAPTER 20
LIVIA

I spend the morning at my desk behind my brand-new paper shade. I alternate between working on a grain order that Nash needs and trying not to think about that kiss last night. Or, rather, kisses, plural.

I'm a strong, independent woman, damn it. So why am I finding it so difficult to stop replaying that moment in my mind?

God. He's a great kisser. And those bossy hands...

"Pussycat?"

I practically jump out of my chair. And when I raise my head to meet his gaze, I'm almost certainly blushing.

"It's noon," he announces. "Instead of a lunch break, I'm heading out to help Matteo pick up a car he bought. You want me to bring back some groceries? I could cook something tonight. Do you have a grill?"

"No grill. But I'll cook," I hear myself volunteer. "You like enchiladas? Bring back some chicken thighs and a package of tortillas."

"I like anything you're making me." He gives me a saucy wink. "That's all you need?"

"Yeah, I've got the rest. Well, except for maybe some ripe avocados and green onions."

His grin widens. "I'll do my best."

I wave him toward the door. "My love to Leila and that hottie of hers. Bet that kid is too beautiful for words."

Nash's eyes narrow. "Why do all the women fall at Matteo's feet?"

"Not all the women," I point out. "Just your sister. Now get gone, and don't forget the green onions."

He gives me a salute, and then he's gone.

Somehow, it's easier not to think about his mouth after he's left the building. Instead, I find myself worrying about Rotty and Razor. I finish out the day in a half-terrified state, darting past windows only when necessary and steering clear of the tasting room.

It's no way to live. But I can get used to anything. I've done it before.

When five o'clock comes, I push all my hair under a cap and take a quick, stealthy trip across the parking lot to the pump-house. In the kitchen, I find the groceries I'd ordered from Nash, and I start on making chicken enchiladas and a salad.

Saucing everything and rolling up enchiladas is fussy work, so I never make this dish for myself. The truth is that I'm a pack animal at heart, and I like having people to cook for.

The kitchen smells like heaven when Nash taps on the door. "It's me."

I hustle over to disengage the hotel lock to let him in.

"The locksmith is coming tomorrow," he says. "Then you'll have a deadbolt."

"Thank you," I say primly. It's a good thing I made him dinner as a thank-you. Because last night I thanked him with tequila and my tongue in his mouth, and that can't happen again.

Nash goes upstairs to shower, and I hear his music start up. Either the playlist was chosen for my benefit, or I'm being egotistical thinking he's chosen it for me. "You Sexy Thing" is followed by "Someday We'll Be Together" and Ed Sheeran's "The Shape of You."

A man doesn't blast Ed Sheeran unless he thinks he can get some. It's just a fact.

Eventually, he comes back downstairs wearing a very tight T-shirt that shows off his rippled chest and his colorful, full-sleeve tattoo. I roll my eyes.

"What?" he demands, opening the refrigerator for a can of beer.

"If the seams of that shirt start to unravel from the stress of the fit, don't come crying to me."

"Wouldn't dream of it. Beer?"

"Certainly. If you leave the grocery receipt on the counter, I'll pay you half."

"Nah. My treat."

I don't like that, because I can't owe this man, and I'm not going to pay off my debts the way he's hoping I will. But I keep silent because I also don't want to argue.

When the food is ready, I make him a big plate of cheesy, gooey enchiladas with diced avocado and scallions on top, and I sit down across from him at the table.

He takes the first bite and moans. Loudly. Then he takes another and does it again.

"Everything okay over there?" I ask, daintily cutting a bite for myself.

"It's really indecent what you can do in the kitchen," he says with a sigh. "Makes me want to get down on one knee and propose marriage."

"That might be almost as triggering to me as being cuffed to this chair," I mumble.

He flashes me a grin, and we both tuck into our dinners. There isn't much talking, but our silence is weirdly companionable, given everything that's happened.

Like that kiss, for instance.

Nash's playlist segues into a song by Noah Kahan, the local superstar. I'm scraping the last bit of cheese off my plate and listening to the lyrics when I hear tires on the gravel outside.

My whole body goes cold.

Nash puts his fork down and reaches across the table to squeeze my hand. "Breathe. You expecting anyone?"

I shake my head.

"All right." He grabs his phone to silence the music, and then we hear footsteps crunching toward the door. I practically hit the ceiling when there's a firm knock.

Nash doesn't panic. He calmly pushes his chair back from the table, walks to the door, and pushes the hideous curtain aside to see who's out there. He unlocks the door and opens it. "Hey, Benito! Come on in."

A handsome, clean-cut guy with shiny, dark hair enters the room. "Sorry. I shoulda called instead of interrupting dinner. But I was driving this way…"

"It's no problem at all," Nash says. "Have you met Livia? She's my father's office manager, and she's stuck sharing the bunkhouse with me for a few weeks."

"My apologies, Livia," the newcomer says with a smile. "You must know my brother, Matteo?"

"Oh, of course." I'd thought Benito's name was familiar, but I hadn't been able to place it. Now I realize he's the younger brother of Leila Giltmaker's partner. "How are Matteo and Leila holding up?"

"They're great. Happy. And tired." He parks his hip against the kitchen counter. "We have a new baby at home, too, so I know how it is."

"Congratulations." Come to think of it, I'd heard this. Leila is friends with Benito's wife. "Can I offer you some enchiladas? I made a lot."

"Or a beer?" Nash adds.

Benito sighs. "Hurts me to say no, because that food smells amazing. But Skye is expecting me at home. I just wanted to let you know that I ran that license plate you asked me about."

License plate. My whole body goes cold, and I shoot an angry look at Nash. *How dare you?*

Nash keeps his gaze on Benito. "Find anything interesting?"

"Well, yeah." Benito taps his chin, a thoughtful expression on his face. "The truck is registered to a business out of Rutland. A garage that services motorcycles."

My heart stutters.

"Now…who did you say was having a problem with this guy?" Benito continues. "Because I gotta say, this garage is known to me and to the drug enforcement unit. They're not good guys."

I'm dying inside. And I'm going to *murder* Nash Giltmaker.

"It's…an employee," Nash says carefully. "This person does not want to involve the police. I think this person is afraid of one or more parties involved."

Benito's eyes travel from Nash to me. And they stay there.

I seethe.

"What should this employee do if the dude comes back?" Nash asks carefully.

"This employee should collect proof of harassment, especially if the employee is a woman." Benito says, watching me. "If things are *very* bad, she should take any previously collected notes on the harassment and ask a judge for a restraining order."

"Oh, for God's sake!" I shriek. "This employee probably knows that a restraining order is less useful than a piece of budget toilet paper. Nash, you had *no right* to invade this employee's privacy!"

Nash flinches. "I was only trying to help. I thought calling the cops was y—" He stops himself. "—this employee's favorite remedy. I just happened to see a cop I know today, when I was picking up his brother. Benito and I were in the same class in high school."

I sink down into my chair and put my head in my hands. "Actually, this employee just wants you to mind your own beeswax."

There's an awkward silence in the kitchen, and then Benito sits down at the table with me. "Can I tell you about my job?"

"Do I have a choice?" I say to the table.

He chuckles softly. "Well, yes. I'll leave if you want me to. But you might find it useful to hear what I do all day."

I take a sip of my beer and look him dead in the eyes. "Go ahead. You came all this way."

Nash opens another beer and passes it to Benito, who takes a sip. "I work for the Vermont State Police on the drug task force. That means I spend all my time trying to figure out who's moving illegal drugs through Vermont, and how I can stop them."

My stomach sinks a little further. Because I think I know where this is going.

"Now, we think those guys in Rutland are near the top of the food chain. So I've spent the last year—longer, actually—making small undercover buys from low-level scumbags to try to get them to roll over on bigger scumbags. It's slow work, but I'm trying to build a case against the Valkyries Motorcycle Club."

Just hearing the name of the club makes me shiver.

I'm sure Benito and Nash notice.

"So," Benito continues, "if I happened to meet someone who understood how that club operates and who could ID all the members, that would be very exciting to me. And if that person was worried that they could somehow be implicated in any of the laws the club has broken, I could probably put that person's mind at ease."

I close my eyes and then force them open again. "That's a really interesting job you have there, Benito. I think I'll stick to bookkeeping."

His eyes widen a fraction. "Did you say bookkeeping?"

Oh my God. "This conversation is over," I whisper. "I'm not about to be your new little informant. I'd only wind up dead."

Benito doesn't get angry. He takes a sip of his beer and gives me a sympathetic look. "I'm going to leave my card in case anyone wants to call me. These guys aren't invincible. Everybody makes mistakes. And when they finally do, I'll be ready."

I believe that. And I believe that Benito is a good man, with honorable intentions. Still—I'm not sticking my neck out for him.

He's going to have to catch them without my help. Razor already wants to kill me. I believe that in my soul. If I help the cops investigate him, he'll make sure I pay.

Benito gets up from the table and makes small talk with Nash for another couple minutes. Then Nash walks him out to his car.

When he returns, I'm still seething. I give him a look so dirty that it might maim a lesser man.

"Aw, pussycat," he says with a sigh.

"Don't call me that."

He shakes his ridiculously attractive head. "I ran into Benny earlier. I casually asked him to run a license plate. I did it because you're scared, and that seems wrong to me."

"It's not for you to decide!" I say. "You're playing with my life, and you have *no right*."

He has the good sense to flinch.

Like an angry teenager, I storm out of the kitchen, march to my bedroom, and slam the door. I fling myself onto the bed and pick up my phone to call my cousin. I need a good vent.

It goes to voicemail. And now I'm trapped in here, and I haven't put away the food or done the dishes.

After five minutes of fuming, I get up and march out to save my enchiladas for lunch tomorrow. It's not like I can even go to the grocery store. With my car locked inside the loading bay away from Rotty's prying eyes, I'm effectively trapped here.

But when I reach the kitchen, the food has already been handled by my smokin' hot nemesis. His muscular arms flex as he scrubs out the baking dish.

So I stomp into the bathroom and brush my teeth instead.

CHAPTER 21
NASH

While I appreciate Benito's help, it's unfortunate that he decided to drop by instead of calling me. Livia is spooked.

And for good reason. I'd imagined that Livia's troubles sprang from a vindictive ex who had a deranged friend who was willing to help him stalk her. I didn't anticipate an entire motorcycle club and drug operation well known to the Vermont State Police.

Although it makes sense, now that I think about it. Livia doesn't strike me as a girl who scares easily. I've only known her for a couple weeks, but I can already say she's one of the smartest people I've ever met.

Now I have more of an inkling as to why she's been so fucking scared. Benito looked *really* interested when she said she was a bookkeeper. And that's when Livia completely lost her cool.

She must have done some bookkeeping work for this creepy ex before figuring out he was a criminal. That's a surefire way to get the upper hand in a relationship—drag your girl into unlawful activity.

What a mess. How's she supposed to extract herself from that? I glance at her closed door. She's hiding here—as if this place were her prison.

———

A few hours later, I'm trying to sleep on the damn couch again. Maybe I'm only the temporary king of the Giltmaker empire, but I won't let one of our employees be menaced by drug lords on our property. Especially when Livia has been busting her ass to look after my father's interests while he can't do it himself.

The couch is too small, and my back hates me. But I finally doze off. I dream that I'm out for the night in a bar, just like the first time I met Livia. She's there, too. She keeps beckoning to me from across the room. But when I try to get to her, she vanishes.

This happens a few times until someone finally reaches out of the crowd and grabs my hand. It's Livia. She pulls me outside a door that appears in the wall, because dreams are handy like that.

I follow her outside and press her up against the wall and kiss the living hell out of her. It's glorious. Her hands are everywhere, and I'm a human octopus, finally able to touch her wherever I want.

We're shameless. I'm just lifting her skirt when I hear the sound of an engine. It draws close enough that I can hear tires on gravel. My hands fall away from her body and form two fists.

That's when I wake up suddenly, my hands actually in fists. And I hear footsteps outside, crossing the gravel lot.

Shit.

I sit up on the sofa, suddenly wide awake, my pulse elevated.

The air pressure in the room changes as I feel the bedroom door swing silently open behind me. I turn to see a freaked-out Livia standing in the doorway, eyes wide, wearing a long T-shirt and not much else.

Rising from the sofa, I pocket my phone. I head for the kitchen door, where my shoes are waiting for me. For the second time tonight, I push the curtain aside and peek outside.

It's pitch dark now. Sadly, the brewery doesn't have any parking lot lighting. My dad's too cheap for that. But the darkness makes it easy to see a flashlight bobbing through the darkness. I disengage the hotel lock and put my hand on the doorknob.

Livia's footsteps sound from behind me. I look over my shoulder and find that she's holding an old baseball bat. One of *my* old baseball bats, unless I'm mistaken. I probably left it here as a child. She offers it to me.

"You keep that," I whisper.

"I have a second one." she whispers back. "Nash, I heard two motorcycles. You don't have to go out there."

"Oh, I'm goin'." I want to know who the intruders are. "Open the window a crack. Call Benito if you hear fighting or if I don't come back in ten. Lock the door behind me."

She looks, if possible, even more freaked out than she did a minute ago.

I slip outside, quietly closing the door. I hear the locks engage.

The flashlight has bobbed its way out of sight, around the front of the building. The intruders have a head start, and I have to follow them slowly because it's hard to stay quiet on gravel.

I pause to inspect two Harleys parked near the corner of the building. I kneel down and quickly open my phone's camera to shoot a photo of the bikes' license plates.

That done, I pocket my phone and sidle around the corner of the building. They've almost made it the whole way across the front lot. They're shining a light inside the building.

As soon as they disappear around another corner, I'm in pursuit. I pick up speed on the mulch landscaping, which absorbs the sound of my footsteps.

My intruders aren't being quite so careful. They assume they're alone. They're poking along the loading bay, shining the flashlight into the windows.

Shit. They'll spot Livia's car. If they haven't already.

So I start running. "Hey! What the hell are you doing on my property?"

The light swings abruptly in my direction, aiming squarely at my eyes.

"Not cool," I snarl, trying to guard my vision with a raised hand. "Put that down. I'm not the trespasser here."

The guy holding the flashlight is the same one who'd interrogated me in the tasting room. He lowers the angle of the light by a few degrees, but it's still held at an obnoxious angle that's meant to frustrate me and maintain the upper hand. "Nobody's tresspassin'," he growls. "Just out for a midnight stroll. I heard this is a good place to park if you want to walk by the river. Some piece of shit told me that."

Aren't you charming. I take a calming breath. "Don't know why you need to look in all the windows, then. River's that way." I point. "And don't bother trying the doors—the beer is locked up tight."

That's not even a lie. The only decent lock in the place is on the walk-in cooler.

"Not here for the beer, asshole. We're here for the girl."

A chill slides down my spine, but I don't react. "Sorry?"

The other guy snorts. He has the same build as his friend— broad and stocky. But he takes better care of himself. His dark beard is trimmed neatly, and he has the kind of muscles that require a lot of hours at a gym. "I know you're hiding that bitch. Where is she?"

"No girls here, man." I manage to sound calm even though I'm raging inside. "The only people roaming my property at fuck-all o'clock in the morning are you two and me."

He doesn't bother replying. Instead, he takes the light from his buddy and swings it up at the brickwork beside us, and squints. I make note of his biker jacket. It's imprinted with a V-shaped insignia. V for Valkyries, I'm betting.

"Nice old place, innit?" he says, still scanning the brickwork. "Hate to see your family business burn to the ground. One Molotov cocktail through the window, and she's just a big torch."

The threat rolls out of his mouth so casually that my blood pressure spikes. Again, I try not to react. "Don't know why anyone would do that," I say quietly. "Don't see the point."

"You make the wrong guys angry, anything could happen," he says with that same casualness. "Don't protect a girl who ain't worth it. Cut 'er loose and nothing bad happens to your smug face or Daddy's business. Be a shame to have all this work go up in flames. You and your little baseball bat wouldn't be able to do much about it."

Now I want to throw down the bat and just throttle him the old-fashioned way. See how he likes it. But he moves the light quickly, searing my vision. And when I slam my eyes shut in response, I hear both of them quickly circling me, running back toward their bikes, kicking up gravel.

Running away, like fucking cowards.

I don't chase them. I go the opposite way, running toward Livia. Clearing the loading bay, I round the building, making myself visible via the pumphouse windows in case she's looking.

The sound of my own heavy breathing is punctuated by the Harley engines roaring to life. They peel out of the parking lot and ride off into the night.

I stand still for a moment, the bat dangling from my hand, my heart pounding with anger. How dare that fucker threaten me.

I take one more calming breath and continue toward the pumphouse. I tap on the door and Livia opens it instantly. One hand swipes at her tear-streaked cheeks and the other grips the counter for dear life.

"Hey. Hey now." I kick the door closed and lock it. "They're gone."

"Did they see my car?" Her voice is high and panicked.

"Well..." I won't lie. "They might have. I couldn't exactly ask."

She crumbles from the inside out. Like all the fear and anxiety suddenly became too heavy to bear. I catch her just as her knees buckle. I scoop her up and carry her through to the bedroom, while she clings to me like a frightened cat. I roll onto the messy bed and gather her close to my chest. "You're all right. It's okay."

"It's *not* okay," she gasps. "Nothing is okay. I have to go. I have to run. Tonight."

She's shaking like a leaf. "Nobody is running," I say, bracing her trembling body against my own. "We'll sort it out."

"I've tried," she whispers. "He's never going to leave me alone. I'm dangerous to them."

"Because you know too much?"

For a long beat I don't think she's going to answer the question. "Yes," she finally whispers. "I did the books for months before I realized they were laundering money. I thought they were just really successful mechanics." She lets out a laugh that comes out more like a sob. "That was his goal—to make sure I was deep in it before I got the full picture."

"Aw, Livia. It's not your fault. I'd have to google money-laundering to make sure I even know what that entails."

"I'm a bookkeeper, though. I should have seen through his bullshit. And his love-bombing and his shifty answers to direct questions. I got played so bad. Now I'll never get out from under it."

"Don't give up," I whisper. "You're not beaten yet."

An owl hoots somewhere in the distance, and she shivers against me. "What did the other guy look like?"

I describe him, and she swallows hard. "What did he say to you? What reason did he give for showing up at two in the morning?"

"Eh..." I'm not sure what she can handle right now. "He didn't even try to lie about it. He didn't name you, but he asked me where you were."

Livia shudders. "And then he threatened you, right? Wait—he threatened the brewery, too. That's how they operate."

"Well, yeah," I admit. "I guess you do understand these punks."

"Sure I do—*now*. When it's too late." She sighs. "I'll get a couple hours sleep, and then I'll go."

"No you won't," I say, running a hand through her soft hair. "That solves nothing."

"Of course it does! If I'm not here, there's no reason for them to bother you."

"But that's not how assholes work," I argue. "I can't prove to him that you're not here, right? I stuck up for you once already. He'll just assume I've hidden you a little better."

Her body tenses up. "God, you're right. I'm toxic now. And it's spreading."

Then she burst into tears.

CHAPTER 22
LIVIA

It's so embarrassing and so unlike me, but the tears flow freely for a few minutes. I can't seem to shut them down.

"I'm…" *Gulp.* "…sorry." I whimper.

"Shh," he says with a tired sigh. An hour ago, the poor man had been asleep on a crappy old couch in what I assumed to be an unnecessary macho gesture.

Then he did a two-a.m. lap around his father's business with a baseball bat, because I led criminals to his front door.

Nash shouldn't be here at all. He doesn't want to run this brewery, let alone chase drug dealers in the dark. He has a whole other life in Boston. But I've *inflicted* myself, like a virus, splat into the center of his life.

And now I'm crying into his T-shirt. And into his very hard chest.

One broad hand smooths my hair away from my face. "He's the toxic asshole, not you," he rumbles. "You gotta let people take responsibility for their own shit. You can't set yourself on fire to keep someone else warm."

Those kind words quiet me down a little bit. I take a deep breath.

"There you go," he says approvingly, as that warm hand slides down my hair again. "Nothing ever looks right at three in the morning."

"Yes, but…" I sigh. "The trajectory of my life won't look rosier when the sun comes up. That's what I get for trusting the wrong man."

"Yeah, well. Win some, lose some."

I can almost hear his smirk, even in the dark. With a single finger, I poke him in the side. That's what he gets for teasing me in a fragile state.

His stomach clenches, and he lets out a surprised laugh. So I do it again, and he catches my hand in his. "Now, now, darlin'. None of that."

"You're *ticklish*," I declare. "That's unexpected."

"Everybody's ticklish," he argues.

"No they're not." I remove my hand from his. But it's just a fake-out. I've seized on the idea of Nash and his ticklish ribs, because I'm emotionally exhausted and overwrought.

The moment he relaxes, I yank his T-shirt up and drag my fingertips across his abs. And—wow—they are beautiful. Taut skin across rippled muscle that contracts instantly.

"Hey!" He laughs then catches my hand again and tugs it away so I can't possibly tickle him again.

The motion destabilizes me, and I fall forward onto his body, arching my back as I fall so we don't knock heads. We end up nose to nose, me pancaked on top of him and blinking down into his now-serious gaze. I stop breathing.

"Livia," he whispers, and I can't help staring at his sensuous lips as he forms the word. "You gonna cut that out?"

"Yes," I whisper, but somehow it comes out sounding like, *YES BABY YES YES YES.*

He releases my hand, and I push myself up. His T-shirt is still bunched above his stomach, and I catch another glimpse of his abs.

Later, I'll wonder what possessed me. I don't tickle him. Instead, I lean down and press an open-mouthed kiss to his skin.

"Fuck," he says under his breath.

My body takes it as an order, not a curse. I drop another open-mouthed kiss to his stomach. And then another.

He grips my hair, and for a split second, I think he's going to push me away. But nope. He just tightens his hold in a possessive way that makes me shiver.

I kiss him again, trailing my lips and teeth across his abs, exploring the dips and dents of male perfection. The scent of his warm skin beckons like a drug. Using my tongue, I slowly taste his skin, and his answering curse urges me on. When I lick my way down to the elastic of his pants, he makes a hungry sound.

And then? With his free hand, he pulls the tie on his track pants with a hum of expectation. It's a very presumptuous thing to do.

Naturally, I enjoy it.

"Yeah, baby," he whispers. "Get after it. You know you want to."

He isn't wrong. My full name should probably be Livia Poor Impulse Control Willis.

I curl my fingers around the waistband of his pants, and his fingers tighten in my hair. Saving time, I tuck my fingertips under the elastic of his boxers. Then I give a nice tug and watch as he springs into view.

And I'm here to guarantee that Nash Giltmaker was wrong a few minutes ago when he said that nothing ever looks right at three in the morning. Because the thick cock that rises up to meet me looks as right as anything I've ever seen in my life.

Which is why I fall on it hungrily, encircling the head with my lips and tasting the tip.

Nash makes a priceless groan that only deepens when I take him against my tongue. The salty scent of him is making me crazy. I glance up at him in a gesture of blatant erotic submission.

Up on his elbows, he gazes back at me with quirked lips and wide eyes. "Called it. I knew you were a good time." Then he gives my hair a little tug, and my nipples tighten.

I close my eyes and relax my throat, swallowing him down. He makes an unrestrained noise of pure lust. And for a few fun minutes, he can't seem to say anything intelligible at all.

After the week I've had, it's such a relief to apply myself to the simple task of making Nash lose his mind. Time and obligation lose all meaning as I work him steadily closer to the edge.

He lets out a sudden grunt of determination and sits up. "Lose the shirt," he says. "Can't let you have all the fun. I need to suck on your tits."

The air whooshes out of my lungs as I hasten to struggle out of it.

"That's my girl." Clasping my waist, he heaves me up and over, until I'm lying on my back against the sheets. When I open my eyes, Nash is straddling me and stripping off his shirt. I blink up at his naked, godlike body above me. Nash bends over me with a hungry groan, both hands on my breasts. "Fuck, lady. *Yes.*" Then he catches my nipple between his teeth.

I'm suddenly drenched for him. And when he runs his tongue across my nipple I whimper and grab his jaw, trying to move him to my other boob.

A dark chuckle. "Patience, baby." He shakes off my grasp. "And you're still wearing too many clothes."

He isn't wrong. With an undignified wiggle, I shuck off my panties. I'm rewarded a moment later when Nash fits his long body atop mine. All that muscle, pressing me into the bed, and the skin-on-skin heat that I crave more than I should.

But instead of lunging for me again, he holds himself up on his elbows, watching me.

"W-what?" I stammer, wondering whether he's just changed his mind.

"Just admiring the view," he drawls. "Thinkin' how lucky I am right now."

I almost make a crack about how much luckier he'll be in a minute, but his expression is so serious that I forget to. Instead, I watch those brown eyes dip towards me as he takes my mouth in a kiss.

And then I forget to think about anything at all. All I can do is experience him. His tongue cruising mine, his hands all over me. Our skin sliding together, erasing the day. Erasing my mind.

I'll probably regret this tomorrow. But the world goes blissfully quiet as we make out. And his touch is magic. It knows the sensitive spot at the base of my jaw, where his kiss makes me shiver. It knows my inner thighs, where dragging fingertips make me shudder with longing.

"Nash," I beg.

"Yes, baby?" he asks smugly.

"*Now.*"

"But what about finding a...?"

"Now," I insist. "I'm covered."

"Yes, ma'am," he says, fitting himself thickly against me. Then he slowly moves his hips forward, and I moan into the fullness and pleasure.

"*Pussycat,*" he whispers. I expect him to make a smug comment, but that's not what happens. Instead, he seats himself completely, then braces his elbows against the mattress and goes very still.

My body tightens around him, looking for more action. Waiting impatiently. I focus my gaze on those caramel eyes and find them smiling at me.

"What?" I gasp. And by that I mean *what's the holdup?*

"You're just so pretty," he whispers. "Can't a man appreciate you for a minute?"

Apparently not, because my gaze slides away. The laser beam of his stare is too much for me. Besides, I'm not here for the compliments. They never last.

Nash kisses my neck and finally begins to move.

CHAPTER 23
NASH

Livia is a goddess, sighing and shuddering into the slow, dragging pace that I've set. A man could get addicted.

I've been needing this since the first time I saw her across a crowded bar. Craving the heat of her body under mine. Desperate to make her pink lips go slack with pleasure and to make those dark eyes lose focus.

Even here, though, she can't let go entirely. Too much eye-contact makes her wary. She's not used to sharing what's inside that pretty head of hers.

And I respect that, I guess. But right this second, I want everything. Every thought, every sensation. Every shiver. My heart beats with a greedy pulse. *Mine. Mine. Mine.*

"Give me that mouth, girlie," I demand.

The urgent scrape of my voice brings an immediate reaction. She sinks her fingers into my hair and kisses me on command.

There's nothing like it. Electricity snaps through my body as I sink into the kiss. But I know a good thing when I've got it, so I take my time. Life is short. Gotta make the best moments last.

That means deep kisses and eye contact until Livia is straining against me, begging me with her body—if not her mouth—to move things along.

"You need something?" I ask.

She growls.

God, it's fun to tease her. But it's also fun to please her. I pick up the pace with long, languorous strokes. "How sturdy do you think this bed is?"

She whimpers in response.

"Guess we're going to find out." I take both her hands and raise them up to the headboard, so she'll have some purchase. Then I up the ante.

"Nashhhh," she moans, and the sound of my name on her lips makes me crazy. I've thought about this so many times already, my inner porn-flick director slotting us into every conceivable position and breaking in every surface of the building.

Plus, the backseat of her crappy little car.

But creativity will have to wait. I'm driving my girl crazy, and I'm too greedy to flip her over or mess up the view I have of her pink cheeks and shiny eyes. Or the "O" of pleasure her mouth makes as I thrust my hips toward heaven.

"Brace yourself, honey," I pant, sliding one of her smooth legs up onto my shoulder.

She gasps as I notch up the pace until the headboard is banging against the wall, and I'm so amped up I might blow like a grenade.

I don't, though, until Livia's gaze locks onto mine, and I lean in for a single, bottomless kiss. Her whole body tightens exquisitely around me, and she moans into my mouth.

Then I'm done for. My body spasms with pleasure, the sound of her climax wringing me out.

And I've literally never been happier in my life.

CHAPTER 24
LIVIA

Nash collapses onto my body with an exhausted groan. Stunned. It's hard to catch my breath.

God, when I decide to turn wicked, I don't hold back.

Beside me, Nash makes a halfhearted attempt to roll off me. Then he laughs.

"What's so funny?" I ask, my defensive hackles rising right on cue.

"Us," he says, his voice muffled by the pillow under his face. "I'd almost like to invite those jackweeds back over tomorrow night to wake us up again."

"Nash!" I yelp, mostly because I hadn't thought about Rotty or Razor for a good half hour.

"*Kidding.*" He lifts an arm and slings it over my body. "I can bang you tomorrow without their help."

"Presumptuous much?"

He lifts his head and gives a pointed look at my very naked, debauched body. "I like my odds."

That shuts me up. Because I never did have any common sense.

I wiggle out from under him and pad off to the bathroom,

giving Nash a much-needed chance to retreat upstairs. Like men do.

But when I come back, he's still there. In fact, he's straightened out the covers and claimed one of my pillows.

I hesitate at the side of the bed. "You don't have to stay. I won't be offended."

"I like your bed," he says sleepily. "Like it even better with you in it."

Too tired to argue, I climb in, arrange myself on the other side, and pull the covers primly over my naked body. "Well goodnight, then," I mutter, curling away from him.

"Goodnight, pussycat," he says. Then he rolls onto his side, reaches out with both arms and hauls me against his chest, making me the little spoon.

I lie very still, but I'm still too wound up to sleep. My brain whirls like a fidget spinner. Meanwhile, Nash's breathing evens out, and he falls asleep. Like a man without a care in the world.

Unlike me. Razor knows I'm here now. They probably saw my car tonight. That means they'll be back. They'll put the whole place under surveillance, and when they've figured out my daily schedule, they'll pounce and drag me away.

There aren't any security cameras at the brewery, and I bet they noticed that tonight. It's probably the first thing they checked.

This is terrible. And I just made it twice as complicated by sleeping with the boss's son. I *pounced* on him. So that's just awkward.

My life is so tangled that I have worries enough to keep me awake until dawn. Except it's strangely relaxing to be curled up against a tattooed hunk who's sleeping. Somehow, it's like anesthesia. Every time his six-pack rises and falls on another even breath, I feel a little bit sleepier.

It's getting tricky to focus on my issues when it's so sleepy in here.

The moonlight creeps around the edges of the tattered curtains, and an owl hoots in the distance.

My last thought before I fall asleep is of Nash's bright eyes as he'd leaned in to kiss me.

———

Four hours later, though, I wake up alone. And that's a good thing, because my first thought is of Nash. *Naked* Nash.

I let out an embarrassing little moan of longing, mixed with a healthy splash of stupidity.

God, what was I thinking? That man is seriously hot, but in a lifetime of bad decisions, he might be the worst one yet. Especially because I'm afraid of what I might do if he walked back into this room right now.

Luckily, he doesn't. And the house echoes with the variety of silence you get when there's only one person inside it.

One very stupid person.

Nash probably agrees with me. Maybe he woke up beside me in the predawn light and had a sudden attack of *what the hell was I thinking*.

Because seriously. Sleeping with your coworker and temporary roommate? Big mistake. Huge.

Maybe we just needed to clear that out of our systems. It's a theory. So then why did I wake up thinking about him?

Oh right. Because I make poor life choices.

I get out of bed and stomp to the bathroom. It takes a cool shower, some deep breathing, and several high-end cosmetics to get my game face back on. I go with a subtle, smoky eye. And I even apply a few dabs of the salon styling products I keep for special occasions, to tame my curls.

"Special occasions" used to mean a night out at the bar or a party. But those don't happen anymore. So I style myself up for a little boost of confidence. Men never notice what you actually do in front of the mirror. They just notice the boost of confidence it gives you.

When I feel more ready to face Nash again, I peer through the curtains of the pumphouse. There's nobody in evidence, so I lock up, shoot towards the back door of the brewery, and then march inside.

The only thing to do is to find Nash and tell him that last night was a moment of weakness for me. That I appreciate all the help he's given me lately, but we can't be having a sexual relationship. My life is already complicated enough.

I'd lay odds that he's busy preparing the same speech for me. He seems like a man who values his independence. When I tell him my thoughts, he'll surely be relieved.

When I find him, he's in the brewhouse, his earbuds in, talking to his dad while he checks the readouts on his batches of Goldenpour. "All right. Let's add some hops," he says. "Tell me what I'm gettin' out of the storeroom."

He listens a second, then runs his hand over his jaw. "Really? All *that?* This is a weird-ass beer, Pops." Then he laughs.

I'm a little astonished. In the first place, he and his dad seem to be having a nice little conversation. In the second place, Nash is a super-attractive man when he's frowning. But when he smiles, it's almost blinding. I feel some warm flutters again, and I don't like it.

Stop it, flutters. You're fired.

I spin around on my heel and head into the office alone. Thankfully, I get very absorbed in some bookkeeping. Eventually, though, I hear Nash's voice outside the window behind the building. He's talking to someone, giving instructions. Something about a ladder.

That's handy, actually. If he's outside, I can duck out there and catch him for a private chat. We need one. Badly.

At the back door, I look both ways before I step outside. Nash is minding a ladder that's propped against the wall. An unfamiliar man is climbing it, and there's a van parked nearby that says *Grunt's Security Systems*.

I don't see anyone else, but I still feel exposed as I step out into the sunshine.

"Hey, pussycat," Nash says, glancing up the ladder, his muscular arms holding it steady. "You okay?"

I swallow and drag my gaze off his body. "I'm fine. What's going on out here?"

"Security cameras," Nash says. "Motion-sensitive lights, too. And a new lock with a keypad."

I blink. "Wait, really? That sounds expensive."

Nash shrugs.

"You know what would be cheaper?" I ask with a slightly hysterical tremor creeping into my voice. "Me leaving Vermont."

"Nobody's leaving," he says easily. "These are basic security upgrades. Shoulda been done a long time ago."

That point is hard to argue. But everyone knows why upgrades never happened. Because Lyle Giltmaker is cheap. "Your dad is really down with all of this? The expense?"

"Eh, he will be," Nash says. "That man is paranoid about somebody stealing his precious recipes. I can sell 'im on the idea. Besides—some of this is on Benito's dime."

The air whooshes out of my lungs when he mentions the cops. *"Why?"*

"He really wants these guys. Could be a big deal for him, career-wise. Hey—I have a name to show you. He traced both those assholes' motorcycle registrations for us. Hang on." He waits a moment for the security company guy to come back down the ladder. After the guy heads for the open doors of his van, Nash unlocks his phone and shows me a message. "These names look familiar?"

The first one is Razor's. Legal name *Richard Sharpe*. It's hardly surprising, but I feel sick anyway. Razor was *here*, right on this property, where I used to feel safe.

The other name also startles me: *Nathan Delrose, age 33. Rutland, Vermont.*

"Nathan?" I yelp. "Rotty's real name can't be *Nathan*. Nathan is your school principal. Nathan is your gastroenterologist."

Nash chuckles. "But there's a driver's license photo. See?" He flips to a picture, and there's Rotty, scowling at the camera in a shaggy beard. "So the name means nothing to you?"

"No. Wait. Show it to me again." I squint at the details and sigh. "Okay, the last name does ring a bell." *Delrose.* "I've seen it before, probably on a document."

"Any idea where?"

I try to think. "There were a lot of papers in that office. It could have been on anything. Like an order for mufflers. But..." I close my eyes and try to remember. "There was one time I saw a filing for one of their LLCs. There was a list of directors. He might have been on it."

When I open my eyes, Nash is watching me with a solemn expression. "Benito wants to talk to you again."

"I bet he does," I say in a grumpy voice. Talking to the cops is about as appealing to me as getting a root canal.

Although I'd liked Benito. He had intelligent eyes and a calm demeanor. Talking to him could be a one-time thing, and there's no reason why I couldn't have a conversation with him and *then* drive like a demon out of Vermont.

I still have choices.

Nash reaches up and tucks my hair behind my ear. We're standing so close to one another. I get a whiff of his clean, piney scent, and suddenly realize two things. One, yum. And two, we're supposed to be having an important chat right now.

"Nash," I say, taking a small step backward. "We need to talk. About last night."

"Yeah," he agrees with a serious nod. "I have something to say about that, too."

That's the best news I've heard all day. "Go ahead, then. Say it," I encourage him. "You go first."

"Fair enough."

Before I realize what's happening, he takes a step closer to me, cups my chin in one rough hand and kisses me. Slowly and thoroughly. And now there's a whole swarm of warm flutters in my belly. And maybe in my panties.

"*Nash!*" I yelp, coming to my senses and stepping back. "We were supposed to be having a conversation, here."

"Oh, we are," he says, his voice like whiskey. "I got a lot more to say on the subject, too. Wanna hear it?"

Confused, I hesitate.

Nash doesn't, though. He steps in and takes my mouth in another hungry kiss. With Nash's banging body pressed up against mine and his tongue licking into my mouth, everything goes blissfully quiet inside my head for a precious moment.

Someone clears his throat. Loudly. With a gasp, I look up to see the security guy holding a camera. "Don't stop on my account. Just step away from the ladder?"

"Sorry, dude," Nash says cheerfully. He gently nudges me out of the way and puts a hand out to steady the ladder.

The guy climbs up and begins installing the security camera. Meanwhile, I suck in oxygen and try to stay on task.

"You look extra hot today," Nash says in a low voice. "Great hair, babe. And that eye makeup is on point."

What the? "Look, let's start over. I came outside to tell you that we can't do it again."

"Do what?" His eyes twinkle.

"You *know* what," I hiss.

He grins. "I can't think of a reason why not."

"I can!" I insist. "A million reasons, actually. We're roommates, for starters."

"That's just convenient." He shrugs.

"B-but…" I stammer. He's got me all worked up. "The power imbalance, Nash! We work together. And not as equals."

"Huh," he says slowly. "I know that can be a thing. But honestly, I'm not afraid that you'll fire me if it doesn't work out. I mean, it's a temporary job, yeah? And if you did fire me, I guess I could live with that."

"Fire *you?*" My head might explode. "You got that backwards. You're my boss right now. You could fire *me.*"

He gives me a look of complete disbelief. Then he pulls out his phone and offers it to me. "Really? Call my dad right now and ask him if I have the power to fire you. Bet you a steak dinner he says no."

Hell. I might actually lose that bet. And I can't afford a steak dinner.

I frown.

He grins. "Got any other arguments, pussycat?"

"Um…" I was so sure this discussion would go my way that I didn't have my bullet points all lined up and ready to go. "I'll think of some."

"You do that," he says. "In the meantime, hide your cute ass inside, just in case your ex comes back with our gastroenterologist."

Having no good argument against this advice, I take it.

CHAPTER 25
NASH

The security upgrade turns out great, but it sets me back half a day. That means my father is blowing up my phone asking to taste this week's brews.

So, after a quick lunch meeting with the brewhouse staff, I ask Livia to help me prep some bottles to sneak into my father's room. "It worked so well the last time."

"Sure. Am I going with you to Serenity Hills?"

"Nah, I'll man up and go alone. You're more useful here."

She gives me a bashful glance from underneath long eyelashes. I wasn't lying when I said she looked hot today. Kinda makes me want to find out whether the office door locks. "All right," she says quietly. "Give me ten minutes to set you up with samples."

A short while later, I'm striding into my father's hospital room, fake kombucha under my arm. I find him sitting on the bed, hooked up to his IV full of antibiotics.

He scowls. "Took you long enough."

"Dad," I say with a sigh. "I'm a busy man."

He looks away, defeat on his face. "I know, because it ought to be me out there. I shouldn't be here on my ass. I should be cooking up a new seasonal brew. Summer's almost here. Wish I

151

could rip this thing out of my arm and just leave. Sitting around is how you become old and irrelevant."

The disappointment in his voice gives me an unwelcome flash of empathy for the old grouch. "I've seen the lines out front during tasting-room hours. Pretty sure you're not irrelevant yet."

"It's a small comfort," he grumbles. "Now let's taste."

I close the door and uncap the first brew.

He sniffs the top. "Goldenpour. Gotta be day eight. Well, let's see how you did."

It's stupid, but I find myself holding my breath while he tastes.

"Mmm. Not bad, kid. Not bad at all."

A very unwelcome spark of pride zings through me.

"We're back, eh?"

"Yeah, you're back all right," I say gruffly.

He tastes the rest and declares them all acceptable, and I rinse the bottles in the sink. Then I sit down in the visitors' chair. "Look, I have to get back to it, but we had a little excitement at the brewery, and there's a couple of developments I need to catch you up on."

"What kind of excitement?" he grunts.

"Turns out that Livia has a nasty ex. He and a buddy have been scouring Vermont looking for her. This week her luck ran out, and they found her."

My father blinks. "She okay?"

"Yeah, yeah. Sorry. Shoulda led with that."

He sits back against the pillows and strokes his chin. "I can see it. That girl is wary. Never talks about herself. Doesn't leave the property much, and she refuses to work in the taproom. So what happened?"

"Dude recognized her POS car in the lot. I was working in the tasting room when he came inside asking whether a woman that looked like her worked there. I lied, because I wasn't born yesterday."

My dad grins.

"She spotted him and practically had an aneurism. I hid her

car and talked her off the ledge. But the asshole didn't buy my story. Came back in the middle of the night to poke around. When I went outside to scare him off, he threatened Livia, me, and the brewery. In that order. Said if I protected her, he'd burn the place down."

The grin slides off my father's face. "Shit."

"Yeah."

"I should be there," he says.

"Twenty-four seven?" I counter. "That's not practical. We need cameras and motion-sensitive lights. So I took care of that today. New locks, too."

He scowls. "How much of my money are you spending?"

"I spent what was necessary," I say firmly. "The place is a tinderbox—full of old wood. And starting over from nothing but ashes is not how a man stays relevant."

Now he looks thoughtful instead of angry, so I guess that's progress. "All right. You call the police?"

"Of course. Benito added a couple cameras to my order—on his tab. Apparently, he wants these guys for some drug deal or something. They're dangerous people. This isn't a drill."

He closes his eyes. "Wish I knew that when I hired that girl."

"Seriously? Tell me with a straight face that you wouldn't have hired her anyway. She's the backbone of your operation."

"Fuck." He blinks his eyes open and sighs. "Yeah, I guess I would have. Just don't need this right now. Sounds complicated. And expensive."

"But you *do* need these upgrades. And Dad? I know how receptive you are to my ideas…"

He snorts.

"But if you ever want to hear a few other ways you could save money by making your operation more efficient…"

"No," he says sharply. "Nothing wrong with my operation."

Right. "Glad to hear it," I say drily.

Some things never change.

CHAPTER 26
LIVIA

"The club is based in Rutland, and I worked out of their offices."

Officer Benito Rossi sits across the table, scribbling notes on a legal pad. And I use the moment to take a gulp of water.

He's not interrogating me by any stretch, but talking about Razor is excruciating. And talking about what I put up with in Rutland makes me feel wildly uncomfortable, even sitting here with a cop in my own kitchen.

"Can you tell me the exact address of the office where they keep the books?" he asks.

I wipe my clammy hands on my jeans under the table and then rattle off the address. "The office is in the same building as the repair shop with a separate entrance in back. Razor lives in the little house next door—to the right, if you're facing the shop. There's a driveway separating the two properties. And the club-house is on the opposite side—to the left of the repair shop."

"Okay…" Benito taps his pen on the pad. "Would you say the shop is busy? Lots of customers?"

"Yes, and no?" I shrug. "There were always a couple of bikes in the service bays. But it's hard to tell how much business gets done, because there are always guys dropping by just to chat. And I wasn't very interested in the repair business."

"Not a motorcycle girl?" He smiles warmly.

I shake my head. It's obvious that he's trying to appear calm and open. Like this conversation isn't a big deal. It is, though. I live for the day when Razor goes to jail, yet my stomach clenches every time I think about taking the witness stand. He's a slippery guy with lots of violent friends, and I'm not sure how this situation can end well for me.

"Let's back up. How did you meet Razor, and how did you end up working for him and the motorcycle club?"

Now we're getting into the meat of the story. "I met Razor in a bar a year ago last fall. He asked me out, and we started casually dating. He was…" I search for the right words. "He was *very* good to me. Attentive. Fun. Flattering. Generous. Now I recognize it as love-bombing."

Benito's pen pauses on the page. "What does that mean to you?"

"Um…" *It means I'm a fool.* "He laid it on thick. Said I was the most interesting woman he'd ever met. Told me I was smart and pretty. The whole package…" I can feel my face burning as I say this. "I fell for it. I wanted to believe everything he said. But he was really just buttering me up. In the spring, my lease was up, and he'd asked me to move in with him. At the same time, he also brought up the possibility of doing the books for the club's Rutland shop."

"You had your own bookkeeping business?"

I shake my head. "I was working for an accounting firm and had a variety of client accounts. The work was steady, and they paid me by the hour, but not very well. When Razor asked me to do the Rutland shop—and said he'd pay me directly—I loved that idea."

"Cutting out the middleman," Benito says.

"Exactly. I was happy to do it, and the books were no more complicated than I was used to."

"How did the business look to you on paper?" he asks. "How did the money flow?"

"Honestly, it looked really ordinary at first. For expenses, they bought motorcycle parts and had a payroll with, like, seven guys on it. For income, they invoiced customers for repairs. It was very straightforward."

"And they were profitable?" Benito asks.

"Sure. Bear in mind that I have never run a motorcycle repair shop. In retrospect, seven guys seems like a lot of manpower. But I didn't have any reason to question it until later."

"I get it," he says. "When did things start to seem weird?"

I let out a sigh. "He's crafty. Don't let the rough appearance fool you. The man knows how to play a long game. He gave me a taste of working on his books and getting paid directly. But he didn't ask me to take on more until later. He waited until I got good and fed up at my regular job."

"With the accounting firm?"

"Right. The owner had a nephew in college who wanted to pick up some hours, so they reduced mine and gave him more. I was mad. But Razor didn't rush in and solve my problems yet. He took me out on a few nice dates and was very sympathetic as my income dwindled and I started to send out my résumé. Then I got an offer from another accountant..."

"And that's when he pounced," Benito guesses.

"Yeah." I heave another sigh. "And it's possible that Razor wasn't just stalling. Before I started doing the books, all the business records were decentralized across his network of operations. No one person could see how the money flowed. He was taking a risk, bringing it all together."

"*Ah.*" Benito scribbles thoughtfully on his notebook. "You ever meet any of those other people? From the other parts of the operation?"

"Sometimes? It wasn't easy for me to tell who was a business associate, and who was just a friend who rode over for some beers. But there was this one dude who helped run the Burlington shop. He was the club member who'd done the books up there. But he wasn't any good at it. The records were a mess. I'm pretty sure that's why Razor needed a change. He was worried about me catching on, but he was even more worried that they didn't have a great handle on the business."

Benito gives another thoughtful nod. "So what was his name? And what was it like when you took over?"

"They call him 'Fish' because his last name is Fishman. First name is John or James or something forgettable like that. He brought me, like, two dozen file boxes. I spent the first month just trying to get a handle on it all. Nothing was electronic—it was all in folders. I moved everything to Quickbooks."

He looks up from his notes. "You still remember the password?"

"Sure. But there's no chance it would still work. Razor is not a stupid man."

Benito rubs his forehead. "Okay. When did you realize they were a dirty operation? What tipped you off in the books?"

"Well, the cash. Lots of deposit slips for cash, and very few credit card charges. But even that didn't bother me so much at first, because bikers can be really old school. They like cash. And otherwise, the paper trail made sense. Burlington was a *much* bigger operation. The garage was busy, with constant income from repairs. But they were also a dealership, with lots of purchases and sales of used motorcycles. And motorcycles aren't cheap, right? A used Harley can go for twenty grand if it's in pristine condition."

"Sure," Benito says. "So how did you know something was wrong?"

"One day I went shopping." I shrug. "Took a day in Burlington with my cousin. We tried on dresses and went out to lunch on Church Street. On my way home, I drove through South Burlington. I don't even know why, but I took a detour off Route 7. I knew the address of the shop. I drove past it."

Benito waits, a smile on his face.

"You already know what I'm going to say, don't you? The

shop is tiny. One step up from a shed. Barely a sign outside. No showroom full of used bikes for sale."

"Yeah, I've spent a few dull nights staking it out. Not a lot of action there. So what did you do then?"

"Went home and asked Razor about it. Shared my confusion." I roll my eyes at my own stupidity. As if this was a funny little thing that happened.

But it wasn't funny at all.

"What did he say?" Benito asks softly.

Before I can answer, the door opens and Nash enters the kitchen. "Hey, kids. Don't mind me. Just need a cup of coffee. Anyone else want one?"

After I shake my head and Benito declines, Nash makes his way over to the coffeemaker and starts puttering with it.

"What was his response," Benito asks me, "when you asked him about the shop?"

"Well…" I drop my voice. "He backhanded me. Then he told me to mind my own fucking business and not to question him."

At the kitchen counter, Nash goes completely still.

"Was that the first time he hit you?" Benito asks.

I nod with as much nonchalance as I can muster.

"And then what happened?"

"He was very apologetic after his, um, outburst. He told me that he was sorry and that I'd triggered him. He said a friend's disloyalty had messed him up when he was younger. That was his exact phrase—'it messed me up.'" I clear my throat again. "Anyway, I didn't ask a second time. I didn't even want to think about it for a while."

"I bet," Benito says kindly.

There's an awkward pause while I wrestle with what to say next. It's hard to account for the next couple of months in my life. I'd known in my gut that Razor was running some kind of sketchy operation, and that I was increasingly tangled up in it.

Even so, I didn't want to believe it. My finances were stable for the first time in my adult life. Razor didn't let me contribute to rent or a mortgage. *I take care of my woman*, he'd said. So I'd been giving a lot of my income to Jennie, who had a son to care for. And to my brother…

"Livia, what was the next thing that made you suspicious?" Benito asks. "I know you eventually left, because you're sitting right here."

"Well…" I glance at Nash's back, wishing I didn't have to explain this in front of him. "I didn't want to admit that I was sleeping with a criminal. And he, uh, was super nice to me for a while. Flowers. Love notes. The whole shebang. But then the revenue from Burlington went bonkers."

Benito's eyes brighten. "Define *bonkers*."

"They netted a quarter million dollars in one month, most of it in cash. Lots of sales of bikes. So I started listening closely when the guys were getting their beers on. They never said a word about selling motorcycles, which I thought was weird."

"Did drugs ever come up?"

I shrug. "Not in a very clear way. Their conversation was more or less encoded. But they kept talking about 'fresh product' in a way that just didn't sound like bikes."

"Why did you think it might be drugs?" Benito asks.

I close my eyes and try to think. "They mentioned 'dealers' sometimes. And it didn't sound like auto dealers. It just didn't. And they mentioned 'drops.' Maybe I watch too much TV, but it gave me a whiff of the drug dealers on *The Wire*."

Benito grins. "Great show."

"Yeah, it was. But I didn't want to live it. And I noticed that the guys who went to 'make a drop' were using their own motor-cycles as transportation. So whatever they were dropping had to be small."

Benito scribbles on his pad, drinking this in. "You ever see any packaging? Vials? Powders?"

I shake my head. "That must happen elsewhere. And Razor was too careful to let anything like that happen in front of me. In fact, he sometimes shushed them when the chatter got too detailed. One time they were planning a drop behind an old CVS, and he came into the room and told them to shut up."

"Interesting."

"So I started poking around in ways I couldn't get caught. I looked closely at their motorcycle sales. Looked up some VIN numbers online. It's not that hard. That's where it got weird."

"Yeah?" He sits forward in his chair.

"The VINs didn't make sense. They were all the right number of digits, but the make and model didn't line up with the details in the ledger book. And it wasn't just one or two sales—it was all of them."

He whistles again. "What month's sales were you looking at? When was the bonkers month?"

It takes me a few minutes to work out the dates. But I'm able to narrow it down to March or April, the months before I escaped. "And pretty soon after that, I knew it was time to go."

"Why?" he asks softly.

My throat closes up suddenly.

Fiddling with the coffee machine, I keep my back to Livia, because I can sense her discomfort. But you couldn't pay me enough money to walk away right now. I need to know what we're up against.

"Do I have to tell you?" she whispers.

"No," Benito says gently. "Especially if you think you'll incriminate yourself. But you should know that nothing you've told me so far puts you in any legal jeopardy."

"Really?" Her voice is pure surprise.

"Really. Just because you did the books for a criminal operation doesn't mean that a prosecutor would ever try to punish you for it. Even if they tried, they would have to prove intent and probably show that you profited off of it."

"But I *did* profit. I cashed their paychecks, which were generous. They paid twice as much per hour as my other employer."

"Yet you had no idea what the racket was when you started, and Razor never leveled with you, did he?"

"Not until the very end," she says quietly. "And only as leverage against me leaving. But I never reported them."

"See, but you left. You made it clear that you never wanted to be part of it. That's why you won't go down for any of this. What led to your leaving? What was the last straw?"

"They, uh, hurt someone." Her voice is so low that I can barely hear it. "I heard Razor's buddy bragging about it. They hired a PI to track a guy down—some associate of theirs. They thought he'd cheated them, so they found out where he'd last used his credit cards, and they staked out a bar in Massachusetts. A couple of club members beat him up."

"You know his name?" Benito asked.

"No. They used a nickname, and I can't remember what it was. But I knew they could do the same thing to me. The way they tracked that guy was sophisticated. So I had to get out of there. Even then, it took me two tries. The first time he came back to the house unexpectedly. He found my packed bag on the seat of my car. My passport was in it. Pretty obvious that I was planning to bolt…" She trails off.

The coffee machine is done, but I'm just staring at the full pot, waiting to hear what she says. I'm not going to like it.

"What did he do?" Benito asks softly.

"He, uh, ran into the house and threw me against the enter-tainment center in the living room. I was so shocked I didn't really have time to react. I went through a glass cabinet, got cut up pretty badly. Then he forced me into the bedroom and restrained me."

All my blood has stopped circulating. And I'm gripping the countertop with two white-knuckled hands.

"How did he restrain you?" Benito asks patiently.

Fuck, how can he sound so calm? I want to flip all the tables.

"With, uh, handcuffs and a chain and the bed frame." Her voice drops to almost a whisper. "He left me there for an entire day. To teach me a lesson. But the only lesson I learned was that I needed to get the fuck away from him."

"Smart," Benito agrees.

"It took another week before he'd leave me alone again for more than a few minutes. He also took my passport and my car keys, but I had a second car key in my duffel bag that he missed. He still has my passport. When I asked for it, he wouldn't give it back."

"That's a crime," Benito says. "Taking your passport is larceny. And it's also a violation of personal liberty—the same as chaining you to a bed. All these extenuating circumstances help ensure that you won't be held liable for his criminal activity."

"Unless he hires every lawyer in Vermont and gets off on a technicality. Then he'll be back for more of this…"

I turn around in time to see her pull up the cuff of her sweater to show Benito the scars on the inside of her forearm.

My friend squints to see the faded, slightly shiny marks imprinted in her skin. "Ouch. That's from the broken glass?"

"He dragged me through it while I screamed."

I can't stop myself from reacting. "He *dragged you?*"

Benito gives me a look that says *cool it*.

But I'm not sure I can. Anger surges in my blood, and if that guy were here right now? I don't know what I'd do. But it wouldn't be pretty.

"Did you happen to take any pictures of the wound?" he asks Livia.

"Yes. He wouldn't take me to the ER for stitches, and he wouldn't, um, let me out of the house for a few days." She drops her eyes to her shoes. "I took photos as soon as I could, but it was a couple days after it happened. I texted them to my cousin. But there aren't any witnesses, and I don't have a doctor's report."

"Pictures are good. How'd you get away, eventually?"

Livia is silent for a moment. "I just waited until he got bored of babysitting me. He went to play some poker a few blocks away, and I didn't waste any time. I spent five minutes packing, then walked out with my remaining car key and drove away. It wasn't that brave."

I can't stay silent anymore. "Well *I* think it sounds really fucking brave."

Livia gives me a flicker of a smile.

"We can build an assault case against him," Benito says. "At least for starters. But I think, with your help, we can get him on something even better. How much proof can you give me that Razor is running a dirty operation?"

Livia shifts in her chair. "I don't know. And I don't want an entire network of bikers to know I'd betrayed their asshole in chief."

Oh, pussycat.

Benito doesn't react for a moment. Then he nods slowly. "I hear you that they're dangerous people. But if you helped me nail Razor and his friends, then you wouldn't have to look over your shoulder all the time. Wouldn't it feel great to be free of this?"

She puts her elbows on the table and drops her head in her hands. "I just don't know if I *can* be free. If I thought it would work, I would have tried it already. His network is vast. He knows bikers all over New England."

"I understand," Benito says kindly. "But would you think it over? I'm not in the business of causing problems for witnesses. Haven't lost one yet."

"Sure. I can think about it," she says. "As if I can think about anything else."

He reaches over and pats her hand just once. "I bet. One last question before I go. Do you know where Razor is staying right now?"

"Um… No?" She looks confused. "Probably at his house?"

"He hasn't been seen there for a couple days. And we can't find Rotty, either. I'm trying to figure out if something big went down, or if they're just off on a joyride somewhere."

She rubs her eyes. "Hold on. Let's try Instagram."

Benito grins. "Bikers like Instagram?"

"Their women do." She pulls up the app and heads to the search screen. "Hey, look. They're on their way to a jamboree. Saranac Lake is in New York State, right?"

He takes the phone, notes the account Livia is following, and scribbles it down. "This is very helpful. Who else should I be looking at?"

She gives him a couple other accounts, and then he pushes back his chair. "I've got to run. But I'm going to follow up on the things you told me. Don't worry too much. If anyone tries to make trouble on the premises, we'll get video evidence of him. Meanwhile, I'm going to go see a forensic accountant who can help me corroborate those bad VIN numbers you told me about."

Livia looks freaked out about this. Still, she pushes back her chair and walks him to the door. Pleasantries are exchanged. Hands shaken. But after he leaves, she slides back into a chair and puts her head in her hands again.

I pour her a cup of coffee—milky, the way she likes it—and set it down on the table. Then I sit in the chair beside hers. And I wait.

Without making eye contact, she takes the mug and gulps from it. "Thanks for the coffee," she says shakily.

"Anytime, pussycat," I whisper. Someone has got to take proper care of this girl, and now that person is me.

And he *hurt her*. It's personal now.

Her dark eyelashes flick momentarily in my direction. "Don't," she says. "Don't make this into a thing. I know you were eavesdropping."

"I do feel a little guilty about that." *But only a little.* "But why don't you want me to know what you're dealing with? This isn't on you."

She gulps. "I don't like attention. And I don't like to play the part of the victim. So this conversation is closed. Thank you for respecting that."

"Hey now—I don't buy that entirely. I think you used to enjoy attention as much as the next girl. But now you don't, because you think a normal amount of attention might get you killed."

She blinks. "That's not a compliment, Giltmaker. No woman wants to hear that she's a diva."

"Never called you a diva. Don't put words in my mouth. But

the first time we almost met, you were different. The woman I saw across the bar last fall is the *real* Livia. She likes a party. She knows how to flirt."

"That was…" She sighs. "That was a fluke."

"Nah," I insist. "Your party vibe isn't the only thing you suppress, either. You're more competent than most people, and probably wouldn't mind a little recognition. But you're hiding in my father's office instead of finding a job that would use you to your full potential."

She rolls her eyes. "Just because you hate working for your father's brewery doesn't mean I do."

"Didn't say that either," I point out. "But you've been keeping your head down for so long that you probably forgot what it's like to go wherever you want and make new friends. Besides—you're at the mercy of this place and this family. Leila asked you to share the pumphouse for a few weeks, and you said yes because you didn't think you had a choice."

She shrugs. "It's fine, Nash. We've been over this."

"Nothing that happened to you is *fine*. And you had to let my ass into the pumphouse as a roommate? It couldn't have been easy for you to open the door to a stranger. Not after…"

She raises both hands, as if to shut me up. "I'm not afraid of you. And you don't have to apologize for *him*."

That stops me in my tracks for a second. Because that's exactly how I feel right now—like the world owes her an apology, and I want her to have it.

Not sure why I think it falls to me. I guess I'll worry about that later. For now, I reach out and lift Livia off her chair and pull her into my lap.

She lets out a little shriek of surprise. "God, warn a girl. I could have spilled my coffee."

"And I would have made you another cup." I wrap my arms around her and bury my face in her neck. "I'm sorry there's an entitled psychopath after you. I'm sorry he put you through a terrible time."

She sighs, but she's still holding herself stiffly. "I appreciate the sentiment. But he's not your problem."

"He is if I say he is."

"What? No," she yelps. "You can't tag me like a deer. That's entitled. That's something *he'd* say."

"Didn't say I owned you. Didn't tell you not to leave. I realize I'm not entitled to get you naked again and have my filthy way with you. That's your call. Although, given the scratch marks down my back, I'm thinking you'll have another go eventually. My pussycat has claws."

She lets out a low growl. But at the same time, her body melts against mine.

"I only said it was my choice whether or not I try to nail the dickhead who's stalking you, and his dickhead friends if they turn up again on my property. I hate bullies. Hope he comes back, so I can show him how much."

CHAPTER 28
LIVIA

I can't help myself. I sag against Nash's chest, because it's strong and warm and also convenient. Although I can't keep leaning on this man. He's going to get tired of me and all my drama.

For the moment, though, he's brushing the hair off my neck and kissing my jaw. Which is not going to solve anything. "Nash, we should go back to work. The beer won't brew itself."

"But you smell so good. Like sunshine and sex."

"I do not," I insist, nudging his questing mouth away from my neck. "I showered."

"Wishful thinking, then."

I laugh in spite of myself. And Nash—that jerk—uses this petty distraction to kiss me. The man has a sinful mouth and generous lips, and the moment his mouth finds mine, I lean into the kiss.

When I kiss him back, he makes a soft, happy sound deep in his chest. Maybe that's why I find Nash so sexy—he's a strong, tattooed beast that is somehow capable of great tenderness.

Honestly, it could mess with a girl's head. It's messing with mine already. Whenever he does this—licking his way into my mouth, his roughened fingertips lifting the hem of my top and then skimming across my skin—I get sidetracked. And I get distracted by the fantasy—that a burly guy with a hot body has arrived in my life to love me and protect me.

But the truth is much simpler—a burly guy with a hot body and good hands has arrived in my life for sex and mutual entertainment. And maybe stress relief.

Not to love me or protect me. I have to do both those jobs for myself. And, frankly, that's easier to do without a man in my bed.

Less fun, though.

Meanwhile, Nash takes my face in his hands and kisses the ever-loving hell out of me. His body is hot and hard beneath mine, and whether I intended to or not, I'm losing myself in the moment.

Until suddenly Nash scoops me up and sets me back down on the chair.

Alone.

I blink, dismayed, as Nash crosses the kitchen to fix himself another cup of coffee. "That'll have to hold us until later," he says. "Tasting room opens in ten, and I'm working the walk-in today. We can't have you in there. Too risky."

"Oh," I say quietly. "I'm sorry about that."

"Not your fault. Catch you later." He turns to go, then turns around again immediately, a thoughtful look on his face. "Hey, Livia? I'm supposed to do drinks tonight with a high school buddy who needs a shoulder to cry on. I can cancel…"

"No—don't worry about it," I say, even as my heart drops. "Go out and have fun tonight."

He frowns, which probably means that I'm not hiding my discomfort as well as I should be. "Benito's guys are going to watch the place. You're not in any danger."

If only that were true. But Nash owes me *nothing*. "Go," I insist. "I don't need a babysitter."

"A babysitter," he repeats slowly. "Now there's an interesting idea."

"What? *No!* I'll be fine. I don't need anybody."

Nash lifts his chin and studies me with an expression that's suddenly serious. "Not true, sweetheart. We all need somebody sometimes. It's just a fact."

I'm just processing this while he gives me a sexy wink. Then he turns and leaves the pumphouse with a powerful stride.

Damn it. The sight of him leaving makes my stomach twist. Like he's taking a little corner of my heart with him.

———

That evening I spend time cooking a big pot of tortilla soup and brooding. And mulling over my options.

Officer Benito wants me to narc on Razor's crew, and I'm terrified to do that. On the one hand, I have a secret stash of evidence against Razor that I took when I left. It's my little insurance policy.

On the other hand, I haven't figured out how to use it and remain breathing. Razor has too many friends, and I didn't spend enough time in his orbit to even know who I ought to be afraid of.

That leaves me two choices—give the files to Officer Benito Rossi, and hope that he's as good at his job as he thinks he is. Or do a runner.

My gut says that door number two is my only real chance. But I'll never really get my life back. I'll always be waiting for the other shoe to drop. I'll always be afraid.

And if the police decide I'm too important to let go, I'll be looking over my shoulder for *them*, too. Maybe Nash meant well when he brought in the cops. But it's making my life even harder than it was before.

After an hour or so of indecision, I pick up my phone and call Jennie.

"Ivyyyyy! What's up with you?"

"Are you okay?" is my first question, even though she sounds cheery. With Razor and Rotty on the loose, I can never let down my guard.

"I'm cool. That dickhead who was looking for you hasn't been back. He must realize that I actually don't know where you are."

My blood pressure drops a fraction. "Good. What's shaking?"

"I miss you. And so does Henry."

The mention of her little boy makes my heart squeeze. If I leave Vermont, I won't get to see him grow up. "How's he doing?"

"Great, actually. He's worked so hard with the speech therapist, and with the OT. I'm really proud of him."

"Aww. That's our boy." I feel a rush of love for Henry. I was the first person to hold him after he was born—a preemie at four pounds, six ounces, but already a fighter. He's five now, with some significant developmental delays.

He also has a twat for a father. Now there's a man who knows how to do a runner.

"The thing is…" Jennie hesitates. And I know exactly what's coming. "I told him he deserved a reward if he could do another ten sessions with the occupational therapist. And he did it without complaining."

"What does he want?" I brace myself.

"He wants to go to Six Flags. His friends have all been."

Ouch. "That's a couple hundred bucks, then." At least she didn't say Disney World.

"Yeah," she says quietly. "And I owe the speech therapist three hundred dollars. But I could pay you back."

As if. "The thing is, I need to trade in my car pretty soon. Before it stops working entirely."

"You told me that thing still had years in it! Did something happen?"

I open my mouth to answer, but then I realize I shouldn't say. Jennie doesn't need to hear my problems. She doesn't need to know that the guys from the Valkyries Motorcycle Club have finally found me.

Or that trading in my car is the only way I can stay in Vermont and avoid detection.

She'll worry.

"How much do you need?" I hear myself ask.

"Five hundred," she says quietly. "Things have been rough."

This is why I haven't saved enough money to escape. This right here. Between Jennie and my brother, someone always needs the cash worse than I do.

"Okay," I say softly. "I'll make a deposit and mail you a check." Most of my money is kept in cash, in case I need to run. But I've been mailing checks to Jennie with fudged return addresses on them. I don't think Razor can trace me from that, even if he got his hands on Jennie's mail.

"Thank you," she whispers. "I wouldn't ask…"

"I know," I say quickly. "I know."

She sighs. "Reading anything good? Wish we could have had our night at the bookstore."

"Me too," I grumble. Meeting at bookstores was my bright idea for seeing Jennie in a place where the members of the VMC would never go. "I'm reading a book on my phone. I just started, but it looks like just the right blend of smart and trashy. If it is, I'll send you the cover."

"Ooh! That's just how we like 'em."

It's true. It's just how I like 'em in real life, too. An image of Nash floats into my mind. I picture him pinning me against the bed… And instantly, I have a case of the warm flutters. That man is exactly the right amount of smart and trashy.

I should never have slept with him.

These are thoughts I keep to myself. And after Jennie and I hang up, I sit down and try to read. It isn't easy, though, because the pumphouse is too quiet without Nash in it. I've gotten used to his presence. He's always here, playing silly tunes and cracking jokes in the kitchen. But tonight, even the creak of the old beams makes my skin crawl.

You're just nervous, I tell myself. *This is Razor's fault.*

As the light fades in the sky, I gather my courage and step

outside, just to make sure the new security systems are doing their jobs.

The moment I do, a bright, motion-activated light comes on. And from inside the house, I hear the ping of the security system announcing that someone has approached the pumphouse.

It makes me feel about ten percent safer than I was last week. So I guess that's something. Back inside, with the doors locked, I open up my laptop and check all the new camera feeds. When I run the clock back a minute or two, I find a crystal-clear shot of myself, along with views of the whole property. If anyone threatens me, I can lock myself in the bedroom and call 911.

Hoping it won't come to that, I sit down on the sofa again and try to read. *This is fine*, I tell myself. Feeling scared is pointless. Feeling lonely is, too.

I'm a few pages into the chapter when my phone buzzes with a text.

NASH

Don't be alarmed if an unfamiliar car pulls up in a few minutes. It's a friend of mine.

Besides, when you see the car, you'll know it's not those assholes.

While I appreciate the warning, his message doesn't tell me what I need to know.

Am I supposed to do something? Take in a package? Let in your friend? Serve drinks?

Do all of that.

???

There's no further response, and I find my irritation rising. Nash ought to realize that I'm a little fragile, here. And his note about the car makes no sense. If Razor wants to kidnap me, he'll drive an unfamiliar vehicle. Because neither of us was born yesterday.

Five minutes later, I hear an engine.

Ping! says the security system.

Thunk goes my tummy.

In spite of Nash's warning, every muscle in my body tenses. I get up and tiptoe to the window, where I twitch the curtain an inch and peer outside. I actually let out a bark of laughter as a car rounds the building toward the pumphouse.

Because Nash was right. There's no way my ex is driving that car.

CHAPTER 29
LIVIA

The car whizzes up to the building before making an abrupt stop. It's a Mini Cooper in hot pink with orange racing stripes.

Razor wouldn't be caught dead in that thing.

Its owner kills the engine and flings open the door. She's a tall, curvaceous woman with wavy hair in several shades of honey blond.

And wait—I recognize her. She's the one who climbed up on the counter and hugged Nash that day in the tasting room. I saw her through the refrigerator window.

Instead of heading for the door, she trots around the car on three-inch heels to the passenger side, where she struggles a tote onto one arm and then pulls another object off the front seat. It's a footed cake plate in a deep shade of pink.

So this woman is *probably* not an operative on a mission to kill me. Or, if she is, her cover is flawless. And so is her makeup.

"Yoo-hoo!" she calls, approaching the door. "Knock knock! I'm Nash's friend, here to make a delivery."

I unbolt the new lock on the door and open it. "Um, hi," I say, because a year in hiding is hell on your social skills. "Come in?"

Her mouth—clad in rosy lipstick—parts in a big smile. "You're Livia, yeah? Nash told me all about you."

"That had better not be true."

The woman tips her head back and laughs so hard that she has to grip the cake plate. She's wearing a smocked, rose-colored blouse with black embroidery around the collar, and kickass silver earrings.

So I hate her a little already, but I'm trying to be polite. "Do you need me to hold anything?"

"Sure! I'm Poppy, by the way. An old friend of Nash's."

I'd bet cash money that "old friend" is code for something else.

This bothers me, even though it shouldn't.

Her smile widens again. "I can see your wheels turning, girlie. And I know exactly what it feels like to fall for a Giltmaker. It's just that Nash isn't my ex. His brother is."

"Oh." *Oh.* Now I feel stupid. "I'm not… I just thought… Do you bring cakes to all your friends?" I set it down on the table.

She cackles. "Not a chance. And this…" She lifts off the cover, and the scent of chocolate hits me. Hard. "Is a dark-chocolate and sour-cherry bundt cake. But it's not for Nash. It's for you and me."

"Come again?" I'm practically getting a contact high off the cocoa scent.

"Nash went out with our friend Corky, who's in a bad way. But he said you shouldn't be alone tonight. And I realized that was a *great* excuse to bake a bundt cake. They make *everything* better. Tonight's cocktail pairing will be…" She rummages in the tote she's holding. "Sour cherrytinis. Citrus vodka, Cointreau, and sour cherry purée."

My mouth waters suddenly, because that sounds seriously good. But there's only one problem. "Poppy, did Nash send you here to *babysit* me?"

She sets her tote on a chair. "Well, babysit is a strong word. He was concerned, that's all. He said you'd had some drama, and you might need a lift."

Good grief. "Did he happen to warn you that the drama involves a scary dude who's trying to kidnap me? Who may be out of town, but also may be on his way over here?" The more I think about this, the worse it gets. I resent the idea that I need a babysitter. And the first rule of being a hot mess is that you don't involve innocent bystanders.

Poppy's beautiful face takes on a thoughtful expression. "He may have said something about that. I can't be sure. As soon as I heard 'new girl in town,' I started thinking about cakes and cocktails."

Huh. "You are an interesting creature."

She smiles, and it only makes her more devastating. "See, it's a *really* small town, Livia. I'm in a bowling league, even though I'm terrible at bowling. But at least they serve beer. And I'm in a book club with all my enemies, because sometimes they're all I've got. You sounded like a nice person, and I like to bake. It's as simple as that."

"*Oh,*" I say slowly. Because, again, living like a hermit is hell on your social skills.

"So maybe you can tell me the whole sordid tale over our first drink?"

Overwhelmed, I pull out a chair and plop down on it. "Okay. You'd better sit. Did you eat dinner? We're going to need some extra calories to fight off my ex if he shows. You want some home-made soup?"

"Already ate. It's cake time. Plates over here?" She heads over to the cabinet, finding them on the first try. She also roots out two forks and a knife from my silverware drawer before returning to the table. "You slice and serve. I need to shake up our drinks."

"Yes, ma'am." I grab the knife, and when I cut the cake, the scent of chocolate practically clobbers me. I cut a thick slice for each of us.

Meanwhile, she pulls out a shaker that's already full of ice and starts pouring vodka and Cointreau into it. Then a splash of fancy cherry juice. She shakes it up with the finesse of Tom Cruise in *Cocktail,* and then pours it into two little juice glasses she pulls from my cabinet. "Not to complain, but we've *got* to get you some martini glasses."

"Hmm," I say noncommittally. "I do enjoy a nice martini glass. But that's not even in the top twenty-five things I need to fix in my life."

"Are you sure?" she asks. "Big problems seem smaller with a nice cocktail in hand. I've had lots of experience with this. Cheers."

I lift my glass and touch it to hers. Then I take a sip of my drink. It's tangy and delicious. I chase it with a forkful of tender chocolate-cherry cake and then gasp. "*God*. This should be regulated as a controlled substance."

"My favorite recipe," she says with a shrug. "For springtime, anyway. I have a rotating collection of seasonal favorites."

"Yes, queen." I take another bite and sigh. "If I were sticking around, I think we could be friends."

She arches a perfect eyebrow. "Nash didn't say anything about you leaving. Does he know?"

"On some level, sure. He's got to realize that having me around is a huge liability. My ex more or less threatened to attack the brewery if he doesn't get his way."

Her eyes widen. "Oh, *honey*. Your ex sounds like a real twatwaffle. Way worse than any of mine."

"It isn't a competition," I tease. "But yeah. The problem is that he also has a lot of twatwaffle friends, and they're all involved with illegal activities. And I'm an idiot, so I stuck around long enough to learn too much about everything. Nash and Benito seem to think they can snare these guys and fix everything, but I think they're high."

She winces. "Okay, that sounds bad. But Benito is almost as smart as he is hot. And the Giltmakers are all very effective people. You're in good hands. Besides—Nash needs you."

"He doesn't," I argue immediately. "I'm the last thing he needs."

Poppy sips her drink as she watches me over the rim of the glass. "The thing about Nash is that he likes a challenge. He grew up in a small town with all the girls falling at his feet. Captain of the hockey team."

"Really?" I blink, trying to picture this. "I thought his brother was the hockey player."

Her eyes dip briefly, and a look of pain crosses her features. "Well, Mitch was a once-in-a-lifetime talent. He overshadowed Nash in the end. But Nash never complained. That man is good at everything he does. Everyone likes him, and he's always loved this town. He didn't even want to move away until his father made this place impossible for him."

"I don't know," I say carefully. "He says he can't wait to get back to Boston."

"That's because Boston appreciates him. But he should be right here in Vermont, carrying the Giltmaker Brewery into the next generation. He just needs a way back in. I think you're it."

"Sorry, but that won't fly." I pick up my drink and take a gulp. "It doesn't even make sense."

"Sure it does." She licks her fork. "He obviously has it bad for you. He told me so today."

"He did *not*," I gasp. "He'd never say that."

She holds up a perfectly manicured hand. "Scout's honor. That's an exact quote. And he even admitted that he's enjoying his work at the brewery." She shrugs. "There's more here for him in Colebury than there used to be, Livia. You just have to convince him to stay."

The vodka must have gone to her head. "That's a nice theory. But Nash and I just met. And if he's into me, I think that's just the sex talking."

She lets out a sigh, and refills both our glasses. "I remember sex. Vaguely."

"It can turn your head," I admit. "It's turned mine before. I've made plenty of bad decisions when the sex was good, but the guy was not."

"Are we talking about your ex now?"

I nod and pick up my drink. "I have a thing for bad boys. They cloud my judgment. I don't trust myself anymore."

"Hmm," she says. "Bad boys come in different flavors, though. Naughty men can be nice. That's Nash, I think. Lots of testosterone, but a heart of gold."

"Sure, sure. But it doesn't really matter. In a month, Lyle will be back in the brewery and Nash will be back in Boston. And lord knows where I'll be." Hiding three states away, probably, hoping Razor doesn't find me.

"Well." She pulls the vodka out of her bag. "That would be a damn shame. So I'd better make us another round, just in case that comes to pass."

"Thank you," I whisper. "Thank you for coming over here tonight. Nash is a pushy bastard, and I don't need a babysitter. But it's a real pleasure to meet you anyway."

She beams. "I hope you still think so in the morning. There's a lot of vodka in this recipe."

CHAPTER 30
NASH

The motion-activated lights blaze as I step out of my dad's truck beside Poppy's car. It's midnight, which is not so late. But it's late enough that the pumphouse apartment is dead quiet when I let myself in the door.

After locking up again, I take stock. There's no sign of Poppy. But there are plates and glasses in the sink. That's unusual, because Livia keeps a tidy kitchen.

Poppy's fancy cake plate is standing on the table, which is a positive sign. I lift the lid and inhale deeply. Then I help myself to a slice of chocolate decadence.

My body is my temple. Usually. But I'm willing to make an exception for Poppy's bundt cakes. And this one does not disappoint.

After I finish my slice of cake, I get ready for bed. But as I'm pacing the house in my boxer shorts, checking all the locks, I can't help but tiptoe to Livia's bedroom to check on her.

She's left the door unlocked, which is unlike her. But she's safe and sound, curled up tightly in a defensive position that cuts me in two. As if she doesn't trust the world enough to spread out and take up space. As if she's been told to make herself smaller.

I'd opened her door just wanting a peek. It's late, and we both need sleep, but I don't leave. Instead, I lock the door behind me. Then I lift the quilt and slide in beside her.

Livia shifts immediately but doesn't open her eyes. Her smooth arms reach out and snake around my chest.

She smells like flowers, and her skin is warm and silky. I take a slow, greedy breath of her. This woman will be the end of me, I swear.

"I'm mad at you," Livia slurs, even as her fingertips explore my abs.

"Yeah? What did I do?"

"You sent me a babysitter. That's sweet, but also con…" She grapples for the word, and she still hasn't opened her eyes. "Condescending. And also dangerous. Poppy isn't the kind of girl who could help me fight off a criminal."

"Poppy is tougher than she looks. But you two were in no danger. I told you Benito's guys were watching the place."

"Pfft," she says drunkenly. "A drive-by every half hour wouldn't save me."

"No kidding. That's why the guy was parked across the way, tucked into that old logging road. I stopped to talk to him before I turned into the lot."

She opens one eye. "Wait. Really?"

"Of course. You think I'd leave you here alone, like bait on a hook?"

She tucks her face into my bare chest. "Maybe. I don't know."

This guts me. I smooth her hair away from her face and choose my words carefully. "You are not alone in this. It's a team effort, pussycat."

"Hrmph," she mumbles. "I've been a solo act my whole life."

"Gettin' that," I murmur. "Poppy got a ride home? Her car is outside."

"Yup. We got drunk." She hiccups.

"You don't say."

She pokes me in the belly. "Poppy got an Uber. Benito's other brother was the driver. They're a good-looking family."

I snort. "I think he's still the only Uber driver in Colebury." And that's why the cop didn't have to come out of his hidey hole to investigate the arriving car. Everybody knows Damien Rossi.

"Mmm," she says sleepily. "There was also cake. *Really* good cake."

"Poppy's cakes are legendary."

"It's *so* good," she murmurs. "It's better than sex. Well, not better than sex with you."

"*Wow*. That's quite a compliment. Because I just had some of that cake and it practically changed my life."

She lifts her head and opens her eyes. "You ate some of my life-changing cake?"

I pull her head back down to my chest. "Easy, killer. There's plenty left. But do you know what this means?"

She gives her head a little shake, and her soft hair caresses my chest.

"Well, by the transitive property, if that cake changed your life, and sex with me is better than that cake, then a good bang from me was also life changing."

"Pfft," she says. "Ego much?"

"It's *math*, Livia. Can't argue with math."

Another shake of her head. "They're both good. Really good. But they didn't actually change my life. Nothing can change my life."

"That's the spirit," I say drily.

"It's just too late to change," she says with a sleepy sigh. "And you shouldn't have come in here. I'm too drunk and too tired for sex."

"Maybe I wasn't looking for sex."

"Sure you weren't," she murmurs.

She doesn't understand how drawn to her I am. But I can be patient. Eventually she'll figure it out.

I settle in, listening to the silence of the night. Until my eyes slide closed, and I fall asleep to the soft sound of Livia's breathing.

————

Six hours later, my alarm starts playing a Rolling Stones tune from somewhere outside of Livia's bedroom.

I wake up slowly, realizing that Livia is still stretched out on my chest. She's not sleeping, though. Instead, she's sucking gently on my neck, while her fingertips skim down my ribcage.

It takes me a moment to arrive at full consciousness. But my dick is already there. As she moves her soft body over mine, I let out a horny groan. "Stop it, woman. I'm supposed to get up."

"Oh, you already are," she says.

"Livia," I warn through a clenched jaw. "My father is calling at seven." And the thought of his grumpy voice in my ear is almost enough to get my body under control.

Almost. But then Livia uses the ultimate weapon. She takes my hand and guides it into her panties. When I feel how wet she is, I forget all about my morning plans.

CHAPTER 31
LIVIA

Nash pulls me into a hot kiss, and I feel about a hundred emotions at the same time.

I'd half-woken a little while ago to find Nash's hard body beside mine. I'd opened my eyes to see his gold skin illuminated by the soft morning light. And I'd been seized with a powerful, irrational thought: *that man is mine.*

For a whole minute or two, I'd been trapped in a waking dream. I'd pictured Nash rolling over to kiss me.

And Nash handing me a cup of coffee.

Nash listening to something I'd explained to him, his expressive brown eyes thoughtful.

Nash laughing.

I'm a practical girl, so it should have stopped there. But dreams are powerful things. So I also pictured Nash holding my hand as we walked outside in the sunshine.

Nash asking me to dance with him in the kitchen.

Nash bending down on one knee, and asking me to marry him…

Okay, seriously. Even when I'm asleep, my dreams don't usually get so far-fetched. So that's when I woke up completely and reminded myself not to be so stupid.

In my defense, Poppy did make me some strong drinks last night. But it's not like me to torture myself like this. I'm smart enough not to daydream about the things I can't have.

And I really can't. Because I'm clearing out of Vermont, for so many reasons.

1. I can't rat out Razor, because…

2. I don't want to die. And…

3. Nash doesn't really need the headache of trying to keep me alive. In the cool light of day, it's obvious that I don't have a choice. Leaving is the right course of action.

That's why I'm seducing Nash. Because I need to touch him one more time.

He doesn't mind. His tongue is in my mouth, and his hand is lodged between my legs.

With every touch, my heart aches a little more, even as my body lights up like a flame. *This is it.* One more wildly intimate moment.

"Baby," he whispers between kisses. "Best wakeup I ever had."

And I've barely even started.

I sit up a little straighter and arch my back as I straddle him. I lift off my tank and toss it overboard, and when my tits bounce, he lets out a hungry sound.

"God, woman." His voice is husky. "Show me. Play with them."

It's easier to obey than to argue. So I tip my head back and pinch my nipples while I slowly ride his hand.

And when I moan, he lets out a string of curses. "Fuck me. You're magnificent."

The truth is that I *feel* magnificent, even if it only lasts for an hour. And what's more, I feel appreciated. And I've always run hot. A woman isn't supposed to admit it, though. You're supposed to be coy about sex, and play the part of the ingenue.

But innocence doesn't turn me on. Action does. Somehow

Nash understands this on a gut level. He gets me, which is why I feel ninety percent fantastic, and ten percent like crying.

I don't cry, though. I put on a show instead. My hands slide across my heated flesh, and he growls before tugging impatiently on my panties. "Take these off before I snap them in half."

"Yes, sir," I whisper. "Right away, sir."

He groans, and I roll off his body to comply. Impatient now, he tightens his grip on the elastic around my hips. And…*whoosh!* That pesky fabric is gone.

A moment later, he's also divested himself of his boxers. There's nothing left between us. "I need to be inside you. And I've only got ten minutes, pussycat."

"Plenty of time," I breathe. And, heck, I think I might even miss that stupid nickname when I go.

With bossy hands, he rolls me onto my hands and knees. "Hands on the headboard."

I moan as I comply.

"Hot damn. We won't even need all ten of these minutes."

I smile as a strong hand braces my hip, and I shamelessly arch backward toward the muscular bulk of him.

"Here, baby. You want this?" My breath stutters as I feel the blunt tip of him against my sensitive flesh. "It's for you. Take it all."

I grip the bed with white knuckles, and I brace my body so I can feel every bump and slide. "*Nashhhh,*" I gasp as he fills me.

"That's right. Say it again."

I try. But he's already moving at a pace that might feel punishing if I didn't need it so bad.

"Such a good girl. So pretty. So willing. And you feel so damn good on my cock."

The praise makes me whimper. He settles into a rhythm, his hands on my body, his breath at my neck. We move together without thought or difficulty. Like we were made to do this together.

And Nash is magnificent. His hands make me want to weep, and the words of praise that fall from his mouth fuel my soul. "Be a good girl and come for me," he finally says. "I need to hear you."

I suck in oxygen and try to find my voice. But he picks up the pace again, stealing my breath.

"Can't hear you," he chides.

Then he slips his hand around my hip and touches the place where we're joined. And I'm so sensitive that I let out a cry of gratitude and surprise.

"That's it, pussycat. Let me hear you purr."

The sound that comes out of me is more like a sob. Everything is sunlight and molten bliss. We rise together to a fevered pitch, and then take the leap together in a final chorus of sound and motion.

I see fireworks, and Nash makes a sound that's so deeply satisfying that I wish I could carry it with me forever.

We collapse on the bed, completely spent, and it's over. I'm still sucking in oxygen when Nash flips me onto my side once more and kisses me quickly. "You amaze me."

I pant, taking in his big brown eyes at close range.

I think I'll miss those most of all.

Nash is truly late by the time we get cleaned up. He vaults out of the shower and into his clothes. Then he runs out of the pumphouse without even waiting for the coffee to brew.

But it's better this way. He'll probably be angry when he realizes what I'm about to do.

That bothers me more than it should, because Nash will assume I'm a coward. And maybe it's partly true. I don't want to face down Razor again—in a dark alley, or a courtroom. I'm afraid of that man.

Although cowardice isn't my only motivation for leaving. It's just easier for everyone concerned. Nash doesn't need Razor breathing down his neck.

You're too much trouble, Ivy, my mom used to say. *Always causing drama.* And that's exactly what's happening here.

So it's time to start packing.

Even though I've been living here for a long time, packing up my belongings doesn't take much time. All my clothes fit inside a single big suitcase. My books fit into a single box.

The kitchen implements are a problem. Most of them are thrift-store finds, and it will be hard to give them up, but packing them all and making multiple trips to my car would be a problem. Someone on the loading dock is bound to ask questions.

With this in mind, and because I still have two bulky items to fit into the car, I wait until the shipping clerk takes his lunch break. When he clears out, I balance my box atop my suitcase and roll everything to the loading dock.

After placing the stuff in my car, I head back to the pumphouse. I eat a bowl of soup and then carefully wash the bowl and spoon. I tuck a box of granola bars into my purse, along with a can of soda water.

I'm stalling now, mostly because I'm sad.

I glance around the place one last time. This little apartment has been my sanctuary. Imperfect as it is, I hate the idea of leaving it behind. Even worse—I hate the idea of sneaking away like a thief in the night. The thought of leaving Lyle and Nash in the lurch gives me a pain right behind my breastbone.

I'll miss seeing Lyle back on his feet.

I never even got to meet Leila's baby.

And I'll never get another one of Nash's hugs.

Ouch. That's what hurts the worst. But Nash would have gone back to Boston in a few weeks anyway. I can't plan my life around him.

After one more deep breath, I make myself shoulder my carryon bag and leave. I lock the pumphouse door and head into the brewery building. In the office, I push the rolling library ladder over to the second bookshelf on the left, and I climb up.

For the last time, I pull down my favorite ledger, the one marked LIVIA'S SUPER TOP SECRET STUFF on the spine, where I've been concealing all my cash. I remove the cigar box from inside and tuck it under my arm. Then I pull a thumb drive out of my pocket and quickly tape it into the ledger before climbing back down.

That's the evidence for Benito. I'll email him where to find it.

The cigar box goes into my carryon tote, and I turn toward the door. It feels wrong not to leave a note. But it's no use writing platitudes, because nobody will truly understand why I need to go.

With a heavy heart, I walk into the corridor, pausing for a moment to listen to the voices in the brewhouse. It's not a tasting-room day, so I only hear the shouts of the brewers over the swish of water flowing into a tank. And the clank of a brush against the metal sides.

Someone laughs, and I recognize it as Badger's chuckle. And then Connor makes a comeback, and they all crack up. I strain my ears, trying to pick out Nash's voice in the mix. But I can't.

I've been happy here. As happy as possible, anyway. Friendships are hard when you have to keep people at a distance. After I leave, they'll forget about me before the snow comes again.

Go on, dummy. Get out of here, before someone asks what the hell you're doing.

I finally get a move-on, taking the back route through the storage room and into the quiet loading dock. I hustle over to the door mechanism and push the button.

With a series of metallic clanks, the door begins to retract toward the ceiling. I hurry to my car, open the driver's door, and slide in. I wrestle my carryon into the passenger seat and grab the keys out of the cupholder.

That's when a hand emerges from the backseat and lands on my shoulder. And I scream bloody murder.

CHAPTER 32
NASH

Whoops. I'll probably be deaf from this day on. "Damn, pussycat," I say, as she whirls around. "Great lungs, babe." It comes out sounding flip, but the truth is that I'm plenty angry.

I can't believe she was going to do a runner.

The screaming stops, but now there's cursing, instead. And vague threats. Then she falls silent, pressing a hand to her heart as she catches her breath. "What the hell are you doing here?"

"That's my line," I growl. "Were you even going to say goodbye?"

A guilty expression crosses her face, followed quickly by sadness. And now I feel like a dick. "How did you know?"

"The goodbye sex. Plain and simple." I roll my shoulders, trying to let go of my anger. "Most times, you try to keep a tight leash on yourself. Doesn't always work, but you try. You don't laugh too hard or show me where it hurts. And you sure as hell won't admit that it makes you happy when I walk into the room."

A flicker of surprise, but then she shuts it down. Like always. And she turns to face the steering wheel. "What good would it do?" she asks quietly. "I know it's not cool to run off without saying goodbye. But I didn't want the argument. And you're leaving, too, you know. In just a few weeks, right? Let's not make this a bigger deal than it is."

Well, damn. My heart gives an unfamiliar stab. It's been a long time since a woman mattered enough to make me this unhappy. But that's what's happening here, and lying about it won't do either of us any good. "Look, I'm trying not to be a dick, but you're selling us short." I put both hands on her shoulders. "You can sneak your suitcase into the car and drive out of here if you want to. I can't stop you. But it's a dick move to say you never noticed how it is between us. I've been drawn to you since before we even met. And I think you feel the same, even if you're too afraid to say so." I run my thumbs along the juncture between her neck and shoulders, and she shivers at my touch.

"I'm not afraid," she lies. "I just don't see the point. You always say how you can't wait to go back to Boston."

"It's Boston, Livia. Not the moon. And when's the last time you heard me say I wanted to go back?"

She has to think for a second, and I get it. Because it snuck up on me, too. In spite of all the drama, I've been enjoying my time in the brewery, and enjoying my time with her.

"I don't remember," she admits.

"Yeah, me neither. But it wasn't recently. And if you leave right now, you'll never know what might have happened between us. What if it's something great?"

"It's already great," she says in a small voice. "Like a gift that was delivered to my doorstep by accident. But sooner or later—No, who am I kidding? It will be sooner. You're going to get sick of the bullshit that follows me everywhere."

Thinking that over, I dig my thumbs into her shoulder muscles, and she lets out an undignified groan.

"I'm not trying to minimize your troubles," I say as her body turns to jelly under my hands. "But you don't get to decide how I feel. Would you put up with that from me?"

She makes an unintelligible noise and sinks a little further into the seat.

"Sorry, I couldn't hear that."

"Your damn hands are magic," she grumbles.

"Just repaying the favor. You had me pretty relaxed this morning. Just saying."

She sighs.

"So what's it going to be? Am I getting out of this car so you can gun it to the state line right now? Or are you going to help Benito?"

Livia pulls out of my grasp and turns to face me again. "You don't understand. I'm not a coward, and this was never an either-or situation. I have a thumb drive of files, and I was going to pass it to Benito. But you wouldn't have to be involved."

That shuts me up for a second. "I don't think of you as a coward, Livia. You're one of the bravest people I know. If that weren't true, I wouldn't be sitting here—" I swallow roughly, because this is unusual for me. "—actually begging you to stay."

She blinks.

We're both surprised. But that's what it's come to, hasn't it?

"I was never running away from *you*," she says. "You know that right? I'm trying to get away from Razor. If I stay, I have to help Benito catch him. Otherwise, I'm just a sitting duck."

"I know it's bad." I reach up and cup her soft face in my hand. "And if I really thought it was safer to run, I wouldn't be selfish. I'd kiss you goodbye and wish you luck. Do you trust me?"

An emotion I can't name flashes through her dark eyes. She doesn't answer, though. Seconds tick by, and my heart starts to sag.

"Yes," she whispers. "I suppose I do."

CHAPTER 33
LIVIA

"Glad to hear that," Nash whispers as my heart beats wildly inside my chest. "Don't go, baby. I'll do whatever it takes."

Air squeezes out of my lungs, because he has no idea how hard that was for me to say. But I *do* trust him. Against all reasonable odds, I finally met a man who's worthy of my confidence.

I just hope that's enough.

His thumb strokes my cheek. "Deep down, I think you're sick of running."

"Of *course* I am." It comes out sounding more anguished than I intended. "I want my life back. I just don't know how to get it. I trust that you'll do your best. But what if he'll never leave me alone? Even from prison, he could still…" My chest tightens.

"Baby," he whispers. "The first step is just to let Benito form a plan. Listen to the man and see what he says. I'm going to make you a promise, okay? If things look hairy, I'll drive you out of state myself."

I swallow hard. "Hope I won't have to take you up on it."

The backseat door opposite Nash opens suddenly, and Connor climbs in next to Nash. "Is this where the party is?"

"We were just…" I press my lips together, when I realize I have no sensible way to finish that sentence. I'm not telling the whole brewery that Nash thwarted my getaway attempt and talked me into staying. It's none of their business.

"I didn't know you two were a thing," he says with a chuckle. "Although, usually couples sit on the same seat when they're getting it on in a vehicle."

"We were just *talking*," I insist. "Jesus."

Connor shrugs. "You gotta admit that's a hot scene in Titanic when they steam up the car in the ship's hold. *God*, I love that movie. And don't you think there was room for Leo on that door?"

Nash and I exchange a puzzled glance. But this is how life works right now—tearing off in unexpected directions.

"Yeah, man," Nash says slowly. "But maybe we should all get back to work?"

Connor shrugs. "Good talk. I thought we were keeping the loading dock door shut, though? You said we didn't want anyone peeking into the building."

"Right," I say, dropping the keys into the cupholder and opening the driver's door. "I'm going to shut the door. And, uh, put away a few of my belongings."

From the backseat, Nash gives me a big smile. "I'll drop by the office a little later. We'll call Benito and do some planning."

My stomach wobbles at this idea. But Nash promised me he'd do all he could. "All right," I say firmly. "We'll do that."

———

Benito comes by an hour later to pick up the thumb drive. "You won't regret this, Livia," he says.

I wish I believed him.

That night, we eat my homemade soup for dinner. Nash puts on another movie, but I'm too distracted to pay attention to the story. My mind keeps inventing terrible scenarios. Like a standoff between the Vermont State Police and the entire motorcycle club. Or a gun battle, with me caught in the middle. Or...

"Baby?" Nash says. "You okay?"

"Fine." My eyes focus on the screen for about three seconds before they drift away again.

Nash leans in and starts kissing my neck. Right around the time he puts his hand up my shirt, I finally forget about Razor.

"You're…really…" It's hard to speak between kisses. "A great…distraction," I breathe.

"The best," he says, unbuttoning his fly. "Let me introduce you to my magic distraction wand."

It's hard to roll your eyes and kiss a man at the same time. But I somehow manage.

He laughs against my lips. Then he plucks me off the couch and carries me into my bedroom. "What do you need?" he asks as he efficiently strips off his clothes. "What would be the most distracting thing I could do to you for the next two hours?"

"Two hours?" My warm flutters flutter a little harder.

"I'd say three, but I figure you need your sleep."

I swallow.

Meanwhile, he's standing in front of me naked, rosy cock pointing right at me. "You takin' those clothes off, or do I have to do all the work around here?"

"Yessir," I say, reaching for my top and yanking it over my head. Beneath it, I'm wearing a sheer, *very* lacy bra. I never wore it for Razor. So now I'm blowing Nash's mind instead. "Fuck me," he says, his eyes darkening as I slowly unzip my jeans. And maybe it's a little silly, but I move my hips a little more than necessary while I wiggle out of my jeans, slowly revealing the itsy-bitsy sheer panties.

"Where have you been all my life?" His voice is a low, hungry rumble. He puts two fists on the bed and hovers over my body, his eyes flaring as he looks his fill.

Heat and expectation shimmer between us like noonday sunshine. But there's something else there, too.

Men have admired my body before. They've looked at me with lust in their eyes. And possessiveness. And hunger. But never with *reverence*. Nash looks at me like it's a privilege. Like he sees more than boobs and designer lace.

Like he sees *me*.

I cup his rough jaw, and he leans into my touch, letting his eyes fall closed for a moment and then opening them to lock his gaze with mine. "Pussycat," he whispers, and it sounds like a prayer. "Tell me what you're thinking right now."

I can't tell him that I'm falling for him. He doesn't want to hear it, and I don't want to say it. So I lie, and say, "I'm thinking I should take off this bra." I drop my hand and arch my back to get at the strap.

Disappointment flashes through his eyes so quickly that maybe I only imagined it. "Don't do that," he whispers.

My hands freeze on the bra strap, and I'm honestly confused. Does he mean that I shouldn't take off the bra? Or that I shouldn't hold back my feelings?

He puts a knee on the bed, and then uses his hands to gently knock mine away. He stretches his big body out on top of mine, pausing on his forearms to study me seriously.

That caramel gaze is almost too much. There's nowhere to hide. But he doesn't look away, even when he leans down to kiss me. Just once. "You're mine for the night, pussycat," he whispers, as if we were in the middle of an argument, and this was his compromise. "Got that?"

I nod.

"Say it," he whispers, dipping down to drag his lips across my jaw. "Whose are you tonight?" Then he licks a line above the lace edge of the bra, and I shiver.

"Yours," I say without hesitation.

He kisses his way down my tummy. "Good girl," he says, and I shiver again. His whiskers tickle my skin as he tracks toward the lace edge of the world's smallest panties. "Good girl. Now hold still. Don't move. But feel free to say my name as often as you wish."

Then he kisses me over the lace, and I part my legs in invitation. He plants one broad hand on each of my thighs. And without hesitation he lowers his mouth to my lace-covered pussy and sucks gently through the fabric.

"Nash," I gasp, and he chuckles against my sensitive flesh.

"That's right. Say it again."

Instead, I moan it.

CHAPTER 34
NASH

I don't know how much time passes. Could be two hours? All I know is that I have a lot of stamina, a long playbook of sexual positions, and plenty of anxiety to burn off in my very favorite way. The bed gets a workout, and the two of us make so much noise we might be frightening the nearby forest creatures.

The first time I get Livia off, she's still wearing her underwear.

The second time, she's on her hands and knees.

The third time she's on her back, staring up at me and moaning my name. And no man can resist that. I practically see stars before collapsing in a satisfied heap beside her.

Now we're cuddling in the bed, bodies loose and tired. The unsettled feeling in my gut has notched down a little bit. Not completely, though.

Livia was going to leave me, because she thought she needed to. I'm still not over it, and it hurts me more than I've let on. I wish it weren't so easy for her to walk away. And I wish she didn't feel unsafe.

This troubling thought wakes me up a little. And when I open my eyes, I find Livia blinking back at me. "You okay?" I ask immediately.

"Yeah," she whispers. "We should get some sleep." She gets up and heads to the bathroom.

A beat later, I follow her for my own round of tooth-brushing. After, I check the security system and tidy the bed. When Livia gets into bed, I'm lying on my back, contemplating the ceiling. It's tempting to reach over and pull her closer, but I hold myself back. Maybe it's selfish, but after our argument in her car today, I need to know that she'll come to me voluntarily.

Whether it's fair or not, I view her as a constant flight risk.

She pulls the covers primly onto her chest as she rests flat on her back. There's a beat of silence that feels long to me.

"Fuck it," she whispers, and then rolls toward me.

But I'm turning, too, and we meet in the middle, her soft arms around me, and I relax against her body. "Good night, beautiful girl," I whisper.

"Goodnight, guy who's too sexy for his own good."

She's joking. But I still smile.

Luckily, our night is uneventful. The security system never pings.

Early the next morning, my father and I mash in another tank of Goldenpour over the phone. He patiently recites the same recipe, and I go along with it. Nobody needs to know that I've written the recipe down and locked it in the safe in his office.

As I stir the batch with the paddle, I let myself enjoy the process. I'm sick of people talking about this brewery as our family legacy, and I'm still annoyed at my father for making it so fucking difficult to care about this place. Nonetheless, I'm having fun.

No other place on earth smells like this. The yeasty air is scented with toasted grains and hoppy topnotes. And I'm wide awake in spite of the hour, because brewing is a physical act. It feels good to make something with my own two hands.

After my father hangs up, I keep at it and mash in an extra

tank of Goldenpour. It took me a couple weeks, but the brewery is finally back to capacity. My father can think whatever he thinks about me, but this place won't go to hell on my watch.

By one thirty, I've been working for hours. So I text Livia.

> Want some lunch? I'm starved.

Her reply is not as food-centric as I'd hoped.

> Benito wants to come over at seven. He wants to plan a sting operation.

Christ, I can practically hear her fear.

> All right. I'll clear my schedule, and I'll pick up some beer in half an hour when I go out to get us burgers.

> I could make us something for lunch.

> Nah I got this. Your job is to just sit there and take calming breaths.

Stashing my phone, I head for the door, unease settling into my gut. Livia is in danger, and all I want for her is to be free of it.

I just hope I'm right about Benito and that he knows what he's doing.

CHAPTER 35
LIVIA

With the ugly curtains pushed open, I see light soften the springtime sky. We're sitting around the little table, beers in hand, while Benito lays out his idea.

And I'm nervous as heck.

"Okay, the first play is getting Razor to admit wrongdoing on a phone call. I'll tape it." Benito points to the thumb drive. "You'll get him talking about everything you found here."

My heart sags, because Razor isn't stupid enough to chat about fraud with me over the phone.

Nash doesn't like this idea, either. "But you have all the evidence Livia saved," he argues. "That should be enough, right?"

"Unfortunately, no. It's enough evidence to nail that dude from Burlington for doing shitty work and faking the VIN numbers. But that won't take down the organization. And the evidence Livia gathered doesn't connect Razor to the money-laundering or the drugs."

"He's too smart to spill anything over the phone," I argue.

"No, he will," Benito explains. "Because you're going to exaggerate what you have. Then you'll offer him the USB. If he arranges to collect it from you, that shows motive. Besides, we can manipulate him even further if we're clever."

"Oh," I say slowly. I suppose it *might* work. "And he'll play along, because he thinks it gives him a fresh opportunity to snatch me, right?"

"No fucking way," Nash says. "I don't want her anywhere near him."

"Of course you don't," Benito says with a grin. "But that doesn't mean it's the wrong play."

"How are you going to keep her safe?" Nash barks. "Look me in the eye and tell me you'd be fine with Skye doing this."

Benito takes a sip of his beer and studies Nash coolly. "I hear where you're coming from. I'd feel the same way if I were you. But if you want this asshole gone from her life, we're going to have to be strategic. The good news is that he's a high-value target. There's a lot of manpower at my disposal."

"Tell me how it would work," I whisper.

He turns to me with a calm expression. He's the only one at the table who isn't freaking out a little right now. "First, you'll call him and offer to give him back all the evidence you swiped. And you're going to exaggerate what you've got."

"Like how?"

"You'll tell him that you made a recording in the bike shop where they thought you couldn't hear them. You'll tell Razor that he's on tape calling the shots. I'll feed you the name of that guy they roughed up in Massachusetts and some locations they use for their drops. He'll believe you."

"Oh, you are a tricky one."

He grins. "I love my job. I spend all day trying to outsmart assholes. It's very satisfying when it goes right."

Nash doesn't smile. He drains his beer and smacks it onto the table. "Let me get this straight—you're going to tell a violent criminal that he has *even more* reason to hurt Livia than he thought he did?"

"Yes, but it's only for a day," Benito says levelly. "Livia will tell him she's leaving town. She wants a clean break from Vermont. He can meet her for the thumb drive, or not. We're going to plan the hell out of this operation, but he won't have that chance. He'll have to show up or shut up."

I'm still terrified, but I really like the way this guy thinks.

Nash seems less impressed. "Livia should not be in any danger, at *any* time. I need your word on that."

"You have it," Benito insists. "The full force of Vermont's drug task force and the tactical services unit will back us up."

"So this isn't just a phone call?" I press. "I actually have to show up."

"The phone call is first. We need that to motivate him. You'll give it to him all breezy—like you're on your way out of town forever. You want to make a clean break and even the score between the two of you. On the call, you'll pick a time and place to meet the next day. You're going to imply that your new man is there with you, and he won't like this arrangement."

"He doesn't," Nash snaps.

"That's going to make him jealous," I say slowly. "So he'll show up himself, instead of sending some deputy asshole."

"Exactly," Benito says. "He'll want to see your face."

"Yeah, *but,*" Nash growls. "If seeing her face were enough for him, I might not hate this plan. Don't forget he's already tried to grab her. He'll try again. She can't actually show up to this meeting."

"No, I have to," I say slowly. "Because he won't show his face if I'm not there, right?" I turn to Benito for confirmation.

"Well, yeah," the cop says with a frown. "We'll pick a spot where he feels he has the upper hand. But he'll be wrong, and we'll grab him. You'll be well protected the whole time."

"No fucking way." Nash's hands are balled into fists. "You can't use Livia as *bait.*"

"Nash..." Benito warns.

"I'll do it," I say quickly. Because I really want this to end.

"Pussycat..."

"Don't start with the cute names," I argue. "I can decide for myself. It's my *choice*, Nash. You asked me to stay here and try to get my life back. I'm doing that."

"Not by dangling yourself in front of that asshole like a worm on a fishhook!" His face is red, his eyes on fire.

"It's going to go fine," Benito says. "We do this stuff all the time."

Nash puts his head in his hands. "I want to be there. Somewhere nearby. So you have an extra set of wheels if shit goes bad."

Benito looks thoughtful. "Official policy forbids me from giving you a role. That said, it's a free country. And if Livia decides to tell you where she's headed, I can't stop her." He winks at me. "Just don't let your hot-headed boyfriend get in my way."

Hot-headed boyfriend. I glance at Nash. That's what he is, I realize. My boyfriend. Whether I wanted one or not.

And he's a good one, damn it. Probably the only good one I've ever had.

I'd better not die right after getting the warm flutters for a really decent guy for once in my adult life.

That would really hack me off.

CHAPTER 36
NASH

The problem with making big, bold decisions is that you have to live with the consequences.

After Benito leaves, I sit down to an inbox full of BrewCo emails and spreadsheets. But I can't concentrate at all. I keep picturing Livia standing on a bridge—like in a spy movie—baiting her ex into showing his face to the cops.

And then, while the cops watch helplessly from fifty paces away, he pulls out a gun or a knife or a baseball bat...

With a grunt of distress, I snap my laptop shut and stand up from the sofa.

"Something wrong?" Livia asks from the bedroom, where she's folding her laundry.

"I'm going for a run. Need to burn off some energy." I move to the bedroom door, and she glances up at me, her expression serene. "After that I'll need a shower. Maybe you'll need one, too?" I cock an eyebrow at her.

Her lips twitch. "Are you implying that I stink?"

"I'm implying that I want to suck drops of water off your hot, naked tits, and then push you up against the tiles." I shrug. "Think it over. I'll lock the door on my way out."

Since I'm racing the twilight, three fast miles is all I have time for. When I drag my sweaty ass back a half hour later and unlock the door, I find a darkened room with a lit candle on the coffee table and a soundtrack playing. It's that song about a guy who runs five hundred miles to see his woman.

I let out a bark of a laugh, and Livia appears in the bedroom doorway. "Cold beer, or hot shower?"

"Who says I need to choose? A shower beer is one of life's great pleasures."

She blinks. "And who knew I made it almost thirty years without knowing that?" She moves toward the fridge, but I'm faster. I've got the can in my hand a second later. I pop the top and then offer it to Livia, who looks startled.

Then she shakes her head. "I was only grabbing one for you. I'm good."

"It's not your job to fetch me a beer. You know that, right? I'm just happy to see your face."

Her brown eyes widen. "Noted."

I step forward and lean in, touching my lips to hers briefly. It's the only kiss I can give her that doesn't involve sweat on her clothing. "Give me a five-minute head start. Then feel free to join me in the upstairs shower. It's roomier than yours."

"Also noted," she says softly as I pass her and head for the stairs.

Twenty minutes later, I've got Livia right where I want her— braced against the tiles with her hips in my hands. Whatever reservations I have about her facing down criminals are temporarily on hold as our water-slicked bodies move in sync together.

"Give me another one," I coax her, my soapy hand roaming her breasts. My knees didn't appreciate spending time on the tile floor, bringing her to climax with my tongue. "You're so sexy when you moan my name."

"Mmm," she whimpers, arching her back. "I don't know if I... ahhh," she moans.

"Give me that mouth."

She turns her chin, and I lose my rhythm on account of our hot, messy kiss. And now the water is turning cold, so I pull out and shut it off. "Let's go, lady. On my bunk. Like summer camp, but dirtier."

"I never went to summer camp," she says, grabbing a towel on her way out of the shower.

"You missed a lot of mosquito bites and charred hot dogs." I nudge her out of the bathroom toward the bunkroom, where my bed is the only one of the four that's made up. "The boys in my cabin always dared each other to sneak into the girls' cabins, but we never actually followed through."

Livia stops and turns around before we reach the bunkbed, and I bump into her naked body. "Are you telling me you were all talk and no action?"

"I was *thirteen*, and they were sequestered across the lake."

She hoots. "What was your teenage fantasy? If you'd actually swum to the girls' cabins and snuck inside?"

I grab her towel and toss it aside. "Pretty sure I wouldn't have even known what to do when I got there. I probably just wanted to see their titties," I say, palming both her breasts. "If one of those girls actually put her hand on my dick, I probably would have straight-up died of excitement."

Livia laughs. Then she puts her hand on my very hard cock, stroking me slowly. And my breath actually stutters. "Now you're living the dream."

"*Nngh*. You joke, but it's true." I kiss her jaw. "You make me happy, lady. I like your style." I nudge her toward the bed. "Now lie down on that bed for me so I can show you how much."

———

The bunkbed barely survives. And the springs squeak so loudly that Livia actually giggles in the midst of my grand finale.

But I am undeterred, shutting her up with one last, steamy kiss as I sink my tired body onto a narrow strip of the mattress and sigh.

Our hearts thump together for a moment as we come down. The bed stops squeaking, and I find myself listening to the night-time silence for reassurance that we're still alone on the property.

"Did you hear something?" she asks tensely.

"No, baby. Just being careful." I stroke her arm. "I know I told you to stay, and I sure meant it. But I'd be a liar if I said I wasn't worried about Benito's big plan."

"But it doesn't matter. I need to end this," she argues immediately. "Tonight, when you went out running, I wanted to put on my shoes and go with you. I'm tired of hiding at home, Nash. I want to *live*."

The anguish in her voice shuts me up for a second, because I hadn't considered all the simple little things she doesn't feel safe doing right now. And all I can do about it right this moment is pull her into my arms.

She comes willingly. "I almost don't remember what it's like not to be afraid," she says. "You were right. If I don't stand my ground, I'll always be looking over my shoulder."

"Yeah. I hear you. But I still worry. I was the one who sat in the backseat of your car and begged you not to go."

She runs her fingertips down my tummy. "Aren't you the guy who told me not to own other people's decisions?"

Oof. I clamp my jaw shut to keep from arguing that point. And it's not like she's wrong—this has to end. So that's what I'll have to focus on. "A week from tonight he could be behind bars. What's the first thing you'll do to celebrate?"

"Visit Jennie. Check in on my stupid brother. Go out for drinks, in a bar, where anyone might see me. Buy tickets for this summer's outdoor music festival. Drive my own stupid car…"

"Can I come along for some of that?" I ask, stroking her hair. "I like the way you think."

She turns her head on the pillow and studies me. "I suppose I could drive to Boston, if my car can make it a hundred and seventy-five miles."

"We have to do something about your car," I say softly, still staring into her eyes.

But my heart says, *we have to do something about those 175 miles.*

CHAPTER 37
LIVIA

The next few days seem to happen fast. In the first place—per their girlfriends' Instagrams—the Valkyries are back in Vermont. When I spot the clubhouse in the background of a new photo, my stomach cramps.

Meanwhile, Benito and his squad are squirreled away somewhere, plotting our sting operation. "I'm staying away from the brewery, just in case they're watching the place," he says during one of our many phone calls. "But I have a bunch of plans to send you. Be on the lookout, okay?"

He wasn't kidding. Every couple of hours, I get a new email. I'm asked to look at maps of various spots on the west side of the state, as they scout out potential meeting places. And I'm asked to review a sheet of talking points for the phone call when I try to convince Razor to meet me.

Still, it all seems like a problem for another day, until I get a certain text.

BENITO

My guys sighted Razor at his Rutland shop the last three days, but I want to grab him before he leaves again. Let's do our phone call at 10p.

Tonight???

Yeah, I find calls at night come off as spontaneous, and less suspicious.

Okay. Better to get this over with, right?

I look at the clock. It's four now, leaving only six hours to panic.

I'm sending an undercover female officer over with a burner phone.

Is 10 okay?

It's not okay at all. And yet it will have to be. I confirm with him and then set my phone down.

Then I pick it up immediately and text Nash.

You around?

I feel gutted when he doesn't answer immediately. And then I want to kick myself for feeling that way. But one minute later, there's a gentle tap on the office door. "Pussycat?"

I rise from my chair just as Nash steps inside. He takes three paces and gathers me into a tight hug. "You okay?"

"Yes," I say, melting against his chest. I am now. "Benito wants to do the call tonight. Ten o'clock."

"Tonight," he whispers. "Hell. That's soon."

"Yeah," I say lamely. "But it's time, right? I'm tired of bullies."

He sighs. Then he cups my face in both hands. "You are a badass."

"On my good days."

He leans in and kisses my nose. "I'm taking you out to dinner tonight."

"What? I thought we were being careful."

"We are," he says. "I didn't say it would be glamorous. We need to get out of the house."

That does sound appealing. "What's the dress code?"

He gives me a sly wink. "Low-cut tops only."

"*Nash.*"

He chuckles. "Wear whatever you want. We're going to invite ourselves over to grill some steaks for Leila and Matteo. Let's get out of here, or I'll lose my mind. Be ready at six?"

"Okay," I say weakly. I can't believe I have to talk to Razor on the phone.

Tonight.

He squeezes my hands. "I'll feed you a good meal, so you're ready to face him. Let me call my sister, and then I'll run out to the grocery store. Any special requests?"

I shake my head. "I could make a dish, too."

"Nah." He touches his lips to mine. "Tonight I'll spoil you. Hang in there, baby. This will all be over soon."

I just hope I'm still alive when it is.

———

The Rossi family owns some of the coolest businesses in Colebury, including the historic brick complex that houses the Gin Mill. Leila and Matteo live upstairs, in a beautiful apartment with comfortable furniture and leaded glass windows.

I've never been here before, and I'm a little self-conscious about being Nash's special guest. So I'm wearing a kickass beaded top and giant silver hoop earrings, just because I need a boost.

It doesn't help that the first person I see after the door swings open is Nash and Leila's mom. She's holding her grandchild in her arms. I've never met Mrs. Giltmaker, but she needs no introduction—I recognize Nash's smile on her happy face. "Look who it is! My long-lost son!"

"I'm not lost, Ma," he says, setting down his grocery sack and closing the door. "I'm just very busy. Ma, this is Livia. She and I have been spending some time together."

Oh God. I can feel my cheeks flushing. Meeting Nash's mom is not the stress-free vibe I wanted tonight. "It's so nice to meet you," I lie. "What a cute baby."

She really is, too, with chubby cheeks and tiny feet that are swaddled in polka-dot socks.

"I'd hand her over, but she just ate, and I don't think you want spit-up on that pretty top." She beams. "Drinks are out on the terrace. Nash, get your girlfriend a glass of wine."

Girlfriend. We haven't formally used that word, and I feel my cheeks heat all over again.

Nash just puts an arm around my shoulders and leads me toward the terrace overlooking the river.

"Hey, little bro!" Leila says from a deck chair. Matteo is sitting beside her, and they're holding hands. They look both exhausted and giddy at the same time. "How's work? Would you believe that I miss that place?"

"It's going fine," I assure her. "Our inventory is still too low, but your father decided to let Nash brew his signature beers. So things are on an upswing."

She laughs, turning to Nash, who's standing at the grill. "I can't believe you got him to share the recipe. What did you say to that stubborn man?"

"Wasn't me." Nash pokes at the grill with tongs. "Dad gave me some bullshit about secrecy, and I left his room, fuming. Then Livia talked some sense into him." He glances up at me and gives me a sly wink. "But she doesn't like to take credit."

"Huh," Leila says slowly. "And here I'd been worrying that you two wouldn't get along."

"We, uh, had a rough start."

"But things are better now?" Leila asks, swigging her soda.

"Oh, *much* better," Nash says with a laugh. "You could even say that we're getting along *smashingly.*"

Leila's eyes widen. She opens her mouth, and then closes it again.

"*Nash*," I hiss.

He shrugs. "Sorry, baby. I happen to like you a lot. Don't mind sharing that with my family."

"Fascinating," Leila says with a little smile. "And here I thought maybe I'd overstepped when I asked Livia if you could stay in the bunkroom."

My face is on fire now.

"What would you like to drink?" Leila starts to rise.

"Don't get up," I say quickly. "We've got it. Are you getting any sleep these days?"

"No," Leila and Matteo say in unison, exchanging a warm glance. "But," Leila adds, "they tell us this part won't last forever."

"Sure hope not," Nash says, moving over to a small table where there's some white wine in an ice bucket and a selection of beers. "Pick your poison," he says to me.

"A half glass of wine, please." I'll need to stay sharp tonight.

"You got it," he says, reaching for the bottle. "Now I've got to set up my veggie skewers."

"I can help," I offer.

"No." He pours the wine and hands it to me. "You sit down for once in your life. I've got this."

Then that jerk leaves me on the terrace with Leila watching me with an expression of amused astonishment. "Wow," she says, sipping her drink. "When Nash falls, he falls hard."

"It's not like that," I say quickly.

"Oh, I think it is," Matteo argues. He raises his glass and clinks it against his girlfriend's. "Kinda fun to watch, honestly. I know you've always wished your brother would move back to Vermont."

"That's right," she says. "But not because I'm being clingy. I think he's hitting a dead end in Boston. His job isn't fun anymore."

"Hey now," I say quietly. "I don't think Nash has any plans to move home. Your dad wants things to go back to the way they were as soon as possible."

Leila makes a face. "We don't always get what we want, though, right? He clearly needs help. Nash has a decade of experience with the business end of running a brewery. My dad is a selfish man, but he's not stupid. I bet he'll figure out how much he needs Nash."

"Maybe," I say politely. But I don't believe it for a second.

CHAPTER 38
NASH

It's been years since I made dinner for my family. I miss these casual get-togethers, if I'm honest.

So I make a nice spread. There's steak, grilled vegetables, and a quick orzo dish with pesto. We eat it at the dining room table in the great room. When little Reina gets fussy in her swing, Leila and Matteo pass her back and forth during the meal.

My sister looks elated. Even the circles under her eyes can't weigh down her smile. It brings me joy to see it. Of the three Giltmaker kids, she's the eldest, and the only one who's settled down.

Maybe I'm next. But Livia and I have a couple of hurdles to clear before we can have that conversation.

I notice she switches to drinking soda, and she eats very little. She's obviously nervous, and for good reason.

My coping strategy is different. I eat everything on my plate, and when the meal is over, I insist that nobody helps me with the dishes. I send the happy couple outside again with my mom and Livia, over everyone's protestations.

Hard work doesn't scare me. It never has.

But losing Livia to Razor? I get the cold sweats every time I picture her luring him to a meeting tomorrow.

My mother wanders inside as I'm hanging up the dish towel.

She paces the room with the baby in her arms, probably because babies find that soothing.

"How have you been, Nash? I've barely heard from you while you've been in Vermont. But that's my fault, isn't it? I've spent these past few weeks staring at my grandchild."

"It's fine, Ma. I've been busy. And if you spent that time staring at *me*, that would just be awkward."

She grins. "I just don't want you to feel like the forgotten middle child."

I laugh, but there's some truth to it. I *am* the forgotten middle child.

"Let's try something," my mother says, walking toward me. Suddenly, there's a baby in my arms.

"Hey, warn a guy." I cradle my niece's warm weight against my chest. "I don't know what the heck I'm doing with babies."

She is cute, though, staring up at me with wide eyes.

"Nobody ever knows what they're doing until the moment they need to learn. But the baby looks good on you, Nash. I think you should have one, too."

I snort. "This feels like peer pressure. Do you have a new grandma addiction?"

"Definitely," she says. "I'll be looking for my next fix real soon."

"At least you're honest about it."

"Oh, I am. But when will you be honest?"

"Me? I'm very honest."

"Not about your own needs," she says quietly. "You pass yourself off as a loner—and happier working in Boston, away from the family who loves you."

"It's not that far down the highway, Ma," I say, just to shut her up. "Stop by any time."

"Livia seems great," she says with absolutely no subtlety. "She has a spark to her that suits you."

"I happen to agree with that."

"So how long have you two been together?"

Lord, she's nosy. But Livia is one of my favorite topics lately, so I don't mind as much as I usually would. "That's the funny thing. It hasn't been very long at all. But I look at her and I see someone I know well."

"Oh honey." Her eyes get dreamy. "I've never heard you talk about a girl like that. Then again, you're usually in Boston, where it's harder for me to be nosy."

"And you wonder why I don't move back."

She laughs. "Touché. Now hang onto that baby a moment longer so I can get out the brownies I brought for dessert."

"All right." I glance down at my niece, whose eyelids are getting heavy. "I'm sorry you're too young for grandma's brownies. They are spectacular."

She gazes up at me sleepily. And I find myself wondering whether Livia wants children.

If I'm lucky, we'll get the chance to have that conversation someday. Because I want that. I want *all* the chances. I only wonder if she'll give them to me.

CHAPTER 39
LIVIA

Nash is very quiet on the way back to the brewery. So quiet that it's making me twitchy. Deep male silences tend to fill me with dread.

"Um, thank you for dinner and for bringing me along tonight," I say.

He doesn't reply. He just reaches across the truck and squeezes my knee.

Hmm. "Hope you had an okay time. I didn't say anything wrong, did I?"

He turns to me in surprise. "Of course not. Why the hell would you think that?"

"I don't know," I say lamely. "You seem…quiet." I don't add that it's the same variety of silence that used to foreshadow anger and violence from Razor.

"Pussycat, I had a great time tonight. But thirty minutes from now you are going to set a trap for your asshole ex, and I don't like it one bit."

"Oh."

Oh.

"Worried that this is too dangerous," he says with a sigh. "I'd feel better right now if you were out of state. Maybe I was selfish.

Need to keep you safe. That's all that really matters. Did I help fuck this up?"

I'm so stunned that I can't reply for a moment. "You didn't," I choke out.

He sighs. "You want me sitting there when you make the call? Or would it be easier if I weren't around?"

Maybe someday it will seem normal for me when a man takes my feelings into consideration. But today must not be that day, because I'm caught off guard. "You can be there. It's fine."

"Not what I asked," he says, putting on his traffic signal to turn into the brewery. "What's your preference?"

"You should be there to listen," I say quietly.

"All right." He pulls into the lot and steps on the brake. "Office, or apartment?"

"Apartment," I say. "Benito wants everything to look normal. And I'm never in the office at night."

"All right." He pulls through and parks beside the pump-house. "Let's do this thing."

———

We set up in the living room on the coffee table. At a quarter till ten, I answer a video call from Benito on my laptop. "Hello, star witness," he says cheerfully. "How was dinner with my brother?"

Sometimes I forget how small this town is. "Nice. They seem exhausted but content."

"Don't we all. You got the burner phone? You feeling steady?"

"Steady*ish*," I say with uncharacteristic honesty.

He grins. "You're going to do great. When you're ready, I want you to mute this Zoom call, but leave the chat open, so I can talk to you. That burner phone I sent you is bugged, so I'll be able to hear and record the call right here…" He picks up an ear bud and puts it in his ear. "Try this—mute me now and call Nash's phone for a second? Let's test our equipment."

I follow these instructions, and Nash's phone rings a second later.

Sitting beside me on the sofa, he answers it. "Bob's Junk Shop. What can we do you for?"

"Aren't you funny," I mumble.

On the computer screen, Benito gives me the thumbs up, and I unmute him. "Could you hear us?"

"Loud and clear," Benito says. "And this is your reminder that the state police are recording this call with the intention that any and all proceedings may be used in a court of law."

My stomach rolls. "Got it."

"Any last questions? Are you clear on the plan?"

I nod my head with a nervous bob.

"And if he tries to change the plan?"

"Then I'll agree to whatever I have to, with the understanding that we might not go through with it if it's too dangerous."

Beside me, Nash puts his head in his hands.

"Right," Benito agrees. "But let's hope it doesn't come to that. Anything else?"

I shake my head, because Benito can't really answer the biggest questions that I have—am I a good enough actor to pull this off? And does it even matter? Razor is probably too smart to get hustled by the cops.

"Okay," he says. "Fire when ready. Mute me first, and watch the chat."

My stomach is suddenly full of angry bees as I mute Benito.

I pick up the burner again, handling it as if it were a hand grenade. After all this time, I'm just going to dial Razor's number, and invite that asshole back into my life?

What a terrible idea this was.

Nash puts a hand on my knee and squeezes.

I open the flip phone and tap in the Vermont area code, 802. Then I take a deep breath and tap in the rest.

It rings. I forget to exhale.

Then suddenly his rasp of a voice is in my ear. "Razor. Who's this?"

For a millisecond, I hesitate. Once I identify myself, there's no going back.

"Who's there?" he demands.

"Ivy," I whisper. "It's Ivy."

That shuts him up for a second, which is gratifying. "Ivy," he echoes eventually. "You run out of money or something? Or maybe you need a good fuck?"

I squeeze my eyes shut and resist the urge to tell him that he was never very good in that department. "No need to be rude, Razor. I just called to tell you that I'm leaving Vermont, and I thought you should know."

"Good luck with that," he says. "Doesn't matter where you go, I'll still be able to find you. Took me a while this time, but I did it, yeah? You're never out of reach, babe. You cross me, and I'll hunt you down. And I'll make it hurt when I find you."

All my blood stops circulating. Nash puts a hand on my back, reminding me to breathe.

I can feel my heart thumping in my throat. "Look," I say, and it comes out sounding shaky. "I called for a reason. But maybe it was stupid."

"What reason?"

"Well, I have some things of yours that you probably want back."

A brief silence tells me that I've got his attention. "Like what things?"

"Like insurance," I whisper. "I took a thumb drive. It shows all the irregular VIN numbers on your books—"

"You fucking little—"

"Bitch? Whore? You can save it, okay?" His anger is somehow clarifying for me. It makes me stronger, and my voice comes out steady. "I wanted out, Razor. So I made sure I had something to trade in case the cops ever came after me."

"And have they?" he demands.

"Not yet," I say carefully. "For a while, I considered revenge. Thought about sending this stuff to them in the mail, with a note. But then I calmed down, and realized I don't know if it's traceable. And I never want to end up in a courtroom. I just want to move away from here and find some peace. So you can have this stuff if you agree to forget my name."

Another silence from Razor.

You're doing great, says Benito in the chat screen. *Seriously fantastic!*

"Not sure I care," Razor says slowly. "Bunch of bad VIN numbers just means one of my guys is a shitty record keeper. It doesn't incriminate me."

I was prepared for this, but my shoulders sag anyway. Next time I decide to date an asshole, I'll pick a stupider one. My heart pounds faster, because I'm about to tell him some serious lies. "Yeah, maybe. But that's why I also parked an audio recorder in the clubhouse. I've got sixteen hours of conversation. You're on a bunch of it."

He snorts. "Sixteen hours of beer drinking and smack talk."

"And your voice, discussing a drug drop in Troy, New York."

My stomach clenches after I drop this little nugget. It's all just grandstanding. I don't have a recording, and I never heard Razor mention Troy. Benito fed me all this from his own investigation.

But if Benito got anything wrong, Razor will know I'm a liar.

The silence drags on until he finally says, "We never use real names, and we never mention drugs by name. You can't prove nothing."

"Maybe," I admit. "But sixteen hours is a long time. There's a lot of conversation, and some names I'd never heard before. I bet there's a cop *somewhere* that would take an interest."

He makes an angry noise.

"But you can have all of it," I say quickly. "I'll give you the recorder, but you have to agree to leave me alone. And also give me back my passport. I need it."

"Where'd you hide this recorder?" he asks. "I think you're bluffing."

A drop of sweat rolls down my back, because he's right to be suspicious. "I put it in the pocket of a hoodie that was hanging on a hook on a wall. Somebody left it there for weeks." *And thank you, Benito, for coaching me on this question.* "It's voice activated, so it only switched on whenever people were talking. Your voice is on there. Maybe you're not the one who actually says what went down in Troy. But you're there, and it's clear you're the boss."

He lets out a quiet curse, while I say a prayer that this seems plausible.

"I bought the device on Amazon," I continue. "Little thing. Looks like a kitchen timer."

"You cunt," he whispers. "Sticking your nose in other people's business."

"You *made* it my business," I argue. "I wanted nothing to do with it."

"Then why did you make *a fucking recording*?" he snarls.

"I had to!" I shout. "I'm *never* taking the rap for your drug deals. I had to protect myself. You want this thing, or not? The data is probably exportable, but I didn't try."

"Uh-huh. You think I'd just trust you about that?" he barks. "Like, you never made a copy of that thumb drive? What's in this for me?"

"I don't *want* this stuff," I argue. "I never did. That's why you had to trick me into doing your illegal bullshit. If you'd been honest with me—that you were laundering money through your bank accounts—I would have never done your bookkeeping. I would have walked right out the door."

"Yeah? Like you're too good for me, bitch? Didn't hear you complain when I took you for steaks at Southside's. Fentanyl paid for those twelve-dollar cocktails you like so much."

BENITO

Boom!!!! Yeah baby!

My shoulders relax by a fraction. "Look, if you didn't smack me around, maybe I could have ignored the fentanyl," I say. "And the scar on my arm? I'll have it for the rest of my life."

"Cry me a fucking river," he says. "Your new boy toy doesn't seem to mind. He know you're leaving the state?"

"His idea," I say quietly. "He got a job out on the West Coast." A location I chose because it's both vague and far away. "Look, I'd FedEx this stuff to you. But I want my passport, because we want to drive through Canada. And it seems like a fair trade."

Another silence. "All right. Tell me where you are, and I'll send someone to swing by and get it."

A drop of sweat runs down my back, because the next minute or so is crucial. "I'm not talking to one of your flying monkeys, and I'm not telling you where I'm staying. I'll meet you somewhere tomorrow. I have to drive to Rutland in the morning to pick up a used car I'm buying. Mine wouldn't make the trip."

He doesn't answer right away, and I stop breathing. "That might work," he says eventually. "Swing by in the morning?"

"No way," I say, allowing myself to sound nervous. "After the beating you gave me? I'm not setting foot on your property. But there's always the parking lot in front of the supermarket. We could meet there. Or CVS? Or even at that Dairy Queen."

"Hang on," he mutters. "I'm thinking."

BENITO

Google the DQ, asshole! You know you want to.

The seconds tick by. There's no way this is going to work.
Although I think I hear the sound of a keyboard in use.

Push him.

"Okay. Yes, or no? Either way I'm leaving town tomorrow. If I can't have my passport, we'll drive through Pennsylvania instead."

Good job!

"All right," Razor grumbles. "Dairy Queen, tomorrow at ten a.m."

"Fine," I snap. "And don't you dare forget my passport."

Then I hang up before he can argue with me about any of it.

Nash grabs me in his arms and kisses me. "Great job, lady. He went for it." Then he leans down and unmutes Benito. "You got him to bite the hook. If you let him run away with the bait, I'm going to haunt your dreams."

On screen, Benito raises both hands in submission. "We're going to have so much coverage. You guys get some sleep, okay? Tomorrow starts early. And Livia—great job getting him talking. His arrest warrant is getting longer by the minute."

"Oh goody."

I just hope I live through tomorrow.

CHAPTER 40
LIVIA

My alarm wakes me up at six. And when it goes off, I find myself tangled up with Nash's naked body. He lets out a groan when I wiggle around to find the phone and shut it off.

"What time is it?" he mumbles.

"Time to catch some bad guys."

His eyes fly open. "You can still change your mind."

I put a hand on his muscular chest and feel the steady rhythm of his heart. "You honestly have no idea how much I appreciate you. But let me just get this over with."

He kicks away the tangled covers. "Then I'm coming, too."

"Nash! Benito isn't going to let you ride along."

"Pussycat." He sits up. "I know they won't put me in the surveillance van. But if you're going to Rutland to catch a crook, then I'm going to be nearby. That's just a fact."

"Wow," I whisper. "That gives me the warm flutters."

"The what?"

"Never mind." I head for the shower. If today isn't a disaster, there'll be time for plenty of flutters later.

———

I put up a good front all morning. But by the time ten o'clock rolls around, my tough-girl veneer is starting to wear thin. I'm sitting in the driver's seat of my ancient Subaru in the parking lot of the Dairy Queen. There's a recording device in my bra.

But I feel very alone, even though Benito swears the area is surrounded by undercover cops, and even though Benito is speaking to me through my phone, which is sitting on the seat beside me.

"Remember—give us as many clues to what's going on as you can. But for now, don't speak to me unless something is wrong," he says. "They probably have eyes on this lot."

"Mm-hmm," I say without moving my mouth. He's told me all this twice before. And last night, the police observed a guy slinking around the DQ lot, possibly planting a camera. Our meetup has turned into a game of cat and mouse.

The minutes tick by, and I'm practically coming out of my skin.

"Eastbound biker on Route 4, headed your way," Benito says, and it's hard not to notice the excitement in his voice. "This could be our guy. We can't see the tag. It's obscured. Bike is a Harley. Black. ETA is about four minutes."

Oh God. My blood pressure spikes, and I realize that up until this very minute, I hadn't believed that Razor would actually show up. He's got to know that it's a trap.

Which probably means he thinks he can outsmart us.

Sweating now, I glance around the Dairy Queen parking lot for the millionth time. It's empty. The place doesn't open for another three hours, which is almost certainly why Razor chose it from the short list of options I gave him.

In fact, this spot is scarily private. Cars pass by every minute or so on the road, but the only human I've seen was when a supply truck rolled into this parking lot ten minutes ago to unload a pallet of canned soda and bottled water by the side door. Then he left with a friendly wave in my direction.

I felt like chasing after the truck and begging him to stay.

"Biker is two minutes away now," Benito says. His crew is monitoring the road by drone.

"Mm-hmm." I lean my head against the headrest and try to look bored.

If only.

When I volunteered to lure Razor to this parking lot, I tried to picture myself facing him in person. The bravest part of me is looking forward to it. That's why I'm wearing a kickass little wrap top and my tightest jeans. I also straightened my hair and did some of my best work on my makeup.

He didn't break me, damn it. I want him to notice.

There's only one problem. Right after he notices how good I look, he'll put his own devious plans into action. And I don't know exactly what those plans are. I do know, however, that Razor wouldn't show up here if he didn't firmly believe he has the upper hand.

"Hey, Livia—there's also a flatbed truck heading in your direction. There are two Valkyries club members in it. They're about three minutes behind the biker, trying to look casual. They're hauling landscaping equipment."

We'd guessed he'd bring backup, but my stomach drops anyway.

"Mm-hmm," I say in acknowledgment.

"Don't panic," Benito says. "We expected this. Black truck. Orange decals on the door."

I groan.

"Deep breaths. Thirty seconds to the biker."

My car windows are cracked open, so I can already hear the unmistakable low growl of his bike. It's a sound that once thrilled me, and now only makes my hands feel sweaty.

"Thumb drive in one pocket. Recording device in the other," Benito says calmly. "Don't forget to demand your passport. It's showtime. As soon as you greet him, I'll give the go-sign to the team at the garage."

Right. A few minutes from now, when Razor and his closest henchmen are preoccupied with me, a team of cops will raid Razor's shop, office, clubhouse, and home. The judge who reviewed last night's phone call—together with the other information I'd provided —has awarded Benito every search warrant he'd requested.

It's great news, but I'm having trouble celebrating as Razor turns into the parking lot, and my heart leaps into my throat.

The bike stops about five paces from my car, and he gets off, looking just as I remembered—rugged and imposing, handsome face scowling.

I exit my car, my movements deliberate, and our eyes meet in a silent clash of wills. Razor keeps his usual scowl, but his eyes flicker with a mix of surprise and something darker as he takes in my appearance.

"Hey," I say, and my voice isn't even shaking. Much.

"Hey," he replies, his tone casual, but there's an edge to it, a hint of the control he used to exert over me. He takes a step closer, the air charged with danger.

But I don't flinch. I'm not the same person I was a year ago.

"You're looking good," he says, eyeing me possessively.

It gives me the creeps, and now I wish I'd worn a potato sack instead of a cute outfit. "Did you bring my passport?"

He pats the pocket of his leather jacket. "Of course. Now show me what you've got."

"Here's the thumb drive." I pull it out of my pocket. "It's all spreadsheets of VIN numbers and fraudulent title transfer dates." Wary of getting close to him, I extend my hand as my heart hammers.

He takes the drive innocently enough, then stares at it in his palm. "What if you're bluffing?"

"What if I am?" I ask, rolling my eyes. "You're still a crook, and I still need my passport back. Did you know you could be arrested for keeping it from me? That's *illegal.*"

His expression hardens, anger making his eyes squinty. I

shrink a little inside, because I know that look all too well. "Let's see this recording thing," he growls.

Trying to maintain my bravado, I pull the gizmo that Benito gave me out of my jacket pocket. "It's here. I even brought you the charge cord. You're going to need it."

"Show me how it works. I want to hear this recording."

Good idea, pal. If only it were real.

Sweating, I press the power button with my thumb. The light comes on. And when I hit the Play button as instructed, the light fades. "You'll have to recharge it." I offer him the device and the cord. "Do you want me to boot up the thumb drive? I have my laptop." I jerk my thumb toward my car.

He squints at my old Subaru, his mouth in a hard line. "Thought you said you were trading that piece of shit in."

"I *am*. Right after I leave here. I didn't want you to see my new vehicle. I mean it, Razor. I'm leaving the state, and I'm not coming back. Are we doing this trade, or what? Show me the passport."

He crosses his arms and stares me down. "I'm thinking."

Shit.

That's when a flatbed truck with orange decals appears, just like Benito warned me it would. Only instead of turning into the parking lot, the truck pulls across the entrance, obstructing both access and sight lines between me and the street.

My heart practically detonates when I recognize Rotty and another biker in the front seat.

"What the hell?" I squeak. "Two of your lackeys are *blocking the driveway*?" God, I hope Benito heard that through the mic in my bra.

Razor doesn't even look in their direction. He just watches me. "What are you playing at, Livia?"

Shit shit shit. I watch, terrified, as Rotty hops onto the flatbed and starts a weed wacker. A very loud one.

If I scream, nobody will hear me.

"What's this?" I shout at Razor. "Can't handle meeting a woman all by yourself?"

He doesn't answer. He lunges at me instead.

CHAPTER 41
NASH

I'm standing in a Rutland parking lot a half mile from the Dairy Queen, where Benito's police unit has set up its mobile command station. They have a couple of drone operators, a K9 unit, and a nondescript surveillance van.

Benito has allowed me to lurk here by my bike while I quietly lose my mind. Livia is the bravest person I know. And while I'd rather smash her adversaries one by one by myself, I'm smart enough to know it's not an option. If Livia wants to be truly free, it has to do be done by professionals.

That doesn't make the waiting any easier.

The doors and windows of the van are all open for easy conversation with the drone operator. I've been eavesdropping from ten paces away.

And when it all goes wrong, I know immediately.

"He grabbed her!" one cop says. "He has a gun."

I cover the distance to the van so quickly that I don't even remember running.

"Your ass is *mine*," Razor hisses through Livia's body mic. "Stupid cunt. Think you can drive away from me? Think again."

I feel my soul leave my body.

Craning my neck to peer around a cop, I see video of the Dairy

Queen. Razor has grabbed Livia's hands behind her back, and he's zip-tying her wrists together.

She valiantly tries to kick backwards at Razor, but he sidesteps her. Meanwhile, the gun glints from his back pocket.

I can't see Livia's face, but there's more tension in her body than anyone should have to bear.

"Fuck!" I yell.

Benito ignores me. A noise that sounds like lawn equipment roars through the mic, making everything more chaotic.

Razor says something, but he's not as close to the mic this time. I think it's, "Where are your car keys?"

"C-cupholder," Livia stammers.

He waves at one of his guys and then points at her car.

"I t-told my boyfriend I was meeting you here," she stammers. This is something else Benito coached her to say. "If I don't call him in ten minutes, he's going to freak."

Razor's reply isn't clear. But on the video, one of the other bikers gets into Livia's car and starts the engine.

"Route 4 units stand by," Benito barks into his headset. At his command, the police will stop either or both vehicles on the road.

It better happen fast. I won't draw a full breath until she's safe again.

But Razor doesn't put her in the truck or the Subaru. I watch, helpless, while he grabs her by the wrists and points her in exactly the opposite direction—toward the back of the lot, and the forested area behind it.

"Aren't we getting in the car?" Livia yelps.

He shoves her toward the back of the lot.

"He's heading east," Benito clips. "Tactical Services stand by."

I stop breathing as Livia drops her head and shuffles away from the camera. They trudge toward the shadow of the Dairy Queen.

"Go soda pop!" says Benito.

My terrified mind can't make sense of that order until I notice movement at the edge of the frame. It's coming from a pallet of soft drinks sitting on the asphalt. An arm shoots from around the pallet and reaches for Razor's ankles.

And then everything happens at once. The hidden cop snags Razor, and Razor starts to topple like a timbered tree. The momentum takes down Livia, because Razor has a hold on her wrists.

"Ow!" she shouts into the mic as she pitches helplessly toward the ground, falling into the dirt.

The cop pounces on Razor's back, and Livia flings herself out of their way. "Watch the gun!" she yells, sitting up.

The cop is on it, though, immobilizing Razor, and more police swarm the property as Benito shouts instructions into his mic.

"Freeze! State Police! Hands up!"

I hear the lawn equipment go silent and the *whoop whoop* of police sirens growing louder.

This is a serious operation. Benito didn't lie. The two bikers who arrived in the truck are in handcuffs already.

And Benito isn't done. Other video feeds in the van show footage from drones in several other locations, where different factions of the motorcycle club are being raided.

But I only have eyes for Livia. Eventually, I see a cop cut the zip ties off her wrists. He helps her to her feet as Razor is being led away toward a cruiser.

My girl sways on her feet, drunk on adrenaline and terror.

But she's also smiling from ear to ear, because she knows she did it. It's really over.

Ten minutes later, a cruiser rolls up with Livia in the passenger seat. I run toward the car, and as soon as it stops, she opens the door and launches herself into my arms.

I catch her. "Good job, baby." I rest my chin on her shoulder. "You schooled him."

"I was so scared," she says, clinging to me. "So scared, but also so ready."

"He didn't win." I brush dirt off the back of her jacket. "You brought down his criminal empire, and you didn't even ruin your makeup."

She laughs. "The first thing he said to me was, 'You look good.'"

"He isn't wrong."

"But aren't you jealous?" she teases.

"Of a guy wearing handcuffs? Not hardly."

Livia steps back, her hand on my chest and a playful look in her eye. "But I only call the cops on men that I like."

We both crack up.

"Hey, kids," Benito says, crossing the clearing to talk to us. "I'll need Livia for a debriefing in my office, and then I'm taking her to a safe house for a couple nights. We're raiding Valkyries clubhouses in four different towns right now. And the good news is that *this* guy wants to talk." He points to a cruiser where the younger biker—the one who'd accompanied Rotty in the landscaping truck—has been handcuffed.

"I remember him," Livia says softly. "They call him Kicker. But I don't know his real name."

"He's going to tell us that himself," Benito says. "He already told me he wants to cut a deal. He said he hates what he was asked to do today—that kidnapping a woman is not what he signed up for. Says he has a baby daughter. So he knows better."

"Huh," I say, squinting at the kid through the cruiser's window. "I guess a little light money laundering is fine for him, but he's not a fan of violence?"

"Something like that." Benito smirks. "I have a feeling he's going to be very helpful."

"Thank God," Livia says, leaning into me. "Maybe it won't just be me testifying against Razor."

"Exactly," Benito agrees. "You did great. Nerves of steel."

Livia smiles down at her boots, like she knows she did well but isn't quite ready to take the compliment.

"We picked up more of Razor's friends in the woods behind the Dairy Queen," Benito adds. "Maybe they don't want to go to jail for attempted kidnapping, either. I'm hoping for all kinds of cooperation."

Livia lifts her face to the sky and smiles. "Let 'em squeal like five-year-old girls at a Disney princess birthday party."

Benito doesn't laugh at the joke, and after a beat I realize he's listening to a flurry of activity over the police scanner. We can all hear it through the cruiser's window. There's a bunch of police codes I can't understand, and then the dispatcher says, "Requesting any available backup. Arsonist heading south on foot."

"What's going on?" Livia asks, her expression suddenly serious.

"Sounds like a big fire," Benito says slowly.

"Where?" she asks.

I hear the scanner squawk again. And the disembodied voice gives an address I know all too well. It's the Giltmaker Brewery.

Later, I won't remember the drive. I think I gave Livia a quick hug before leaping onto my bike and roaring away. I practically flew back to Colebury.

When I come tearing onto the property, it's like looking up at a hellscape. The entire south end of the brewery—where the loading dock leads to the brewhouse in the center—is engulfed in flames. Firefighters have surrounded the place with trucks, hoses, and a safety barrier.

In spite of their efforts, the fire is busy licking its way across the roofline toward the office on the north end. Like a hungry beast that won't quit.

Badger comes running toward me across the gravel lot, and I

drag my gaze away from the burning building to look him over. His face is covered in soot. "Nash! I'm sorry."

"Jesus. Is anyone hurt?"

He shakes his head. "No, thank God. Connor was the only one in the loading dock when the guy threw the thing through the window—a Molotov cocktail. Landed near the cardboard packing cases. Lit up like a flare. Connor started shouting, and I ran in there. Grabbed the extinguisher. But we couldn't beat it back." He puts his grimy face in his hands. "Dude, I'm *so* sorry. Can't imagine who'd do this to you."

"I can," I mutter, staring at the antique building. The flames form a corona that's so bright my eyes are stinging. And wouldn't you know? This is the first moment of my adult life when the words *family legacy* really click for me.

God damn it, but this hurts. Like a wound on my soul.

And my poor father. He'll never get over this.

CHAPTER 42
LIVIA

The first thing I do when I wake up is listen. That will never change.

Fortunately, I'm napping at Benito's safe house, and Razor is in prison. So there are significantly fewer things to panic about than there were a few days ago.

Still, old habits die hard. And my heartrate revs when I hear a car outside.

I sit up on the couch and wait until I hear the knock. Then I rise and walk noiselessly to the front door to peer through the peephole.

Since Razor's arrest thirty-six hours ago, the cops have been on a tear, charging over a dozen criminals and interviewing a dozen more. With every passing minute, the threat against me retreats, but I'll probably spend the rest of my life being cautious about opening doors to people.

Benito stands on the porch, waving at me from the other side of the steel door. "Anyone home?"

He knows I am.

"One sec!" I call, needing a moment to hastily finger-comb my hair and pinch some color into my cheeks. I've spent the last couple of days crying, and it shows.

When I'm good and ready, I open the door a crack. "You're alone, right?"

"It's just me and this pizza."

I open the door all the way. "Thank you for the pizza."

He steps inside. "You are very welcome. Did you speak to Nash today?"

At the mention of Nash's name, tears threaten again. "No," I mumble.

Benito chooses his words carefully. "You've got to talk to him eventually, right? The longer you wait, the harder it gets."

I say nothing, because I'm not going to argue with him. I don't know what to say to Nash. Or any of the Giltmakers. The brewery is gone, and it's my fault.

The only saving grace is that Nash had to go to Boston yesterday. It wasn't until Benito told me that he'd left town that I could finally sleep through the night. I've been so heartsick that I can barely close my eyes. Every time I do, I see images of the brewery burning. They're all over the TV. Bright orange flames. Black smoke.

The worst clip of all is from the moment when the hundred-year-old ceiling fell in. They're calling it a total loss.

That's what I did to the Giltmakers—caused a *total loss*.

Benito crosses to the dining table and sets the pizza down. "Hey, have a seat?"

I pull out a chair and sink down into it. The pizza smells good, but I'm not hungry. I haven't really been able to eat much at all.

Benito leans back in his chair and sighs. "Honey, nobody blames you for the fire."

Oh please. "They should."

He shakes his head. "Razor had a guy listening to the police scanner. They planned the whole thing ahead of time. When he heard the clubhouse got raided, he threw a Molotov cocktail through the window on the loading dock. And that was that. If anyone is to blame, it's me."

That's a lie. But I know he's only putting it like that to make me feel better. "Did you get the guy who did it?"

Benito's eyes brighten. "Took an entire day, but we found footage of the perp buying gasoline in a small container the day before. I got a plate number and found he's a Valkyries member. Arrested him this morning. Get this—he googled 'how to make a Molotov cocktail' on his phone. The tab was still open on the browser."

I smile for one split second. But then I remember that it doesn't matter if the perp goes to jail. The brewery is still gone. Decades of love and labor, literally up in smoke.

I brought that trouble to the Giltmakers' door. It will never be okay.

Benito pushes the pizza box in my direction. "Come on now. I cooked this myself."

"You did not," I argue, and he smiles. "Want a slice?"

He eyes the pizza. "I shouldn't. Gotta watch my diet. I'm just here to give you some good news."

"What kind of news?" Unless the brewery magically healed itself overnight, I'm not sure how good it could be.

"Kicker—his real name is Chad—"

Chad?

"—gave us even more dirt than I'd been hoping for. He corroborated some major drug deals from the past three years."

"Wow." That really is surprising. "I'm happy for you. Kicker always seemed gentler than the rest of them. Not like that's setting the bar very high. But I wondered if you'd get any more traction."

"We did. After Kicker started talking, it got easier to cut deals. We got more guys to flip."

"What will happen to them?" I ask. Somehow my slice of pizza is disappearing quickly.

"Kicker will get the best deal—a new identity. He'll be relocated somewhere out West, probably. He has a young family to think about and doesn't mind starting over somewhere."

"Starting over," I sigh. "I'm pretty familiar with that myself." But I'm so tired. I don't even feel like trying.

Benito considers my sad face from the other side of the table. "Look, Livia. I know you're hurting. The brewery didn't have a sprinkler system, and that's Lyle's fault. But they did have insurance."

Having nothing else to think about for the past thirty-six hours, I've already considered this. "Insurance isn't going to get their business back on its feet anytime soon. I'm grateful to you that Razor and his crew are getting what they deserve. But the Giltmakers won't be. They showed me kindness and protection, and I'm literally responsible for burning everything they have to the ground."

Benito opens the pizza box and pulls out a slice. He takes a bite. "I know you feel terrible about the brewery. All of Vermont feels bad."

"Right. Because we lost a treasure. And I'm the match that set the whole thing on fire."

"If that's how you want to look at it, I would like to point out that you're *also* the match that set a drug ring on fire. You're the one who gave me enough to arrest Razor on assault and money-laundering. Which got me a broad judicial warrant and a new material witness or ten. After two years of working this case, *you* cracked the whole thing open. Tomorrow you can walk out of here. There's no more target on your back."

"That's good news," I say woodenly. "Thank you for that."

He sighs. "Razor is already behind bars. Not only are you safe, but he can't abuse any more women. That's important, isn't it?"

"Yes. It's a start."

He eats his pizza slice thoughtfully. "It's been an incredibly productive couple of days. The most arrests I've ever made in a single week."

"That's extraordinary," I say with as much enthusiasm as I can manage. "I hope they give you a huge promotion."

"Straight to God's ears," he says. "Baby needs new shoes."

I form my mouth into a smile, but it almost hurts to try.

Benito looks at his phone. "Sorry, I'm just waiting for confirmation of one more arrest in Brattleboro."

Somehow my first piece of pizza has disappeared, so I pick up a second one.

He watches the screen for another moment, and I'm just about to offer him a soda when his phone chimes with a text. "All righty. Suspect in custody. Do you know what that means?"

I shake my head.

"You're done." He grins. "You can walk out of this place unafraid, because that was the last arrest. All the drug runners are in custody. Even better—they know through the grapevine that Razor effed up and walked into our trap and that bikers close to Razor flipped for the prosecution. This isn't on you anymore. Nobody wants you dead anymore. You're free."

Free. It's all I ever wanted. I spent a whole year wishing I could walk around Vermont unafraid. And now I'd give it all back if I could prevent the brewery fire. I really would.

Benito gets up to wash his hands in the kitchen. "You stay here one more night, okay? Maybe life will look rosier in the morning."

"Maybe," I agree. But I know it won't.

You ruin everything, my mother always said. And I'm afraid she was right.

Benito plucks his jacket off the back of his dining chair. "In other news, now that you're no longer in danger, this isn't a safe house anymore. It's just a house."

"Cool," I say dully.

"Yup." He heads for the door. "That's why I just texted Nash the address."

"What?"

With a hand on the doorknob, he shrugs. "Yeah, you two clearly need to work some things out. And he's on his way back from Boston. He'll be here any minute, I think. Night, Livia!"

"Benito!" I'm up out of my chair and panicking already. "Now hang on—"

The door closes behind him.

"Shit!" I scream. I can't face Nash. I'm not ready.

I will *never* be ready.

CHAPTER 43
NASH

I've barely slept in three days. Coffee is my best friend.

Maybe my only friend. Badger and the rest of the brewers are suddenly out of a job. Livia isn't taking my calls. My dad is an inconsolable ball of rage.

And then there's my brother Mitch in the passenger's seat, staring glumly out the window. He's been in a bit of a mood since the minute I picked him up from Boston's Logan Airport.

I reach across the gear box and give him a poke. "What are you thinking so hard about over there? Distract me."

"This place," he says quietly. "Seems like yesterday I was an eighteen-year-old kid heading for the woods with a pony keg in the back of my truck, thinking that was the height of excitement."

"It was at the time. But listen, pal. It's not your turn to be all quiet and broody. Take a fucking number."

He chuckles quietly. "At least I'm here, right? Ready to do what I can. I'll stack up sooty bricks or whatever."

"Your only job is talking Dad off the ledge. He always liked you best." In the cupholder, my phone beeps. "Can you tell me who's messaging me?"

"Sure. Happy to be your secretary. Wait—do you have an actual secretary?"

"I have an administrative assistant." I slow down to let a deer cross the road.

"She hot?"

I snort. "I'm sure her husband thinks so. But I honestly don't give a damn about that. It would impress me more if she did her damn job."

"Is her name Melanie?" he asks, gesturing with my phone. "Because someone named Melanie wants you to know that the shipping cartons haven't arrived yet, and somebody named Chip is mad. Why are they texting you at eight p.m.?"

I let out a low groan. "Please reply to Melanie that she needs to stop fussing over her manicure, pick up the damn phone, and sort it out with the vendor herself."

"All right." He starts tapping on my phone. *"This is Nash's hotter brother. He is driving right now but he asks you kindly to…"*

Mitch seems very pleased with himself after he sends the message. "It's cool you have an assistant. Your job is more glamorous than mine."

"On what planet?" He's a professional athlete, so I reach across the gear box and poke him again. "Don't patronize us normal people."

"No, I meant it." He shrugs. "You overestimate the glamor of my job. But it's literally just… practice rink, jet, game night, jet… and repeat."

"Sorry you got knocked out of the playoffs," I say, slowing down for a fox to cross the road.

"Me too." He leans his head against the seat. "I thought we could go all the way."

"Maybe next year."

A deep silence from the other side of the car seems ominous. But he doesn't say anything more, and I don't ask, as per the Giltmaker way.

"Thanks for picking me up," he says eventually. "Sorry you have to."

"It's fine. I showed my face at work. Went to a couple meetings, picked up some things from home. But, seriously, why is your driver's license expired?"

"Because I forgot to renew it."

"Don't you have people for that?"

"Again," my brother says patiently, "you seem to overestimate the glamor of my job."

I glance at Mitch. When I look at him, I'll always see my baby brother—the kid who once believed our house was haunted by a glowing skeleton named Jingles because I told him it was.

The rest of the world sees Mitch differently, though. *A generational talent*, said *Sports Illustrated*. His nickname in sports media is Goalmaker.

And it's hard to believe my baby brother is thirty now. "Happy Birthday, by the way. Hope it was a fun one."

He lets out a little grunt of displeasure. "Thanks. But I'm past the age where landmark birthdays are a cause for celebration."

Okay, touchy subject.

"You have another message, asshole. From Benito Rossi. How is that dude, anyway?" He chuckles. "He sent you an address on Pine Lane. Is this for a party?"

I step on the brake and pull over to the curb. "An address?"

"Yeah, but watch the whiplash? This body takes enough abuse at my day job."

I grab the phone out of his hands. Then I tap on the address to see where it is on the map. "Hey—help me navigate."

"Why?"

"That's where Livia is." I push the phone into his hand and pull onto the road again.

"I thought you were taking me to Dad's place?"

"You'll get there eventually," I tell him.

"Wow, this girl has you messed up. One clue about her whereabouts, and you're pushing down the pedal."

He isn't wrong.

"If she ghosted you," he says slowly. "Why are you chasing after her?"

"She didn't *ghost* me." It comes out sounding defensive. "There's some trauma here, Mitch. Her ex burned down the brewery, and she's freaking out."

"Sure, but..." He sighs. "She doesn't sound stable. Even if this girl is hurting, this isn't a good sign. Haven't you heard the saying—hurt people hurt people?"

I have, in fact, heard that saying. And it troubles me more than I care to admit. Especially because Livia might not even deny it. She'd told me early on that her ex had done a number on her and that she wasn't in the right headspace to have another relationship.

Yet, I didn't listen. I'd gone and fallen for her anyway. Not that I'll admit it to anyone, but I'm truly angry at her for ghosting me right now.

Maybe she told Benito she was ready to see me. That's the hope I'm clinging to.

"What's she like?" Mitch asks.

"Hmm?"

"This girl who has you so wrecked. I've never seen you lose your shit over a woman. What's so special about her?"

"Everything," I mumble, turning on the high beams. "She's smart. Sexy. Knows her own mind. Doesn't play games. She's a grownup."

"And yet she's not taking your calls?"

I sigh.

"Just...know your worth, bro. You're a catch. If she can't figure that out, then maybe you need to let her go."

Hell. There's a truth bomb in there that I'm not really ready to hear. "In my gut, though, I *know* we're not done." I've known it since that first night when she gave me the slip at Speakeasy.

"Fox," he says.

She is, I think, just when I realize my brother meant an *actual* fox. I slam on the breaks just as the little fucker runs off the road.

"Ow," Mitch complains.

"I thought hockey players were tough."

"But my season is over."

It's not a great joke, but I laugh because it's so good to have him home.

———

"This is it," Mitch says ten minutes later when we find the little house on Pine Lane. "Kinda dark in there."

My heart sags, because it *is* dark in there. I park and get out anyway. I trot up to the front door in the fading light and knock.

Silence.

Shit.

After a few minutes waiting here, I duck around to peek in the garage window.

No car.

My stomach falls. I can't believe she's done a runner. I go back to the front and open the screen door so I can try the handle. Something flutters off the door and onto my shoes.

It's a note.

Nash—

I'm so sorry about the brewery. It will never be okay. So it's better if I go, like I meant to do before.

Once you have a little while to consider it, I know you'll agree with me. Try to picture me at the Thanksgiving table with your family. Yeah, I can't either. Nobody wants to pass the stuffing to the person who brought ruin to the Giltmaker legacy.

I'll <u>always</u> be the person who did this to all of

you. You'd probably forgive me eventually. But I don't want to ask that of you. It's just so unfair.

I'm sorry. And I already miss you so much. But it's better like this.

Love,

Livia

"No fucking way!" I shout.

"Whoa," says Mitch from over my shoulder. "She bailed?"

"No," I bark. "That's not how this ends."

"So what are you going to do about it?" my brother asks.

That's the right question.

CHAPTER 44
NASH

I drop Mitch off in front of our dad's house. He's not allergic to cats. "Here's the keys." I toss them. "See you in the morning."

"Hey! Aren't we seeing Dad tonight?" he asks.

"He'll have to wait. Or you could call someone else for a ride over there."

"Nash!"

But I'm already getting back in the car. Before I drive away, I ask my phone to call Benito.

"What's up?" he answers.

"Livia did a runner," I bark. "Where can I find this cousin of hers. Or the brother?"

"You know I can't give out citizen's private details," he says.

"I'm not asking you to run their license plates, Benny. I could google their last known locations, but why should I when my high school buddy has recently looked them up himself?"

Benito sighs. "I'm a very disciplined law enforcement officer. If I knew the whereabouts of Jennifer Witcomb of Arby Lane in Vergennes or Brady Willis of 300 Weaver Street in Winooski, I wouldn't tell you."

"Vergennes," I mumble. "Where's that."

"Google it for fuck's sake," Benito says. Then he hangs up.

I decide to try the brother first. Winooski is only a quick drive, and I watch for Livia's car on the road ahead of me. But I don't find her.

The house on Weaver Street is old—and broken up into a host of apartments. I step inside, find the door marked WILLIS and knock.

A voice calls out a greeting from the other side of the door. "One second, hot stuff." Then the door jerks open, and I'm face to face with a skinny young man whose face contracts into a grimace. He has Livia's eyes, though, and they're the most attractive feature on his face. "Wrong apartment, pal," he says.

"I don't think so. I'm looking for your sister."

The grimace deepens. "You're the new boyfriend? You just missed her. Told her it was a bad time. I'm expecting company, okay?" He looks behind me into the vestibule, which is empty, then tries to close the door.

"Hold up," I say, blocking the door open with one quick motion. "Your sister turned up here looking for your help?"

"Well, yeah. But she looked okay to me." He shrugs. "I got a small space. No room for guests. She understood."

Fury rises in my chest. "Did she tell you about the fire? Her place is a crime scene."

He shrugs again. "That's rough. But again, not a problem I can solve."

"Where did she go?" I growl.

"How should I know?" He throws his hands in the air. "Ivy takes care of herself. She's better at it than most people. It's her special gift. You want to find her so bad? Maybe try Jennie's place. I got plans."

I stare down at him, probably with murder in my eyes. Because he starts to look scared. "Your sister's special gift is keeping her shit together while the world takes potshots at her. Then she comes to you for help, and you're too busy?"

He looks away. "Yeah, well." He clears his throat. "She wasn't exactly surprised when I wasn't helpful, okay? So I assumed it wasn't that bad."

I want to grind him into the rug. But unfortunately, I don't have time. "Thanks for nothing, punk. If I catch up with her before she hits the state line, I'll tell her you said hello."

And here I thought *my* family was dysfunctional.

Cursing to myself, I'm back in the car a minute later and navigating toward Vergennes. It takes me a while to find the right street, so I lose time getting lost in a town so small there's no traffic light.

But I finally pull up in front of a house with children's toys on the lawn. What I don't see, though, is Livia's car. So I already have a sinking feeling as I make my way up the narrow walk and knock on the front door.

I hear motion on the other side of the door. But whoever's there doesn't say anything.

"Sorry to bother you, Jennie," I say, trying to sound friendly and nonthreatening. "I'm Nash, a friend of Livia's, and I'd like to talk to her before she leaves the state. It's important." I knock again. "Please, is she here?"

The door opens a crack to reveal a woman with curly hair and a frazzled look in her eye. "Shh."

"Sorry," I whisper.

She opens the door wider, and I get a glimpse of a man sacked out on the sofa inside. She steps out onto the little stoop and closes the door. "I don't think Livia wants to see you," she said in a low voice.

I perk up immediately. "Is she here?"

Slowly, she shakes her head. "She came by. My husband had just got home from work, though." She flinches. "It was bad timing. Livia has caused some trouble for us lately. My husband didn't react too well to seeing her. He asked her to leave."

"*Seriously?*" My heart drops as I picture Livia driving from one relative to the other, getting pushback everywhere she goes.

"I feel terrible," she whispers. "She does a lot for me. But he works two jobs." She hooks a thumb in the direction of her husband. "He wants peace and quiet when he gets home. I told her to come in, and we'd figure something out. But she, uh, read the room, and said never mind. She'd figure something out."

Livia can't catch a damn break. Which means neither can I. "Look, do you know where she'd go? If her brother told her to take a hike, and then your man did, too?"

Her eyes get wet. "I don't know. She doesn't have much money. And that car of hers…" She shakes her head. "I'm sorry. When you find her, tell her to call me. We'll find room for her somewhere."

"Sure. Thanks," I mutter before walking away.

I'm practically shaking with frustration as I stand beside my father's truck, unsure what to do. Vermont is one of the smallest states. But it could feel really big and lonely to a woman with few resources and fewer supportive people in her life.

I only wish I knew where to look.

Getting back into the truck, I start the engine.

She doesn't have much money, Jennie had said.

And now I think I know what I'm supposed to do.

CHAPTER 45
LIVIA

"Let me get this straight," Poppy says.

We're sitting on her enormous sofa, eating cookies. *Because trouble calls for cookies*, in Poppy's words.

"You want me to break into a dangerous building, where the ceiling might fall in at any moment, to help you recover cash from a crime scene?"

I set my cookie down onto my plate. "Well, when you put it that way..."

"I'm in!" she says brightly. "I love a good caper. But I'll only do it if you explain to me why you can't just ask Nash for help."

"Because I can't do that to him. There's police tape everywhere. I've dragged him as far into my messy life as he needs to go, and it's best if I just get my money and get on the road."

"Hmm," she says, nibbling a cookie. "Seems like he'd want to be asked."

I shake my head vehemently. "And you don't have to break the law, either. You're just my lookout. Or, you know, the one who calls 911 if the ceiling falls on me."

She looks alarmed. "How much money did you leave in that cigar box?"

"A few thousand dollars. But it's all I have left in the world. And all my clothes and jewelry were in the pumphouse."

"Not counting your fabulous friends." She grins. "Let's do this. Let me just change into something more suitable for a stealth mission than this." She waves a hand in front of a low-cut top, a terrific pencil skirt, and a pair of spike heels.

"Good plan."

When she returns a minute later, she's wearing a close-fitting top and jeans—all in black—and a pair of pink Air Jordans. "All right. Let's get 'er done so we can have a cocktail in town before you leave."

"I shouldn't drink and drive, Poppy. And I should get on the road."

"Fine—we'll make yours a mocktail. But I insist, since I'm going to be breaking the law for you."

"Fair."

"Also, you're staying here tonight. On my sofa bed. If you're so hot to leave tomorrow, you can get an early start."

My shoulders drop with relief. "Thank you. I appreciate that more than you know."

She grins. "Okay. Let's do our James Bond thing so we can have a cocktail after. I'm raring to go."

The moment we pull into the parking lot on the brewery property, all the air leaves my lungs. "Holy..." I gasp, because it's so much worse in person. A hundred years of history transformed into a charred skeleton.

Many of the brick walls are still standing, but their leaded glass windowpanes are blown out, leaving only jagged glass teeth and angry-looking soot in their wake. And through the missing parts of the ceiling, I can see moonlight.

I've never seen a more heart-wrenching sight.

"Breathe," Poppy reminds me.

I try. But now there are tears running down my cheeks. I slowly sink to my knees.

"Oh honey." Poppy crouches down beside me. "It's awful, I know. But this is just a setback."

"A *setback?*" I yelp. "It's a *tragedy.*"

"Have you seen the GoFundMe campaign? Another brewery started it. There's a hundred grand in there already, and it's only been twenty-four hours."

"That doesn't matter," I whisper. "You can't get back time. Lyle spent his whole life in this building, crafting the most famous beer in America. It would take him, what, two years to get it up and running again? He can't even leave the rehab center yet."

"Get up. Come on," Poppy pleads. "I think I heard a sound."

"It's just the building groaning."

She shivers. "Please don't go inside there. You can't use the door, see?" She points to indicate the caved-in front entrance.

"I have to try. It's four thousand dollars. If I die, I need you to call the ambulance. Also? If they find my Kindle, take it or burn it. The password is *livia69*, all lowercase."

"Bitch, please." Poppy makes a choking sound. "Just do me a favor and don't die, okay? I don't mind getting arrested, but helping to kill you is a hard limit for me."

"Fine." I wipe off my cheeks and reflect on what a shame it is that I have to leave Vermont, because Poppy and I would have been a great duo. "I'm pulling myself together. Help me find a window that I can climb into without cutting myself up too badly."

We edge around the corner of the building. Now we're standing beside the office. The building is in decent shape here, but getting in will not be easy.

"Hey—this window is open a little bit," Poppy says.

"Oh yeah?" When I look, I see that she's right. And when I wiggle my fingers into the opening and shove hard at the sash, I manage to lift it about ten inches before it won't budge any further. "Help me push this up?"

Working together, we get the window to open another half inch or so. But that's all. "I don't think this is going to work out," Poppy says.

"No, it is. Just help shove me through that opening, I'll make it."

"Okay, okay," she mutters. "Here, use my leg as a step." She braces it against the bricks.

I grab the window ledge and carefully step onto Poppy's thigh. But this looks so much easier in Cirque du Soleil. I'm having trouble lining my head up with the partially opened window.

"Oh shit! A car!" Poppy yelps.

I jerk my chin around to try to see it, but all I get is a blast of headlight glare. "Who is it?"

"No idea," she whispers. "Better hurry, though."

"Okay, okay." I angle my head through the opening as Poppy grabs my hips. "Push!" I close my eyes and prepare to topple onto the office's wood floor. It's a good thing I kept this place clean of debris.

"This is like birth, but in reverse," she mutters. Then she pushes me… right into someone's waiting arms.

Even in the dark, I'd know his scent anywhere. "Nash!" I squeak.

He lets out a low chuckle and pulls me all the way in, easing me to the floor.

"What are you *doing* here?"

"Getting your cash," he says, cupping my face in his hands. "I realized you'd left it behind, and I didn't want anyone else to find it."

"Oh." His body is like a big, warm magnet, and I feel the pull on a cellular level. That's why I have to take a healthy step back. "Why didn't you say something?"

"Watching you and Poppy is really fucking entertaining." He chuckles again. "What's on your Kindle, anyway?"

I make a frustrated sound. "Stop being so nice to me, okay? This is hard enough. I have to get my cash."

He reaches over and grabs something off a shelf. It's my cigar box full of cash. He hands it to me. "Here."

I take it, blinking at him in the sooty darkness. "How did you get in here, anyway?"

"Ladder into *that* window." He points toward the back of the building, where I can make out the inky rectangle of a window sash opened to a Nash-sized height.

"Oh. Well…thank you. Listen…"

"Psst!" Poppy says from outside. "I don't want to interrupt this reunion. But I see someone wandering around in back."

"Do they look threatening?" Nash asks.

"Well, no. Just curious."

"All right. Let me know if you need help," he says. Then he puts his hands on my shoulders. "You were saying?"

The warmth of his touch makes me ache inside. "I'm so sorry, Nash. If I had any idea this would have happened, I would have left the state when I had the chance."

He tilts his head, considering. "You think if you left the state, then there's no chance the brewery would have burned? Who's to say they wouldn't have done it anyway? They fucking told me to my face that if I didn't turn you over to them, this could happen. And then they did, which is a fucking shame. But they went to jail for it. Instantly. So I wonder who regrets it most."

"Well…" He's got me there. And it's a little confusing. "Still. I brought this trouble to your door, and I don't think I can ever look your father in the eye again."

"That's bullshit," Nash says, squeezing my shoulders. "How come you blame yourself, and not Razor? You ran away from Razor and hid for a year of your life, because you were unwilling to go down for his crimes. You told me that yourself."

"Yeah? So?"

"So why are you going down for his crimes now?" he asks. "He burned this place. Not you. But you're punishing yourself."

"Because I gambled your family's future on mine!" I shout. "I should have known right from the start that hiding here was a bad idea. I should have foreseen that it would blow up in all our faces."

Nash doesn't even look upset, which is weird. He just shakes his head. "I get why you think this way. Had a little chat with your brother tonight. And Jennie, too. Nobody ever has your back, do they?"

"You talked to my brother?" I gasp. "Now, there's a waste of time."

"Exactly." Nash actually smiles, and his teeth glint in the darkness. "My family can be tough sometimes, but they have my back when it matters. If I showed up on any of their doorsteps with nowhere to go, I know they'd take me in. Even my dad, and he's a cranky fucker."

"Damn right," says a hoarse voice from the back window.

I gasp. But Nash turns around slowly to look over his shoulder, where a face has appeared in the inky dimness. "Sorry I called you a cranky fucker," he says.

"I am a cranky fucker," Lyle replies. "Is the safe still there? I came to get my recipes."

"How'd you get here?" Nash asks.

"Got Mitch to bring me. He's waitin' in the car."

There's a small sound of distress from the direction of Poppy.

"I'll get your recipes in a sec," Nash says. "Livia and I have more to discuss."

"We don't," I whisper. "I appreciate your forgiveness, but it's better if I go."

"That's a damn lie," Poppy mutters from outside.

"She's not wrong," Nash says. "I love you, and it will hurt me if you leave. That's just the truth."

Everything inside me slows down while I try to take that in. *I love you*, he'd said. Those aren't words I've heard very often in my life.

"She still breathing?" Poppy asks.

"Not sure," says Nash. "Let's give her a minute."

"*Nash*," I gasp. Then I gulp oxygen.

"Still breathing," he says cheerily.

"You are..." I struggle for words. "The best man I have ever met. And you are someone that I could love, under easier circumstances. For example, if I hadn't just ruined your family's financial stability and future happiness."

"But you didn't," comes Lyle's gravelly voice. "I did that all myself."

"Wait, what?" I ask. Nash and I turn to gape at the shadowy figure in the window.

"I knew this place was a tinder box," he says with a sigh. "It's not up to code. That's why I haven't made any improvements to the building. Like that canning line Nash wants to fix up. I would have had to move a wall, which is a structural improvement..."

"Which would've demanded that you bring the place up to code," Nash says slowly. "The fire marshal was probably on your ass to make improvements."

"Right," Lyle mutters. "But I didn't want anything to slow me down. It was all about the beer."

"Plus, you're famously cheap," Poppy chimes in.

"There's also that," Lyle says drily. "So now there's no beer at all. Because I didn't want to shut the line down for a month and make the place safer. Livia is tryin' to take the blame for a burnt-up old building, and I'm just lucky nobody died." He sighs.

I'm so busy trying to absorb all this new information that I don't object when Nash steps closer to me and folds his arms around me. "Baby, don't leave. My dad is going to want to rebuild. And he's so cranky that nobody else will help him with that but you."

"That's half right," Lyle says. "Gonna need Livia's help. But Nash—I need yours, too. If anyone can figure out how to get this place back on its feet, it's you. So long as you don't fiddle with my recipes..."

Nash laughs, and I can feel his body shake against mine. "Like I'd *dare* touch your recipes. Dad, if we're going to work together, you're going to have to be honest with me. And think before you snarl."

"Yeah," he says grudgingly. "You know a lot about the beer business. You did a hell of a job keeping this place together for me."

"All for nothing," I mutter against Nash's chest.

"It *wasn't* for nothing," Poppy pipes up. "Not if Nash moves back to Vermont and the brewery doubles in size."

"Agree to disagree," I argue. But, strangely, I haven't disengaged myself from Nash's hug. Instead, my arms have snaked around his sturdy body.

This is why I didn't call him or see him these past couple of days. I knew I wouldn't be able to let go.

Nash kisses me on the head. "Come on. Let's pull Dad's recipes out of the safe. Then you're coming home with me."

"Home? Where are you staying?" I ask as he releases me.

"On Poppy's pull-out sofa."

"What?" I yelp. "She didn't mention that when she offered to let me sleep there tonight."

"Oh, didn't I?" she asks. "My bad. And you still owe me a cocktail, hon. I'm holding you to it."

"I'll treat you both," Nash says. "Livia, help me open the safe." He guides me carefully toward the corner in the dark.

I crouch down, my mind still whirling with all that's happened. I thought Lyle and Nash would resent me, even if they didn't blame me. But that doesn't seem true at all.

Even though I'm distracted, and even though it's very dark, the safe clicks open on the first try. I've always been good with numbers.

"Nice job, pussycat," Nash says.

"Pussycat?" Lyle scoffs. "I thought you were allergic to cats."

"Oh, I am." His hand finds my hip in the dark. "But some of them are worth it, sharp claws and all."

Then he kisses me. And I'm not too stupid this time to wrap my arms around him and kiss him right back.

"Let's go to Speakeasy," Nash says. "I'm going to stand on the same side of the bar as Livia."

"Of course. Why wouldn't you?" Poppy asks.

"Long story," I murmur. And then I kiss Nash again.

CHAPTER 46
NASH

Three hours later, we're alone at Poppy's house.

I'm lying on top of Livia on the pull-out couch. Luckily, this couch is located in the guest room. And luckily, this guest room has a lock on the door.

Luckiest of all, we're both naked. It wasn't even my idea. Livia started stripping off my clothing the minute we reached this room. Now we're kissing like the world might end before morning, and we're both trying to leave this earth with our mouths fused together.

Honestly, it wouldn't be a bad way to go. Her smooth hands are reacquainting themselves with every inch of my body. And if I'm lucky, I'll wake up with fingernail scratches on my back.

But we haven't reached that part of the evening. In spite of my body's predictable enthusiasm for lying naked on top of Livia, I'm trying to slow my roll.

"You know..." I say between kisses. "That night last year at Speakeasy? I thought it would end like this. But the wait was worth it."

"Good to know," she says as her fingertips take another journey across my chest. It feels amazing. "Maybe it *was* destiny. Even the bartender remembered that night."

It's true. When we appeared together at the bar a couple hours ago, Archie had a good laugh. "Well, strike me pink! Didn't expect to see you two turn up together. What's the story?"

Livia had admitted to calling the cops on me the second time we met, and Archie had another laugh and comped us our drinks.

I expect we'll be seeing a lot more of Archie now that Livia can socialize again.

Right now, though, her hands are socializing with my body. Her fingertips edge down to my belly, while I try my hardest not to feel ticklish.

I fail and end up twitching in a way that's not exactly sexy.

She lets out a gleeful laugh. "Be honest—where else are you ticklish?"

"No place," I lie. If she wants to tickle my feet or the backs of my knees, she's going to have to figure it out for herself.

"Uh-huh," she says, unconvinced. Smiling, she captures my face in her hands and sighs. "Nash, I just want to tell you that I'm sorry."

"For tickling me?" I tease. "You should be. But please don't apologize for the fire, Liv. We've been over this."

"I wasn't," she says with a wistful smile. "I'm apologizing for trying to leave without saying goodbye. That was cowardly."

Oh. "Well, you were…" I hesitate. "You were in some pain, and I get it. I was really mad at you for a minute there. But it's been a while since life gave you a break, so I'm trying to understand."

"But you give me all the breaks," she says, mussing my hair. "Until I met you, I was pretty down on the human race. So thank you for that. And I'll try not to panic the next time something goes wrong."

"I know you will." I kiss her jaw. "I've got your back, honey, and I know you've got mine, too. You can remind me of that when I go in to quit my job next week."

Her eyes widen. "That sounds stressful. Will they be pissed?"

"Yeah, probably. It won't be easy to replace me. That's not ego; that's a fact of the job being difficult."

She kisses my shoulder. "Come on, it's ninety percent the job, but ten percent ego."

"What? No." I laugh. "Baby, nobody can return an email like I can. You'll see. Since we'll be working together to rebuild the brewery, you'll even get a chance to see me make a flow chart." I grind my hips against hers. "It's *very* sexy."

"Oh, baby," she whispers. "Show me your boxes and arrows. Talk flow-chart to me."

"Step one," I whisper. "Who's the *man*? If Nash is the answer, then give me that mouth. Otherwise, go back to step one."

She must be great with flow charts, too, because I get another bottomless kiss.

CHAPTER 47
A FEW MONTHS LATER
NASH

Pia, the architect for the brewery reconstruction, steps back so we can all see the laptop resting on the tailgate of Dad's truck. "Let's take a look inside the tasting room, shall we?"

We lean in as a crow caws at us from the branches of a nearby tree.

It's a late summer afternoon here in the parking lot of the family property. It was cleared of debris a month ago, and since then, earth movers have been hard at work prepping the site for the rebuild.

The four of us—Dad, Livia, the architect and I—have weekly design meetings. Today Pia is using the "walkthrough" feature of her design software to show us how the interior of the new building will look.

"I've filled in some of the features you asked for last week. The display case is here, behind the bar." She points at the screen. "I need to fine tune the dimensions. What's going in the case? Trophies?"

I speak up. "Trophies, framed awards, and hopefully some mementos from the old building. Can you use any part of this? I saved it and stashed it in Dad's garage." I open my phone and flip to a photo of the original door frame, which was slightly charred in the fire. "When I was a kid, we all soldered our initials into the wood."

"Cool!" she says. "How much of the frame did you save?"

"All of it," Dad pipes up. "We thought you could cut a piece and use it in the display case."

"That could work," Pia says. "But if you have the frame, I could reuse the whole thing. Doesn't matter if it's charred. I can still make it work."

"Hell, yes," my father says, staring at the screen. "Didn't realize that was legal. I assumed it would be against code. Seems like *everything* is against code."

Livia and I exchange an amused glance. My father is still a grump. That will never change. But he isn't a control freak anymore. The fire seems to have burned that right out of him.

"Maybe it was an exhausting way to live," Livia said the other night when we were discussing him over dinner. "And he finally realized that if he didn't want to rebuild the entire company all on his own, then he'd have to bend a little."

She must be right, because Dad's new attitude isn't even an act. He seems more relaxed at the core. As if the thing he dreaded most in the world actually happened, so now he doesn't fear it anymore.

"The bar is twenty feet long on the tasting side," Pia says, as a computer-generated image of the room whirls across the screen. "And ten feet long on the retail side. But we'll accommodate an extra set of taps on the retail side, for special events."

Maybe it's too soon to say it aloud, but rebuilding the brewery is going to improve the space by leaps and bounds. Every room will be updated, easier to use, and easier to maintain.

And don't even get me started on the brewing equipment. We're getting a state-of-the-art setup on our production line. The beer will still be made by hand, every step of the way, but the setup, cleanup, and canning processes will be modernized.

Dad didn't even fight me on this stuff. All I had to do was drag him out to see another award-winning brewery in Burlington. "I dare you tell these guys that they don't make these beers by hand, just because their new hopper lifts the grain up to the mouth of the masher."

"Yeah, yeah." Dad had chuckled. "Go on. Get the new hopper if it means so much to you."

It's going to be amazing.

Pia's virtual tour moves through the brewhouse. "You guys need to finalize the width of the aisle between the fermentation tanks," she says. "Is five feet wide enough?"

My father frowns at the screen. "Can't I just see it on paper?"

"Sure," Pia says smoothly, because she's used to this by now. "I'll just grab the blueprints out of the car."

My dad still loves his paper. Although Livia is forcing him to computerize their accounting now. All their old ledgers are either sooty or soggy. It's taking Livia months to secure and transcribe all his old records and tax filings.

The architect returns with the blueprints and consults my father on his floor plan. Leaving them to it, I tug Livia a few steps away before wrapping an arm around her and kissing her on the cheek. "What do you say we have a picnic after this?"

"A picnic?" She gives me a curious look. "In the middle of the workweek? I thought you were going to take a conference call while I drive us back to Boston?"

I'm still working at BrewCo for another few months. They wanted a long transition, and I gave it to them because paychecks are nice, and the brewery construction is going to take some time.

Meanwhile, my dad is making small batches of Goldenpour at the Speakeasy brewery in town, and in another brewery's spare tanks, in order to keep the beer alive during the interim.

Livia is still employed by Giltmaker as Dad's assistant. But she's been working from Boston where she's staying with me. Every week we drive up here and spend a night or two in Poppy's guest room, so Dad and Livia and I can work on brewery details together face to face.

It's a little chaotic, but somehow it works. Life is good. Which is why I have a plan to make it even better. "I've decided to reschedule that conference call. Let's get some sandwiches. I have a destination in mind."

She shrugs. "Okay. If you want to blow off work today, I'm not going to stop you."

"Good. Now let's have some deep discussion about the spacing between fermentation tanks, so we can get the heck out of here."

CHAPTER 48
LIVIA

After the architect's meeting, we stop at a deli for sandwiches and lemonade.

"It isn't a picnic without lemonade," Nash says.

"Really? If you say so."

"Trust me, babe. The Giltmakers are beverage experts." He taps his credit card against the scanner, even though I'm pretty sure it was my turn to pay.

Being with Nash these past few months has been amazing. Sometimes I still have to remind myself to relax and just take things as they come. Razor made me doubt everyone's intentions. I wasn't sure I could trust a man again.

It's just that Nash makes it so easy. He likes having fun, and he likes having it with me. Most of the time it's that simple.

With Nash, I never have to look for an ulterior motive. He's always upfront about his intentions. Like right now when he says, "I have a destination in mind. Can I take you there?"

"Sure."

He looks over and gives me a smile that's pure Nash—sixty percent warmth and forty percent naughty.

I love that smile, but I also trust that smile. It's not only a nice way to live, it's a revelation.

After we leave the Colebury Deli, Nash heads up a country road outside of town that's unfamiliar to me. A half mile or so up the hill, the road turns from asphalt to gravel.

But our car can take it. These days we're driving a new-to-us Subaru that we bought together after trading mine in. When we drive back and forth to Boston, I no longer fear the engine falling out on the road.

"The turnoff is up here," he says, guiding the car past a meadow. "See that mailbox? The driveway is just past that."

"We're having a picnic at somebody's house?"

"Hold your questions for a second." He reaches the drive and turns. I see a rolling green lawn and a cute, white, two-story farmhouse. There's a wraparound front porch and a peaked roof.

There's also a For Sale sign on the lawn. "Nash?"

He chuckles. "I found this listing online, and I've been staring at the pictures all week."

"It's gorgeous," I agree. "But Nash—we can't buy a *house*."

"Can't we?" He shrugs. "I'm a couple weeks away from listing my Boston condo for sale. And Mitch said he'd float me the cash for the down payment in between the closings."

"He…really?" My mind is blown. I can't imagine having that kind of cash. And I can't imagine buying a house.

"Let's look inside. The realtor opened it up for us. Nobody lives here right now. The owner is a retired couple. They moved to Atlanta." He gets out of the car and brings our lunch with him. "Come on, pussycat. You know you want to."

He isn't wrong. I'm ten different kinds of curious about a house Nash would like. So I get out of the car and chase him up the walkway. On that gorgeous front porch, he sets our deli bag down and then opens the front door. As if he owns the place.

I follow him inside, and then try not to sigh. Whoever owns this place has taken *very* good care of it. The walls are freshly painted, and the wood floors shine. It's light and bright, with views of the meadow across the street.

"It's...very pretty," I say haltingly. "But I can't afford a place like this, Nash. I thought we were going to find a rental."

"We can, if that's what you really want," he says, opening the coat closet to peer inside. "But this house won't last. It's in perfect shape. And I thought we have enough of a project on our hands with the brewery. Wouldn't it be nice to live in a house where everything already works?"

"Well, yeah. But..."

"But..." He puts an arm around me and kisses my head. "Do you hate it?"

"No! Who could hate it? Oh wait—I know. My bank balance hates this idea a lot."

"What if your bank balance doesn't get a vote?" He shrugs. "We're going to live together somewhere, right? If you want to split it fifty-fifty, I suppose we can do that. But why should we?"

"Because that would be fair."

"Livia!" He puts both hands on my shoulders and gives me a gentle squeeze. "Life isn't always fair. You know that as well as anyone."

Too true.

"We're going to work really hard over the next couple of years to get the brewery back on its feet. Why shouldn't we live in a nice place while we do that? I can afford this place." His brown eyes are begging me. "It doesn't have to be this house, if it's not to your taste. But let's not waste time. What's that saying? Living well is the best kind of fuck-you?"

I laugh. "That might not be the exact saying."

"Whatever." He grins. "You get the idea. Can we finish the tour? There's three bedrooms upstairs. And then we need to look out back. I saw a hammock in the photos."

"Oh. Well." I feel a rush of love for this man. "Why didn't you lead with that? If I knew there was a hammock, I might not even be arguing."

An hour later, we're lying side by side in a hammock that stretches between two old maple trees, while the afternoon sunlight dapples the green leaves overhead.

Nash is playing with my hair and telling me how it would all work. "After the sale of my condo, I'll pay off the bridge loan to my brother. And then my monthly mortgage payment on the house would be almost the same as it is now."

"I get it," I say grudgingly. But after upgrading the car, I'm cash poor again. And there's no way I'm getting a raise until after the brewery is back up to speed. "I just wish I could contribute in a more meaningful way."

He snorts. "Every time you talk my dad off the ledge, and every time you solve some problem for my family business, you're contributing in a *very* meaningful way."

"You know what I mean," I say, and then I roll to face him. Or at least I try to. But the hammock sways violently, and I end up clinging to him with my whole body like a frightened cat.

"So I guess hammock sex is off the table," Nash says. "But that doesn't dampen my enthusiasm for this house. What do you think? Be honest."

Be honest. It's harder to be honest with myself than it is with Nash. "I feel about this house the same way I feel about you. It's impressive. It's amazing. I love every stick of it, and I can't believe it's here in front of me."

Nash blinks his brown eyes at mine. "Aw, baby. Let me buy us this house. I love it so much."

"Okay," I whisper. "I do too. And Nash—I love you even more than this house. You know that right?"

He grins. "Yeah, baby. You just told me. Every stick of it."

"That's right."

"So glad you love my stick." He wiggles his eyebrows.

My laughter unsettles the hammock again, and I end up clutching his T-shirt like a Titanic passenger on a life raft.

"We'll have to work on our hammock game," he says easily. "I want lots of practice time."

"You got it, Giltmaker," I tell him. "I'm all in."
And I mean it.

**THE
END**

ALSO BY SARINA BOWEN

ALSO IN THE GILTMAKER SERIES

Good as Gold

TRUE NORTH: the original Vermont series!

Bittersweet (Griffin & Audrey)

Steadfast (Jude & Sophie)

Keepsake (Zach & Lark)

Bountiful (Zara & David)

Speakeasy (May & Alec)

Fireworks (Benito & Skye)

Heartland (Dylan & Chastity)

Waylaid (Daphne & Rickie)

TRUE NORTH SPINOFFS

Roommate (Roddy & Kieran)

Boyfriend (Abbi & Weston)

BROOKLYN HOCKEY / BROOKLYN BRUISERS

Rookie Move

Hard Hitter

Pipe Dreams

Brooklynaire

Overnight Sensation

Superfan

Sure Shot

Bombshells

Must Love Hockey

Shenanigans

Love Lessons

THE COMPANY

Moonlighter (Eric Bayer's book)

Loverboy

THE IVY YEARS

The Year We Fell Down #1

The Year We Hid Away #2

The Understatement of the Year #3

The Shameless Hour #4

The Fifteenth Minute #5

Extra Credit #6

GRAVITY

Coming In From the Cold #1

Falling From the Sky #2

Shooting for the Stars #3